1

MAISIE – MAY 1944

'Rain, rain, rain,' Maisie Miles muttered as she tied the ends of her headscarf beneath her chin. 'Where's my umbrella?'

'Here.'

It wasn't usual for Carole Thomas, Maisie's lodger, and mother of a three-month-old baby to follow her out into the hallway. She'd been a bit quiet over breakfast, which Maisie had put down to her baby daughter, Paula, having disturbed during the night.

Looking pensive, Carole swung the umbrella on one finger.

Sensing something was wrong, Maisie frowned. 'Is everythin' all right? You're looking a bit peaky.'

'I've been thinking...'

'About what?'

In that moment, it seemed to Maisie that Carole held her breath before dropping the bombshell.

'I've decided to have Paula adopted.'

Maisie had been about to open the front door. Suddenly it seemed too far away to reach. Yet she had to. It was Friday, the last full day of the working week at the W. D. & H. O. Wills tobacco factory, in East Street, Bedminster, Bristol. She had no wish to be late. She was never late. But Carole's words stopped her in her tracks. Her jaw dropped, seeming only to be held in place by her headscarf tied beneath her chin.

She took a deep breath before finding her voice.

'Carole, I think you need to think carefully before making such an important decision.'

The slender young woman, only four or five years younger than her, pushed a tress of blonde hair behind one ear. 'I have said it before.'

'Yes, but only in passing.'

'That's not true.' Carole's blue eyes blazed. 'I meant what I said.'

'You need to give yourself time.'

'She's three months old and it's best she's placed sooner rather than later.'

Maisie bit her lip. It was true this wasn't the first time Carole had mentioned having Paula adopted. But Maisie had always talked her out of it, or thought she had.

And I'll do it again, she assured herself. She plastered a smile onto her face and said glibly, 'Let's talk about it tonight, shall we? You might feel different then.'

By tonight, she might have forgotten about it. That's what Maisie hoped.

Carole folded her arms and said nothing. Nothing signified agreement to Maisie. She fussed with her hair, dark and curly as opposed to Carole's light blonde, pushing as much as possible beneath her headscarf. Her eyes too were dark, her figure slight and she was shorter than Carole.

'Good. Good,' said Maisie, hoping her dismissive attitude would wash the problem away. 'I'll see you later then.'

After pulling the door shut behind her, she paused for a moment on the doorstep. The weather was foul, and she should really go back inside to fetch her umbrella which she had forgotten

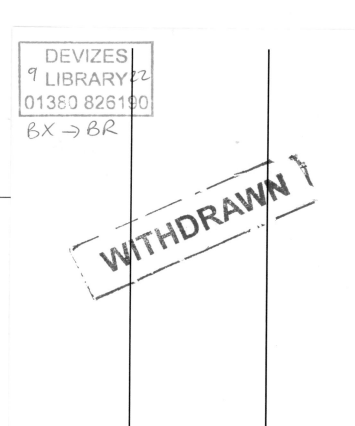

This book may be returned to any Wiltshire library.
To renew this book, phone your library or visit the
website : www.wiltshire.gov.uk

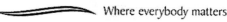

Wiltshire Council

Where everybody matters

First published in Great Britain in 2022 by Boldwood Books Ltd.

Copyright © Lizzie Lane, 2022

Cover Design by Colin Thomas

Cover Photography: Colin Thomas

A CIP catalogue record for this book is available from the British Library.

Paperback ISBN 978-1-80048-526-6

Large Print ISBN 978-1-80048-525-9

Hardback ISBN 978-1-80483-653-8

Ebook ISBN 978-1-80048-528-0

Kindle ISBN 978-1-80048-527-3

Audio CD ISBN 978-1-80048-520-4

MP3 CD ISBN 978-1-80048-521-1

Digital audio download ISBN 978-1-80048-522-8

Boldwood Books Ltd
23 Bowerdean Street
London SW6 3TN
www.boldwoodbooks.com

to take from Carole. But if she went back in, Carole might yet again mention having Paula adopted. This time she might try a more determined stance. Best to leave things as they are, Maisie thought. Leave it until this evening.

* * *

Carole was left staring at the closed door. She turned disconsolately away and went upstairs. Alone in the house, she looked down at Paula. She'd just been fed and was sound asleep in her cot, her downy head all that showed above the bedclothes. Having no one else to talk to, Carole addressed the baby.

'She doesn't understand. I hope you do. I hope you'll thank me in years to come.'

It wasn't Carole's habit to read newspapers, but on one Sunday shortly after Paula had been born and feeling low, she'd picked one up. After reading the front-page news concerning the war, she had flicked through advertisements for corsets and Bovril, until she'd come to the classified ads.

Kindly aunt in need of baby niece. Good permanent home assured. Write P8345 Sunday Dispatch.

She'd written as instructed. A meeting had been arranged, but she was not yet ready to tell Maisie. Maisie would talk her out of it and she was prepared to lie, to say she was going out with a friend and to pretend that she was happier than she felt. Anyway, it wasn't her fault she'd got pregnant, but it was for her to do something about it. After all, Paula was her baby and the decision was also hers.

2

It was tipping down with rain, foul weather for the time of year. As far as Maisie Miles was concerned, the bus couldn't get to the bus stop in East Street quick enough. Every seat was taken by wet and miserable-looking people and the smell of damp clothing was accompanied by coughs and clearing of throats.

The woman sitting next to her took up more than half the seat – not quite two thirds, but certainly more than she was entitled to.

Bite your tongue, Maisie told herself. It wasn't often she got into such a foul mood, but what with the weather and Carole yet again mentioning having Paula adopted, her mood sat heavy on her shoulders. *Think of something pleasant, anything but the smell and sound of a journey to work on an unseasonably wet day in dear old Bristol.*

Through the misted windows, she could see umbrellas bobbing along and those people without them bending against the slanting rain, coat collars turned up, hat brims shielding faces against the deluge.

She drew the outline of an umbrella on the steamed-up window and glanced at the woman sitting next to her. Droplets of water were falling from the woman's hat. A sodden feather drooped over her face. No matter how many times the woman's yellow-ended fingers pushed it back, down it fell again. Normally Maisie might smile or make comment. Today, all traces of humour had been wiped out that morning.

Surely Carole couldn't really mean what she'd said this morning. Her stomach churned at the thought of it. The house would seem so empty without Carole and her baby, though she understood her reasoning. An unmarried mother had a tough time in the world. She understood that. All the same she couldn't bear the thought of Paula being brought up by strangers. Her heart would be broken. So too might Carole's.

There were the usual grumbles about the weather exchanged between passengers, who on other days wouldn't bother to make comment.

'Ruddy weather! It's that Adolf Hitler's to blame.'

Hitler, Maisie mused, got the blame for everything, perhaps rightly so.

First her feet were soaked, then her legs as she stepped down from the bus. Water from overflowing drainpipes and the unrelenting downpour lay an inch deep over the pavements.

Never had she felt so relieved to see the red-brick tobacco factory rising like a Gothic castle along one side of the road. On the opposite side were ordinary shops, selling everything from sweeping brushes to crockery, tripe to turnips.

Even this early in awful weather, queues had formed outside the butchers, grocers, and greengrocers. Food was still rationed, and queues formed at the slightest rumour of something scarce suddenly being available.

The rain seeped into Maisie's headscarf, and she dreaded taking it off. She knew how her hair would look underneath its feeble protection. Her dark waves would have turned into a mass of unmanageable frizz.

No umbrella of course. That's what came of lingering over a baby. Not her baby of course, but Carole's baby, Carole Thomas who had moved in with her some time ago. Her pregnancy was a result of rape. She'd had nowhere else to go, no one else to turn to.

Maisie had considered herself lucky that she owned her own house, left to her by her grandmother. In the absence of Phyllis and Bridget, her very good friends, both serving their country, she had felt a little lonely. It took her no time at all to offer Carole a stable home.

'Lousy, rotten weather,' she said to no one in particular.

'More like November,' grumbled a fellow workmate as they bustled their way to the ladies' cloakroom. Beyond that, the clocking-in machine awaited the insertion of their individual cards.

In the crowded cloakroom, coats steamed, umbrellas were shaken out and tousled hair was combed or patted into some kind of order.

Maisie shook out her headscarf, then took off her coat and hung it up. Her big toe felt uncomfortable, and she guessed what the problem was. Prepared for it, she eased off a shoe and emptied out the water that had found its way in. The soles were of cork – fine in sunny weather but not so good in wet. Roll on the day when shoes were once again properly made with soles of leather.

Just as she was about to slide her foot back into her shoe, Maisie pulled her stocking a little tighter around her toes and...

'Blast.'

A ladder shot up from the hole her big toe had made and ran all the way up the front of her leg.

She grimaced. It wasn't exactly the end of the world, but stockings were precious. If you laddered one, all you could do was keep the other. When another pair laddered, the good one was kept for pairing to the one already languishing in the bedroom drawer back at the house in Totterdown.

'When's this blessed rain gonna stop,' said Ida Baker, who now sat where Maisie's dear old friend Phyllis used to sit before she'd joined up and found herself serving on the island of Malta, one of the most bombed places on earth.

'June perhaps,' muttered Maisie. 'That's when summer's supposed to start.'

Ida gave a brief nod before carrying on. 'Luckily I don't 'ave far to come. And I've got a brolly. Ain't you got one? You look soaked.'

'I'm soaked through, and I've got a ladder,' grumbled Maisie.

'At least you got 'ere. I 'eard tell there's some roads blocked off around the Yank air fields. Troop manoeuvres, so our local copper said, but 'ow would 'e know anything?'

'They reckon it's the same on the trains,' said another woman whose husband worked on the railways. 'My Stan says a lot of rolling stock's being diverted. Said 'e saw a whole train of flatbeds carrying field guns and tanks.'

'Something big 'appening, I reckon.' The speaker was Betty Bennet. 'I can feel it in me bones.' She hissed through her teeth and rubbed at her aching hips and knees as if to emphasise the point. No one disagreed with her, though it had little to do with her knees.

'I look forward to the day when the invasion of Europe finally 'appens,' said Maisie and meant it.

So much had happened since she'd first walked into this factory. Meeting up with Bridget Milligan and Phyllis Mason had been like finding a new home complete with friends who made up for the sisters she did not have. She missed them dearly and couldn't wait for the day they were reunited – whenever that might be. In the meantime the war dragged on.

'My Shirley's old man told 'er that all leave 'ad been cancelled. Bloody Adolf.'

Maisie determined to talk about something else. It was always the war, the bloody war! Once they were seated and working in the stripping room, conversation began to buzz.

'Anyone been to the pictures lately? Seen any good films?'

Betty finished sticking plasters on her fingers and began stripping leaves.

'*Mrs. Miniver*'s on again at the Gaumont in town. I've seen it four times but wouldn't mind seeing it again. Made me cry, it did.'

Maisie said that it had made her cry too. She'd already guessed that *Mrs. Miniver* would be the prime choice for discussion. Everyone loved its stiff-upper-lip heroism of a woman who confronts a downed German pilot in her kitchen. Everyone knew the plot off by heart and loved Greer Garson and Walter Pidgeon and Maisie was pleased. Listening and taking part in a familiar conversation meant she could carry on thinking her own private thoughts. What would a world without war be like? Not the big things, but the little things in her life such as looking out on streetlights, with light from a living room pouring out, without having to worry about pulling across the blackout curtains. She couldn't wait to burn those!

The colour of Greer Garson's hair was mentioned.

'Auburn. I read she's got auburn hair,' declared Betty.

Maisie made comment. 'If you read it, then it must be true.'

'Hard to tell with a black and white film,' added Ida.

Auburn hair. Just like Phyllis, thought Maisie. She'd been struck by its colour on their first meeting, as well as by Phyllis's overall glamour. For only the second time that morning, Maisie smiled. The times Phyllis had been told off for wearing bright red lipstick. She smiled to herself.

Always immaculately turned out, Phyllis had had ambitions. Getting married to Robert Harvey had been a wrong move. Getting out of it had been difficult, but it now seemed that donning a uniform had got her what she'd wanted; her letters gave the impression it had.

Mick is the one. He really is. I feel so relaxed with him. I can be whatever I want. There are no rules.

As for Bridget, the third one of the friends, she'd been the bookish type and thus had always had an opinion. She'd married an American, Lyndon O'Neil, the son of the owner of a tobacco plantation. Phyllis's letters came from where she was based with the RAF in Malta. Bridget's from each of the hospitals she'd served in.

Maisie Miles, I always knew you'd keep the home front going for when we return. Missing you. Heard anything from Sid?

Yes, thought Maisie. *I have.* The thought made her smile but then another came to her which made her sad - dear Sid was still incarcerated in a Japanese prisoner of war camp.

Sid had been a very casual date, not much more than a friend, yet since he'd been away their written communication had in some way brought them closer. That day of the tobacco workers trip to Weston Super Mare was more vivid now in her memory than it had ever been. Dear Sid, scoffing sandwiches on top of buying fish and chips wrapped up in newspaper, the smell of malt vinegar mixing with that of a salty incoming tide.

Ida interrupted. 'What you smiling about?'

'Was I?'

'You were looking all dreamy-eyed. Got some 'andsome man in yer life, 'ave you? You going out with a Yank?'

Maisie laughed. 'Now there's a thought. I could do with a new pair of nylons. Wouldn't mind some chocolates either.'

'I wouldn't mind a tin of Spam,' said Ida. 'It ain't bad fried in

5

When Maisie got home from her half-day Saturday shift, Carole had a slice of bacon, egg and fried bread waiting for her.

'You dashed off without any breakfast this morning, so here it is, breakfast in the middle of the day.'

The smell of frying bacon and bread drew Maisie into the kitchen. 'I didn't realise I was so hungry. You look nice,' she said. Carole was wearing a pale blue jacket with a pleated skirt. The skirt was made from a check fabric that was roughly of the same shade as the jacket. Maisie suspected the friend was male. She hoped it was. 'Your friend must be special.'

'I haven't seen her for such a long time. Anyway, I've always liked to look nice. That's why I loved being a visitor's guide so much. I got to wear a suit instead of an overall.'

Her sharp retort was a bit hurtful. Maisie had always worn an overall.

'I've fed Paula. She won't need another feed until three or even four.'

'I can do that. I'm not completely useless,' said Maisie.

'No. Sorry. I know you can cope.'

'Of course I can. Now run along. Go and enjoy yourself.'

Carole waved a cheery goodbye.

A sudden thought crossed Maisie's mind. What if Carole really was meeting a young man? What if she married someone? If that happened, she would no longer see so much of Paula. Was it wrong to not want her to leave? The girl was entitled to some happiness.

Maisie decided to make herself a cup of tea.

Weekends were usually the time she set aside for housework, but not today when she had Paula to herself. Instead of dusting and polishing or clattering around with the carpet sweeper, she smiled down into the pram, marvelling at her downy hair, her round face. She'd convinced herself that Paula had smiled at her first, not her natural mother, and felt favoured.

'Now aren't you the pretty one, Paula Thomas.'

Time and time again, whenever she got the chance in fact, she touched the delicate little fingers, smoothed back the wispy hair and never stopped smiling at her.

Whilst sipping a most welcome cuppa, Maisie thought back on the months Carole had been living with her both before and after Paula had arrived. Carole had been dour from the start, crying how life was so unfair, not wanting the baby, and wishing what had happened had never happened. She'd seemed to accept Paula, had sometimes looked at her in wonder, seemingly unable to believe the beauty of the tiny human being cradled in her arms. At other times, she had purposely avoided picking her up, clamping her hands over her ears so she wouldn't hear her crying.

Someone had told Maisie that new mothers did sometimes suffer from moods following the stress of childbirth. She told herself that in time all would be well. Carole would adapt to her new life.

She leaned over the sleeping baby, wanting her to wake up, even if it meant a bout of crying. As it worked out, she didn't need to about the London train. A pencil pushed behind his ear wobbled as he shook his grey-haired head.

'You could have a long wait, me love. We're doing our best. Signal failure so we've been told.' He tapped the side of his nose and winked. He was insinuating the excuse might be otherwise, but it was lost on her. She was here for a reason and although she felt sick inside, she kept reassuring herself that it was something she just had to do.

Resigning herself to the fact she might have to wait for some time, Carole headed to where she'd been told to go.

The other more populous platforms were left behind. Soot and silence were all-pervading except for the sound of her footsteps echoing off the subway walls.

A gust of cold air hit her as she came up out of the subway and onto the platform which had a bleak and neglected look, a far cry from its Victorian heyday.

Paint was peeling and a skewed sign creaked above the waiting room, the words faded and barely legible. Tufts of grass almost obliterated the remaining and little-used railway tracks. This was only a meeting place. Mrs Lavender would arrive on the London train on a different platform. *The old platform will lend us privacy,* she'd said in her letter. *I hope to arrive by three o'clock.*

Carole didn't need to glance up at the station clock to know that she had a long wait. Temple Meads Station wasn't usually this chaotic in normal times, but these times were not normal.

There's a war on.

How many times had those words been repeated since the outbreak of hostilities in 1939? A lot. Too many. She sincerely hoped it wouldn't be long before they were never heard again.

Despite it being late May, Carole felt cold. The rain had only eased off yesterday evening, but deep inside she knew it wasn't the rain making her feel so cold. Could she really go through with this?

What would people think of her? What would Maisie think of her? Maisie was the kindest person she'd ever met. She'd looked out for her from the very first time she'd reported for work at W. D. & H. O. Wills and she'd been happy there. But her life had been thrown upside down. To her mind, it made sense to cut all ties with the city where the worst possible thing had happened to her. Once it was done, she would depart for a new place, London perhaps, or even further away. Perhaps she could join up. Maisie too would then be unencumbered with her and her illegitimate child. It would be a fresh start for all of them.

For most of last night, she'd laid awake telling herself she was being sensible and that both Paula and Maisie would adjust. It didn't stop her feeling guilty. She trembled at the thought of telling Maisie that she'd lied and wasn't out meeting an old friend, that she was meeting a woman to whom she would hand over her baby.

The door to the waiting room was stiff. Her shoulder, already bruised from all the pushing and shoving of crowds, ached a bit more with the effort of forcing it open.

The room was semi-derelict and only one of the wooden benches was still upright. One was enough. She needed to sit for a while and steady her nerves. She also wanted another chance to read the instructions she'd been sent.

It smelt of old dust and damp and the draught from outside disturbed ashes from a long dead fire in the ancient grate. Cobwebs thick with flies hung ragged in front of windows that hadn't been cleaned for years.

Despite the dirt and debris, Carole dusted off the rickety wooden bench and sat down.

Mrs Lavender had stipulated that she carry a folded-up copy of the *Sunday Dispatch* under her arm. Picking up the newspaper had been the first step to being here today. She unfolded the newspaper had imagined. She was wearing a fox fur, more suitable for January than May. The brim of her hat from which a feather trembled was pulled low, hiding one half of her face. Gauzy black net hid most of the rest of it.

For a moment, the statuesque figure slowed her steps, speeded up and then stopped, almost as though she was considering she was in the wrong place at the wrong time.

Although it was difficult to see her face through the black net, Carole fancied she saw a puckered brow. Heart racing, she decided to make the first move.

'Mrs Lavender?'

Her voice seemed to bounce off the dirty walls and disturb the creaking sign for the waiting room.

Mrs Lavender shrugged her shoulders so that the fox fur rippled like a live creature and settled anew on her shoulders. There was a wariness about her, though stiffly she stood, casting her eyes around, searching for something. 'Miss Thomas?'

The tone of voice was as sharp as the nasty jaws that clamped around the fox's tail. Carole had always thought fox furs distasteful. After all, it had once been a living creature, yet here it was, just the fur with all the insides taken out.

'Yes.'

Lips now pursed in what Carole perceived as aggravation, Mrs Lavender's head twitched in each direction, then over Carole's head to the waiting room.

'Ah! The baby is in the waiting room,' said Mrs Lavender, sounding greatly relieved. 'I thought for a moment you hadn't brought the baby with you.'

Carole was immediately flustered. 'No. I haven't. I thought I had to sign the forms first and then you take her later...'

'Later?' Mrs Lavender's sharp voice now bordered on a shriek. 'On the nail! Everything done today. That's what I stipulated.'

'But I thought...' Carole instantly realised that she'd been in more of a fluster than she'd realised.

Mrs Lavender half turned away, then stopped and turned back to face her. 'Silly girls like you don't think. That's what got you into trouble in the first place.'

'It wasn't like that!' Carole felt her face grow hot. Innocence had been her only fault when she'd stupidly entered the house of a man she thought she could trust.

Mrs Lavender's red lips curled into a sneer. 'That's what they all say.'

'But you have to help me. I've given you twenty guineas already.'

'That was a deposit. And before you ask, it's non-returnable. Goodbye and good luck. You're going to need it.'

'Please,' Carole called to the retreating back of Mrs Lavender. 'This childless couple. I really want them to have Paula – if you're sure they'll love her.'

'Too late.' Mrs Lavender waved her hand in a dismissive fashion, the heels of her smart shoes already tapping the beat of retreat. 'You've got me here on false pretences. I have my expenses to consider and another train ticket here costs extra time and money.'

'I can pay you the balance – and more. My father is a wealthy man. He's in business.'

At mention of receiving a sum above that demanded, the retreating tapping of Mrs Lavender's shoes came to an abrupt halt and she spun round.

'I do have more,' said Carole as she rummaged in her handbag. For some reason, finding the money was somewhat elusive. Just when she wanted to swear, a single thought invaded her mind. *Don't pay up unless the goods are on the table.*

Surprised by the thought, she stopped rummaging and considered who had said it. Realisation was not long in coming. It was what her mother, a good-time girl if ever there was, used to say. She never did anything for anyone – especially men – unless she was paid up front. Neither did she pay out anything unless she was certain of receiving what she'd paid for.

Her mother had been far from perfect. Unmarried, she'd given birth to Carole in a Salvation Army home for single mothers. For some reason only known to herself, she'd not given Carole up for adoption. Up until this moment, she'd never questioned her mother's decision. Like her, she'd been young. Could it really be that her mother's heart had been less selfish than her own?

Carole set her jaw in a firm line. *Everyone has a price* – another of her mother's pearls of wisdom. 'I'll give you another twenty guineas now. The rest when you collect my baby.'

Carole wasn't to know, but Mrs Lavender had a lot in common with her mother. They shared the same profession, had survived a tough upbringing, could read what people wanted and how far they were likely to go. She recognised desperation when she saw it. The girl standing before her wanted her life back, wanted to go out and have fun with others of her age.

Sharpness buried for the sake of expediency, she allowed an amenable smile to stretch her lips. 'Well, I suppose I could make another journey.' She looked at her watch before looking back at Carole, letting her dangle as she gave it some thought. On coming to a decision, she nodded. 'I'm willing to accommodate you, but at a cost. I have to bear extra expenses in mind. Let's say... an extra fifty guineas.'

'Fifty?' It was more than Carole had expected.

'Hmm. Perhaps that's a bit much. I like you so will make an exception. Thirty. That's one hundred and thirty overall – guineas of course.'

'Pounds.'

Mrs Lavender took her time thinking about it, but money was money. A guinea was one pound and one shilling. She was being paid more than normal. 'Hard little mare, ain't you,' said Mrs Lavender, superior accent gone, her words doused with the accent she'd grown up with. 'All right. It's a deal.'

They shook hands.

'When,' asked Carole, holding onto the gloved hand; gloves of snakeskin.

'Two weeks' time.' The sharp voice was back. Mrs Lavender took out a notebook from her handbag which looked to be made from genuine crocodile skin. She scribbled something with a tortoiseshell pen. 'Let's say Tuesday the sixth of June at eleven o'clock in the morning.'

Carole nodded. 'I can manage that.'

Mrs Lavender smiled. 'Right. I must be off. I'll see you then. Eleven o'clock in the morning. Remember to bring the baby – and the money of course.'

BRIDGET

Training to be a fully qualified nurse was hard work but enjoyable. London was busy despite its battered appearance, the tumbled wreckage of once handsome buildings, the houses in the East End that had borne the worst of enemy bombing. It was possible to find a few things in the shops and even dine out if you didn't mind too much what was on your plate.

Shopping or dining out could be fun, but in the quieter moments, when all Bridget wanted to do was unwind and connect with someone who wasn't in uniform, she wrote to one of her friends – specifically Maisie or Phyllis.

A snatched moment off duty finally occurred. Tired but determined, she put pen to paper.

Dear Maisie,

I hope Carole gets to appreciate just what a brick you are. Nobody I know is as strong-minded as you. If anyone wants a true friend, Maisie Miles is it, and I for one am very happy that I know you.

No matter what happens, both her and the baby have a

good friend indeed. Wish I was there too. I'm presuming your sewing and knitting skills are improving, but if you need any help don't hesitate to call round to my mother. She'll love helping out. In fact, she keeps asking me when Lyndon and I are starting a family. I keep telling her not yet, not until my training is over and I can finally tell the hospital that I'm married. As I've already told you, nurses are not allowed to be married – at a time when nurses are needed more than ever! Crazy! I'm hoping that things will have changed by the time I finish my training.

I'm learning the hard way that nursing isn't all about a starched uniform and laying a cool hand on the head of an injured man. It's also about scrubbing bedpans, giving bed baths and staying one step ahead of what would be a ward sister in a civilian hospital but in Queen Alexandra's is actually a major!

Sometimes at night I lie awake in bed looking out at the moon and fantasising of the day the Three Ms are together again. I like to think it will happen. You, me and Phyllis, the tobacco girls reunited. I will continue to scrub bed pans etc., until that lovely day.

In the meantime, let me know what you decide about Sid's proposal. What a romantic man he is.

Love, Bridget.

In her letter, she maintained a light-hearted tone, preferring to write about things Maisie could relate to and not giving her cause to worry. The truth was that training was hard. At times, Bridget wished she was back working with the wonderful Mr Gillespie, the surgeon who had recognised her natural suitability for a job in medicine. Things were different here. The training was more regimented, and as trainees, Bridget and the others got the worst jobs.

'Milligan. You're on sluice duty for the next two hours. I want

The underground stations were functioning normally, so Bridget's journey from the hospital to the flat she shared with Lyndon met with no lengthy delays. The main reason was that no longer were Londoners hiding from air raids that had so battered the city back in the Blitz.

Before having a bath, she made a cheese and potato pie ready for the oven.

Once in the bath, she closed her eyes and lay back. Lyndon popped into her head. It worried her that he no longer served in a lecturer/admin mode but had become a navigator in a B17 Flying Fortress stationed in the flatlands of Lincolnshire. But it was what he'd felt obliged to do.

'How can I look some of these young guys in the eye and tell them about England. They're younger than me. I feel obliged to do my bit.'

So off he'd gone not too long before they'd got married. Their wedding had been nothing fancy. Just a three-day pass and a few close friends in attendance. Neither of their parents had been informed until after the event. She could still see her mother's look now when they'd visited Bristol to tell them, a mix of shock and disbelief. Her father had merely accepted it as what she wanted. Lyndon's parents, whether at their home on the Virginian tobacco plantation or their palatial apartment in New York, had so far been silent on the subject. She wasn't of their class, didn't have their wealth. 'In time, they'll come round,' Lyndon had said. 'My dad has, I think.' He'd not gone on to mention what his mother thought. Bridget could guess from his silence that she had not and perhaps never would.

Once out of the bath, hair towelled dry, she fondled the wonderful set of lingerie she'd found in Harrods. In the past, she would never have been able to buy underwear made of silk, but Lyndon had left her with money, telling her to spend it on herself.

The habit of being frugal when growing up was difficult to shift. He'd seen the look on her face and gave her an added incentive to go out and spend, make herself look beautiful. 'Do it for me. Surprise me when I get back,' he'd said to her.

'I will indeed,' she said now, caressing the soft silk camisole top and knickers with one finger. How soft it felt – and exciting.

A squirt of French perfume – also acquired at Harrods – wafted in a fragile mist onto her neck and the inside of her wrists. Stockings, a mint-green light wool dress and she was ready for him. All she prayed was that there would be no hold-ups in his travel plan.

Folding her arms, she looked out of the window, above the leafy treetops and up into the sky. The yellowish smoke of a factory chimney dirtied the sky. Above it, there was only blue. Some way in the distance, she could see what first seemed a company of black dots. The black dots became crosses, a whole squadron of bombers with accompanying fighters. The windows rattled as they flew over but were close enough for her to see the big white star on the side of each of them. Friendly aircraft on their way to enemy territory.

Dry-lipped, she prayed that Lyndon wasn't involved, but, if he was, said a silent prayer. She often did – in fact every time he went up, she prayed for him. Sometimes she prayed whilst at work bustling between the beds, fetching bedpans, turning out lights, seeing things in the shadows that were only there in her mind. At night when she was off duty, she knelt beside her bed just as she had as a child. At other times, she sought solace in the cool darkness of a Catholic chapel near to the hospital where icons and plaster statues added splashes of colour to sepia walls and low lighting.

As the last rumble faded, she clasped her hands together, raised her tear-filled eyes heavenward and pleaded, 'Please keep him safe. Him and everyone.'

A candle flickered and for a moment they seemed to move. Not true of course. They were only plaster, but in her heart, she wished them life in the hope that they could really intervene. 'We've taken marriage vows. Grant us a long life together. In the name of the Father, the Son and the Holy Ghost.'

* * *

That night was everything she'd wanted it to be. Lyndon had arrived home and held her so tightly, she thought her ribs would break. For her part, she really wished that their bodies would melt into one. They were two sides of the same coin. They belonged together.

Together again. At times, she'd dared hope. At times, she'd plunged into fear. He was doing a dangerous job, but here he was. Still alive. Hard flesh tight against her.

They said nothing, just holding each other, her face against his shoulder, his buried in her hair.

'I've made a cheese and potato pie. And I found a bottle of wine in the sideboard. Will that be all right with you?'

He traced his fingers down her face and, smiling, shook his head. 'I don't want it.'

'Okay. How about we go for a drink first at the Bunch of Grapes?'

The pub was a favourite of theirs, very traditional and overlooking the river at Rotherhithe. She was hoping he said no. The truth was, she wanted to go to bed with him right there and then. But best to let him set the pace.

'Too far.'

'It's a fine night for a walk,' she said a little hesitantly, her eyes locked with his.

He shook his head again. 'I don't want a drink. I don't want cheese and potato pie – tasty as I'm sure it is. I just want you.'

'You're not too tired?'

He grinned. 'Are you kidding? Thinking of you got me through. We're ruling the skies now, but you rule my heart.'

Pulses racing, their eyes locked in mutual desire. Absence in their world really did make the heart grow fonder. Not for them food, drink or dancing until gone midnight. All they wanted was each other.

Their clothes – his uniform, her mint-green dress that she'd purposely selected for this evening – ended up in two crumpled heaps. Her stockings, unfurled down to her ankles, her underwear, so carefully chosen to entice – as though he needed any enticing. She could see from the way his underwear hitched on his growing desire before being tossed to the floor.

The bedroom was dark; the cotton sheets cool at first until infected with the warmth of their desire, so intense and undiminished by time. Every time they made love was like the first. Bridget sometimes wondered if the hunger she felt for him would ever be assuaged. She hoped not. She hoped to feel like this forever and ever.

He smothered her cries of delight with his mouth. Lips slightly parted, he moved south over her neck, licking her throat, the indents of her collarbone, her breasts, around her nipples and down over her belly. All the time, his fingers were tangled in her hair.

Earlier she'd prayed for his safety. Now, in this private moment, she prayed for this moment to last forever.

Hips lifting to meet his, she gave one last cry and, chest heaving in the aftermath of passion, fell back against the pillow.

Finally spent, she lay in his arms, gazing intently at his face as they whispered their devotion to each other in the time-honoured way. I love you. She lost count of how many times they said it.

Her fingertips traced the softness of his eyelids as they began to close.

'Rest, my love,' she whispered. 'Rest.'

Muttering wordlessly, he buried his head in the pillow and rolled over. She felt his fatigue but also his joy as he slept soundly, the warmth of his body cupped against hers.

Nestling her face between his shoulder blades, she breathed in the scent of masculinity and strength. Lightly, so as not to disturb him, she traced the full length of his spine, closed her eyes and thanked the almighty that he was here. This was the body she wanted to feel beside her forever.

She had no regrets about marrying him and neither did her family – not now anyway. Her mother had been reticent at first, though Bridget had never quite worked out the reason why. All her life, she'd been closest to her father. He was the one to whom she'd tell her closest secrets. They'd read books and newspapers and discussed what was going on in the world. He loved her very much and she loved him.

However, on the day she and Lyndon had visited the house in Marksbury Road to tell her parents they were married, her father had smiled sadly. His comment had stuck in her mind. 'I knew the day would come when another man would come between us. A chick is only on loan. It's only natural that one day they'll fly the nest.'

Smiling to herself, she snuggled more closely into Lyndon's back, determining that all her dreams tonight would be of their future together. In the meantime, she was careful that nobody at the hospital found out that she was married. She so wanted to continue playing a part in all the new medical developments going on. The war, she thought, had done some good in that direction, encouraging a flowering of more research into all branches of medicine. New procedures and medicines were being constantly developed. And she wanted to be part of it – for as long as circumstances allowed.

As her eyes began to close, Bridget forced her mind to veer towards happy dreams. It was something she'd always been able to do and dreaming of their future and how it would be made for a contented sleep. She would like three children – no, four, a nice even number.

The sound of yet more aircraft flying overhead burst her happy bubble, reminding her that Lyndon was on active duty and the day after tomorrow would report back to his base in Lincolnshire. The moment for sleep was past. In its stead, a frightening reality threatened.

Squeezing her eyes shut, Bridget stroked his shoulder and buried her face in his back. 'Tomorrow and tomorrow and tomorrow,' she whispered. 'I want us to have all those tomorrows.'

9

PHYLLIS – MALTA

Phyllis looked up at the sky, which was very blue and very empty. It hadn't always been that way. Since 1941, hundreds of enemy aircraft had attacked the island in numbers that had turned a blue sky dark with menace. There were ruins everywhere. Honey-coloured stone, warmed by the Mediterranean sun, still lay in heaps waiting to be rebuilt. Passing footfall and the wheels of vehicles sent clouds of dust up into the air. Before the great destruction, the dust had been mortar holding the honey-coloured stone together.

Someone waved to her from the beach. She waved back, not quite sure who she was waving to. The thing was, she'd met so many people, more than she would ever have met back home in Bristol. The world had changed, and she had changed. So had Malta.

The raids had ended and the atmosphere in Malta was becoming less dour, more like the summer sunshine that was just around the corner – glimmering and fresh, a bright portent of better times to come. Better times were round the corner, it seemed, but the dry docks of Malta were still busy repairing and reprovisioning ships heading through the Suez Canal or the straits of Gibraltar and home.

Night-time too had changed. For the first time in a long while, the blackout wasn't so dense. Flames from candles and oil lamps flickered behind slatted shutters and from cafes and bars cut into the city walls. There was more beer and even more food, though mostly pasta and tomatoes. Sometimes rabbit meat. More often fish. The coastal waters were flecked with the lights from fishing boats, spangling the water like sprinkled confidence. There were minefields round the island, but the fishermen were a canny lot. They knew the local waters, their skill passed down from one generation to another. It was as though they navigated by instinct alone, like bats finding their way in pitch darkness.

Having dinner in a nice restaurant had always been a big joke on the island. Back in the bad days of bombings, new arrivals, not quite taking on board how bad things were, asked where they could get a decent meal. The response always floored them, along with the laughter from a Maltese gunner or a British corporal as they waved their hand in the direction of a pile of tumbled masonry. 'That used to be the best place on the island. Don't hold your breath waiting for it to reopen, though they will do – once they can get hold of some food to cook.'

Now the siege was over. Italy had surrendered the previous year and the German army was besieged at Monte Cassino. The sea route from the Atlantic via Gibraltar was no longer so dangerous. More ships were getting through carrying much-needed provisions. What with them, the brave fishermen and the slow breeding of goats and the swifter recovery of the rabbit population, things were beginning to look up.

A party. Everyone wanted a party. The weather being mild, a number were held outside. Like everyone else, Phyllis was glad to get out of uniform and into a dress that positively hung on her due to the amount of weight she'd lost.

'I look like a scarecrow,' she said to Mick.

'You look grand to me,' he countered. She asked him to repeat it, purely because she loved his Australian accent.

Mick was a reconnaissance flyer, a whizz of a photographer, besides being a very capable pilot. She'd been smitten from the start, and fell apart when he'd gone missing, presumed dead when flying reconnaissance over Sicily. By some kind of miracle, he'd survived, rescued by Sicilian partisans, and came back from the dead.

Mick, she'd decided, was the man she should have married, though without this war they would never have met. She would have stayed in a conventional marriage to Robert and been gradually worn down by both him and his dominating mother, but that was in the past.

She'd done her best to clean and brush his uniform. 'No jacket,' he said. 'Shirtsleeves only.'

'What if an officer is there?'

His eyes twinkled. 'I'll just tell him I'm an ignorant colonial who don't know any better.'

She pretended to admonish him, slapping him gently on the shoulder. There was no getting Mick Fairbrother to conform to anything and because he was so good at his job, nobody bothered him much.

Her playfulness was equalled by his. His lips were everywhere and if she hadn't been dressed already, things might have gone further – and she'd have let it.

'We're going to be late,' she murmured between hot kisses.

'We'll have our own party. Here, just the two of us.'

It was difficult saying no, reminding him that they'd promised to be there.

He gave in with a smile on his face. 'Later then.'

She nodded. 'Later.'

There was an air of hope and new beginnings. The alcohol might be a bit watery, the food a bit lacking in taste – no smoked salmon, that much was for sure. But nobody cared much. There was fruit and dried fish, olives, honey and fresh bread. The Royal Navy bakery, slightly damaged a while back, was baking again. Someone had even lit candles along the sea wall overlooking St Paul's Bay, named after the saint who was said to have been ship-wrecked there. People were still nervous about lighting up. The blackout had been in operation for so long. It felt wicked doing so, dangerous too, or at least it had been. Now was a time of read-justment.

There was a good deal of bread and plenty of honey.

'No butter I'm afraid,' said Phyllis as she handed her darling Mick a thick chunk of bread dripping with honey.

'That should go well with this beer. The brewery's up and running again. Victory is ours,' he shouted, raising his glass on high in one hand, his hunk of bread and honey in the other.

Other voices relayed the best news a group of hardened fighters could possibly hear. The hearty toast was accompanied by the clinking of beer mugs, tin cans and glasses – any receptacle that could hold liquid and didn't leak.

Beer, it seemed, was the yardstick on which victory was based, at least to those who had borne so much hardship. Beer was normality.

Mick refilled their glasses, leaned close and kissed her long and pleasurably. 'To us, sweetheart.' The glasses clinked. He kissed her again, then licked his lips and beamed broadly at her. 'You taste of honey.'

'So do you,' she laughed.

Her heart was bursting with love, and she couldn't take her eyes off him. This man made her feel so good. He didn't care much about formality. Life to him was an experience to be savoured and not just by the day, but every hour, every minute squeezed until the pips squeaked.

Once the honey topped bread had been washed down with the third beer, they danced a while, the sea breeze cooling their faces, Mick led her away to a rocky promontory. Waves surged over a small shingle beach. Green fronds of weed ebbed and flowed like a mermaid's hair.

They toasted each other. Toasted the allies. Toasted the Italians who'd had the good sense to surrender. Their voices rang off the rocks. The moon shone a silver path across the water.

They kissed of course. His lips tasted soft and cool. His tongue flicked between her teeth. There was a moment of stillness between them when their lips parted. Their breaths mingled, so close did their lips remain.

His fingers traced the shape of her cheeks, of her jaw. His eyes were fixed on her. He looked thoughtful.

'So, what next?' she said, licking the last of the honey from her lips.

He took his time answering just as he had when he was off on the reconnaissance mission from which he hadn't returned for some while. A dangerous mission that still chilled her blood.

Not again, she thought. *Please. Not again!*

A fist of fear tightened around her heart.

'What is it, Mick? Are you off again? Is it a mission?' Her voice faltered and despite the humid evening, she felt a sudden chill. She covered her eyes with one hand. Suddenly she had a headache.

For a moment, his features were still, unsmiling. It was gut-wrenching to see the intense blueness of his eyes. There was something he had to tell her.

'You're not off up north to Italy...'

'No. No.' He took hold of her shoulders and smiled down into her face. He ran his hands up and down her arms. 'I've been offered a training job. Not just the flying, but training others to use new photography reconnaissance equipment. They reckon I'm the man for the job.'

'Surely you're not the only one who can do it?'

His eyes fixed on her face. 'Reckon I am.'

She saw the sea beyond his silhouette, where diamonds of light danced along the path to the moon. Very pretty, but he filled her eyes, more important than a pretty scene, more important than anyone she'd ever known. There was one question above all others that she needed answering.

'Where? Please don't say it's Monte Cassino.'

A triumphant look lifted his expression. 'No. Not Monte Casino. It's England, darling. I'm being posted to England.'

She gasped. 'When?'

'They want me over there pronto.' He looked away again as though there was something difficult he wanted to say, something he felt awkward asking.

Phyllis felt the warm breeze on her face turn cold. He was leaving her. Yet again, he was leaving her. Okay, it was England and safe, but all the same. They'd be apart.

She shook her head, felt the silkiness of her hair around her cheeks, but there was also anger. 'Mick, I don't think I can take it. You were taken from me once. I don't know that I can face that again. Can you... Will you turn it down? For me? I mean, is there a chance that you might...' Her voice faltered.

'No.' His response was sharp, yet still he smiled. There seemed more he wanted to say, and whatever it was he was nervous about it. He dropped his voice to a whisper, his conversation closed to everyone else around them, all those laughing, singing and talking just a little way away. 'I think something big is coming down. I think it's finally going to happen. That's why they want me over there.'

All flippancy vanished. His look was serious.

It was enough detail for Phyllis to read. Talk of the second front had been going on for a while now, especially since the successful invasion of Italy. The enemy was falling back. The time was drawing nigh when the rest of Europe would be liberated.

'I understand that, but don't you realise how much I will miss you?'

'No, you won't. I'd like you to come with me.'

Hope suddenly soared. 'I might be able to get a posting back there. After all, I've served here longer than any of the other girls. I deserve to go home!'

'You most definitely do.'

'If there's a chance...' Her thoughts whirled and she was filled with joy.

'There's more than a chance if you come back with me as my wife.'

She gasped. Her breath caught in her throat and in that wonderful instant, she felt as though she was drowning.

'We'll get married here in Malta. I've made enquiries. No problem getting a special licence. I've given the padre a date, time enough for us to brush off our uniforms and arrange a bit of a shindig. Alex Dimech, that gunner chap mate of mine, has agreed to be best man.' He looked a bit sheepish. 'Hope you don't mind that I asked him before you'd even agreed for us to get hitched.'

She laughed and shook her head. 'No. Of course not.' This was the most wonderful thing, and she didn't care who came to the wedding. She didn't even care if nobody did. As long as Mick was there. That was all that mattered.

Back in Bristol she'd had a proper wedding with a reception, family and friends. Robert had insisted. His mother had insisted. It had been expected of her, but a wedding with white dress and cake, plus presents and congratulations, didn't make a marriage. A marriage really was a bond, an agreement between two people; that was her view.

He beamed. 'Great! I'll leave the bridesmaids to you. You'll all need flowers for a bouquet, but I'm sure—'

'Mick Fairbrother! You were sure I would say yes.'

He nodded, then drew her head onto his shoulder, kissed her hair and fondled her breast under cover of darkness.

'Yes.' She closed her eyes. Nothing she had ever experienced could match how she felt now. 'Yes,' she said. 'Yes, to everything.'

'That's it then. You're throwing in your lot with old Mick Fairbrother.'

'Yes,' she exclaimed, voice bubbling with delight as he kissed her forehead and felt the warmth of his hands running down her arms. 'I'm going to be Mrs Mick Fairbrother.'

He cupped her face in his hands. His grin was contagious. Like a Cheshire cat, she thought as she did the same. 'You might need to ask permission of your commanding officer...'

'If she doesn't OK it, then I'm going AWOL. Give me the date and I'll make sure I'm there.'

* * *

Before parting company, they sat on a low stone wall above the party that was still going on down on the beach.

Leaning her head on his shoulder, she asked him to tell her again about Australia: what it was like, the house he was going to build, the view through its windows to miles and miles of vines twisting over the earth.

He went into detail, even suggesting how many kids they might have.

'And the sky's always blue,' he finished. 'I promise you that.'

'There's only one promise I really want you to make. I want you to promise me that you'll survive and don't do anything rash, like going up whilst we're still in Malta.'

He kissed the top of her head. 'Don't worry yourself, darling. It's safer now.'

She sighed, rested her chin on his shoulder and looked up at him. 'It's wise not to tempt fate. Stay put on the ground. Promise?'

He promised. 'Though I might have to go up now and again to get the cameras balanced. But mainly it's about teaching young bloods to use the new cameras. Whatever happens next in this war, we need information on enemy forces and territory. The top brass insists that I'm the man for the job. Can't say no, can I?'

The moonlit path across the dark water yet again drew her attention as she considered a return to England. It had been so long since she'd left. She was due a great deal of leave which had been offered her over the years, but she'd always refused because she had no home to go back to. Her only regret was being away from her old friends, the tobacco girls.

A thought occurred to her. 'Would you mind if we got married twice?'

'Twice?' He laughed.

'I mean, get married here and then have another ceremony with my old friends back in England. Even if it's only a party – though I wouldn't mind walking up the aisle twice – if it's with you. Would it be too much to ask?' She looked up at him hopefully.

His finger touched her lips, then traced first the upper lip and then the lower. He smiled. 'You can have whatever you want. I'm a man of the world and I know what I want. I want you, Phyllis. Get it?'

She nodded. 'Yes.'

'Phew,' said Mick, wiping his brow with the back of his hand.

'I've been on tenterhooks all day worrying about whether you'd accept. I need a drink.'

Grabbing her hand, they left the stone wall and made their way to where a lot of laughter, singing and dancing was going on.

Mick dashed into the middle of the party, dragging Phyllis behind him. He took the needle off the wind-up gramophone, which resulted in a din of protest. 'I've got an announcement to make.' His loud voice drew everyone's attention. A whole host of faces turned their way. 'Pour me a drink someone.'

A glass of beer was thrust into his hand, which he raised to the throng awaiting whatever it was he had to say.

'Let me introduce you to the future Mrs Fairbrother,' he said, raising the glass in Phyllis's direction. 'We're getting spliced, and then we're off to England. After that, it's home to Australia with the most wonderful wife in the world.'

Congratulations abounded, along with the sharing of more beer before the gramophone was once more blaring out something jazzy.

In the small moment between the celebration and parting of ways, they found a flat rock hidden from view. The rock had retained the warmth of the day. Beneath a canopy of stars set in an indigo sky, they made love with a new gentleness. The urgency born of the fear of living for today had lessened. Peace was on the horizon and with it a new future for them both.

* * *

Phyllis fell into bed that night, cocooned in the sound of the other girls sleeping and happily looking forward to telling them her news in the morning.

Morning couldn't have come quickly enough and when it did, she bounced up early and blurted out the news. 'Me and Mick are getting married. The date's booked. The padre's booked. All I need now is to invite a handful of guests.'

'Only a handful?' Her old friend Vera acted taken aback. 'Sorry, love. You'll just have to make do with us'

Mariana, one of her colleagues in the plotting room, a pretty, dark-haired Maltese, offered to be a bridesmaid. 'If you want me, that is.'

Phyllis hugged her. 'I would love you to, though I can't offer you a pretty dress for the occasion. It'll have to be uniforms for all of us.'

Mariana frowned. 'No, it doesn't. I've got my little sister's communion dress. My mother made it from an old pair of net curtains. It's very pretty and with a bit of letting out, it'll fit me fine.'

'Oh, how wonderful.'

As she said it, she thought of Mariana looking pretty in lace and her in uniform.

'I don't have a wedding dress. Perhaps we should stick to uniforms for all of us.'

'Not strictly true, darling.' The speaker was Beth, an elegant girl who seemed to know everyone who was anyone on the island and seemed related to quite a few of them. Wives of officers and civil servants were more numerous nowadays. It hadn't been the norm to have wives around during the siege, but as the situation on the island had improved, a number of goodly types had appeared, their upper-crust accents as crisp as their cotton dresses and stiffly styled hair. 'Lady Dartfield has offered her wedding dress to any woman serving in the military.'

Phyllis eyed her reluctantly. In her mind, she visualised something in heavy brocade and very dated. She so wanted to see a flash of appreciation in Mick's eyes.

Beth saw her expression and brayed like an excited donkey or horse; it was commonly known that she was fond of both. 'Stop looking so worried. It's cream satin and would fit you a treat. And there's a veil. Put a few flowers in your hair and you're all set. It'll be fine. No excuses. We'll take a look at it tomorrow. I'll ask her if we can come for tea, crumpets too if we're lucky. And butter, I bet.'

The thought of meeting a titled lady filled Phyllis with dread. After all, she was just a tobacco girl at heart. 'Will I have to curtsey?'

That loud braying laughter again. Beth never took no for an answer and always hammered her ideas home. 'Leave it all to me. We're going to tea tomorrow.'

Oh, my goodness, thought Phyllis. That night, she dreamed of crumpets piled so high with butter that it melted and ran down her cheeks. The scene changed to one where she was curtseying, got her feet tangled up in the train and fell flat on her face.

10

MAISIE

Something wasn't right. She hadn't meant to peer into the biscuit tin where Carole kept her money, Paula's birth certificate and other confidential items. She'd only meant to place Carole's clean underwear into the top drawer. In doing so, she'd knocked off the lid of the tin. Inside was the bundle of money Eddie had brought last Saturday afternoon, along with a page of classifieds from an old newspaper. Maisie's heart flew to her throat as she read the advert Carole had circled in pencil. *A couple in need of a baby.*

A cold shiver ran down her spine. Surely not!

She slumped down onto the bed, holding the piece of paper tightly, so much so that it became even more creased.

It was gone seven at night. Carole had gone out with a friend. Maisie considered facing her with the hard evidence when she got back. Paula was presently asleep, not yet due for another feed.

What should she do?

She read the complete advert again and felt sick inside. But the feeling of sickness was soon replaced by anger.

'Just wait until you get home, Carole bloody Thomas.'

She'd tackle her. That's what she would do, tell her in no uncertain terms how callous she was being. Of course she couldn't give up her baby.

So distressed was Maisie, that the pie she'd made remained untouched on the cold slab in the larder. She just couldn't face it.

Leaving a cup of tea to go cold, she thought about of what she would say.

'You cannot possibly give Paula up just like that... What are you thinking of, you wicked, cruel, young woman!'

She stopped herself. Was it really warranted? What if nothing had yet happened? It was just a piece of paper dated a few weeks ago.

As she sat staring into the gathering dusk, Maisie contemplated the consequences of being too harsh, of even being entirely wrong. If she could just control herself and not fly off the handle, Carole might tell her anyway. Difficult as it was for her to hold back, she had to give the girl a chance. Maisie didn't want to upset her so much that she moved far away. Eddie could facilitate her doing that.

Maisie wiped away a threatening tear. The worst thing in the world was Carole moving out and taking Paula with her. Her world would turn upside down if that happened, so for now, she would let sleeping dogs lie.

* * *

Just in case. That's what Maisie kept telling herself as The Council House on College Green, newly built and very imposing, loomed ever nearer. She was doing this in case Carole decided to have Paula adopted. She'd been quiet on the subject of late but Maisie feared the idea was still there, not spoken of but festering just beneath the surface.

She'd determined to do something, so here she was in the

pouring rain heading for the Children's Welfare Department and feeling as jittery as a cat on a hot tin roof.

Droplets of rain dripped from her umbrella. Water seeped into her shoes and her stockings were soaked. She gave no account to either. It was what she was about to do that filled her mind.

She didn't like people in authority at the best of times. First came the inquisitive look. After that, followed one of contempt once informed of her origins. She reminded herself that she now lived in Totterdown, quite a distance from the Dings and Old Market. And in her own house. Her life had changed greatly since her grandmother had left her the house plus money and a valuable piece of land in Avonmouth. Surely that would act in her favour. She could only hope that it did.

Ida, the closest nowadays of her workmates since the departure of Bridget and Phyllis, had asked her why she was taking the afternoon off.

'Things to do,' she'd replied, unwilling to give anything away. 'I've got holiday days due. Might as well take it while I can.'

Ida had arched an overplucked eyebrow. 'You got some fancy man you ain't told me about.'

'Why, you jealous?' Maisie had retorted.

They'd laughed.

Maisie had voiced the lie she'd already decided to tell. 'I've got a leak in the roof. Need to be there for the bloke who reckons he can fix it. And Bert Higgins is no fancy man, I can tell you. Yellow teeth, greasy cap and lets the wind blow free – if you know what I mean.'

There was a Bert Higgins matching her lurid description, but that certainly wasn't her reason for having the afternoon off. Paula was the reason and the sickening fear that Carole might indeed still consider adoption. So, she'd made the decision to be prepared and here she was standing in front of the new building on College Green, a grand building with a unicorn on the roof at each end.

Calling it The Council House, made it sound as though it was the only one in the country. There were few that came close to looking so grand. Construction of it had begun before the war but faltered once the bombing had started. Now, with the prospect of peace growing ever nearer, building had resumed.

Clutching her handbag in front of her with both hands, Maisie took a deep breath, tucked the closed umbrella beneath her arm. At the entrance, she was confronted by what seemed a never-ending list of departments, piled up one on top of the other, black lettering on white backgrounds. She was that nervous each and every one of them seemed to be bouncing up and down in front of her eyes.

'Get a grip. Read them alphabetically,' she murmured to herself. She took a third deep breath and scrutinised the list yet again until she found what she was looking for. Once assured of where she was going, though fearful of what might transpire, she ventured up the creamy marble steps and into the curving atrium.

More signs pointed her in the right direction. Children's Welfare. Was that typewriter keys she could hear tapping, or just the echoing of her heels? Perhaps even her heart tapping in Morse code that she was a fool to be here.

Finally, the tapping of her heels led her to a sign saying Children's Department and a door saying Waiting Room. She pushed it open.

There were just four iron-framed chairs with canvas seats and backrests in the room. The floor was well polished but being brown did nothing to aid the little light coming through the wire-enforced window. The walls were bare. A bespectacled woman with iron-grey hair was hitting the typewriter keys with unrestricted energy. The metallic noise was nerve-rattling.

Swallowing her nerves, Maisie stood in front of the desk. At the ping of the typewriter carriage return, the typist finally looked up.

'Yes?'

'I need advice about adoption.'

With unflustered efficiency, the woman reached for a pencil and opened a navy-blue ledger. 'Name?'

'Maisie Miles.'

'Have you applied before?'

'No.'

'Take a seat.'

She said all this with her eyes fixed on what she was writing, and once it was done went back to bashing the typewriter keys.

You don't know who I am, thought Maisie. *I could be anyone coming in here and asking this.*

Ten minutes later, the woman's eyelids flickered just once in her direction before getting up from behind her desk. She knocked at the blonde wood of the door behind her. Without waiting for an answer – or at least none that Maisie could hear – she went in.

In just a few minutes, she was out again, the door held slightly ajar behind her. 'Miss Warburton will see you now.

The inner office Maisie entered would have been as stylishly officious as the waiting room if it hadn't been for an old Victorian-style painting of rosy-cheeked children. One of the children was playing with a puppy, another with a ball, a third was blowing bubbles. The sky at the top of the picture was a perfect blue and a profusion of flowers spiked the scene between them and the thatched cottage at their rear.

Miss Warburton, her hair a fluffy mass of pale grey, smiled and with a wave of her hand indicated one of the two Rexine-covered chairs reserved for visitors. 'Please take a seat, Miss Miles. It is Miss, isn't it?'

She looked pleasant enough and her voice was warm.

'Yes. Yes. It is.'

A knowing look came to the kind eyes, coupled with a faint jerk of her chin – almost as though she already knew her reason for being here. 'I can't offer you any tea, I'm afraid. We're rigidly rationed to staff only. But never mind. Make yourself comfortable and ask me anything you want. I'm here to help.' The children's welfare officer smiled, sat back in her chair and clasped her hands together at a point just below her ample bosom.

Although she was all warmth and smiles, Maisie felt uncomfortable, afraid she might not get the advice or assistance she needed. It suddenly occurred to her that the receptionist had not asked her for her address. It seemed odd.

'It's about adoption,' Maisie began. 'I wanted to find out more about the procedure.'

The kindly look and motherly smile intensified. 'I will help you in any way I can. That's what we're here for.'

Maisie felt herself relaxing. This wasn't so bad. 'I don't quite know what's required and how to go about it.'

'My dear,' said Miss Warburton, moving her clasped hands onto the desk and leaning forward, 'your secret is safe with me. Anything you tell me will be in the strictest confidence. You may have noticed that my receptionist only asked for your name. All other personal details are confidential until you have made your decision. And that decision, my dear, is yours and yours alone, though it has to be said that keeping a baby born out of wedlock can ruin your life. I thoroughly recommend having it adopted. Is it a boy or a girl?'

'A girl. Her name's Paula...' Maisie suddenly realised she was stammering, her tongue tripping over the details. There was something quite odd about this questioning.

Miss Warburton began scribbling something in the ledger in front of her – a larger ledger than the one used by her receptionist.

'And the father? Is he still alive?'

'No.'

Suddenly bringing Reg Harris to mind made her blood run

cold. It didn't matter how he'd died. It was the way he'd lived, what he'd done to Carole that sickened her.

'Was he in the forces?'

Maisie shook her head.

Miss Warburton sighed. 'And he left you no assets of any kind, no maintenance?'

The penny dropped along with Maisie's jaw. Her gaze met that of the person on the other side of the desk. Her countenance was still convivial, her lips and eyes still smiling. 'I think you've got it wrong, Miss Warburton. I haven't come here to have a child adopted, I've come to find out how I go about adopting one. A child that's known to me, whose mother may very well wish to let her child go.'

Her statement resulted in the tweed-attired woman looking surprised and sitting upright. The top was returned to the tortoise-shell pen. She then placed it neatly between the inkwell and the blotting pad. 'Oh!' She looked surprised.

'Oh indeed. It seems you misunderstood. Let me explain,' Maisie added, feeling more confident than she had done. 'A dear friend has been left with a baby. She's unmarried but is very young and is considering having the child adopted. I love that baby and am willing to give it a home. I want to know if I can do that.'

It seemed to take a moment for what she'd said to sink in. Finally, Miss Warburton apologised. 'I'm sorry. Looking at you, well, I thought... Never mind. Blow the rationing; let's have a cup of tea.'

There was something surreal about sitting there, drinking tea and talking things over with Miss Warburton, who assured her once again that everything she told her would be in the strictest confidence.

Maisie began to unburden herself. 'It was a terrible thing to happen, so I can understand why my friend wants to give up her child. But, you see, I love that baby so very much.' Maisie shrugged but was unapologetic. 'I have my own house and am quite well off. I also have a good job. I know it won't be easy, but if there is a chance I can adopt her, I would very much like to. Can I do this? Would I be acceptable?'

A spoon rattled in the saucer as Miss Warburton set down her teacup, got up and went to the window. She stood looking out, hands clasped behind her back, which was turned towards Maisie.

'We're becoming overwhelmed with orphans and babies up for adoption. There are presently more children in need of care than there are parents willing to adopt them. However,' she said, turning slowly round, 'recent guidelines mean we still have rules to follow. There's still a market for unauthorised adoption agencies, even though a law has been passed to outlaw their activities. Some are good, some reasonable and some purely in it for profit. In time, they'll be stamped out, but this war... We haven't the resources. It's proving a slow process.'

As she sat back down, she shrugged and spread her hands, a signal of helplessness.

'I understand,' said Maisie, setting her own cup and saucer back onto the tray. 'This war has caused a lot of bad things to happen. I'm thinking that once it's over good things will happen more and more.'

Miss Warburton smiled. 'So do I, Miss Miles. In the meantime, I do hope we can do something to make adopting easier for you. Ideally, we prefer children to be placed with married couples. In our view, it gives more stability. In time, things might be different, but for now we are abiding by the rules despite a growing problem.'

Maisie's laugh was somewhat brittle. 'So I need to find a man willing to take on both me and another man's baby – not even my own.'

'It would put your application in a more favourable light. Do you have anyone in mind? Sorry, I don't mean to be personal.'

'There is someone,' she replied. If only Sid was here. That was her first thought. Her second was that if she wanted to adopt Paula she couldn't afford to wait for his release. Maisie felt herself blushing. Sid was always in her mind, but he was a long way away. Much as he would be ideal for her purposes, there was no chance of him being back in time to carry out her plan.

Miss Warburton smiled and nodded. 'I wish you success. Now I must get on. I've appointments all afternoon. You were lucky we could fit you in.'

Maisie thanked her for her help and the tea. 'It's the first decent cup I've had in ages.'

The conversation they'd had stayed with her all the way down Park Street. It amused her to think of shouting out if there was a man there who would like to marry her. There were plenty of prospects around, men in uniform, some in office suits, plus working men in dungarees, flat caps and wearing work-worn faces. How many would offer? she wondered.

Smiling at her mad thoughts, she made her way across what was still called the Tramway Centre. Tramlines had been blown up by enemy action a few years ago. There were only buses there now. Who would have thought the trams would have come to such an abrupt and destructive end – thanks to bombs blowing up the lines?

And who would have thought I would contemplate marrying a man I barely know, just for the sake of a child? It was crazy and quite improbable. She'd not had a serious relationship with a man, even with Sid. All around her, girls were getting married, many of them far younger than she was.

'You'll end up an old maid,' Ida had remarked.

Her retort had been instant. 'I'll take my time for now. If I'm still unwed at thirty, then it's meant to be.'

But if Carole does make the fatal decision, then I need to be married.

Needs must, Bridget used to say. Maisie hadn't been quite sure what it had meant, but she certainly did now.

* * *

Bootees, nightdresses, napkins, a little knitted bonnet decorated with pink ribbon, a dress decorated across the chest with pink smocking; Carole folded each item with loving precision. Tears weighed heavily in her eyes. She bit her lower lip to stifle each threatening sob. There was still room in the woven suitcase for a small teddy bear Maisie had bought for Paula. More clothes too. Warm clothes. She couldn't bear the thought of her baby being cold.

Once the case was full, she shut it and pulled tight the green leather straps that held it closed. The woven suitcase was where she kept most of Paula's clothes and would arouse no suspicion if Maisie found it.

After Paula's case, Carole turned to packing her own. She wouldn't take much, just enough to tide her over a week or so. London was where she was heading. Paula was going there too but separately with Mrs Lavender. She knew it was a big place and although she was unlikely ever to bump into her daughter, being in the same city, the same part of England, made it seem closer.

She placed both suitcases inside the wardrobe. On the date of the handover and once Maisie had left for work, she would place both in the wire carrier beneath the pram. Paula would go off on one train and she would travel on another. The truth was that she couldn't bear to stay under the same roof as Maisie. Carole preferred to run away – to anywhere in the country really – rather than face Maisie.

She forced herself not to go into the other room where Paula was having her afternoon nap. Instead, she stared out of her bedroom window, watching the rain running like tears down the panes and over her reflection. Only the tears running down her face were nothing to do with the rain. She had no alternative but to harden her heart and keep to her plan. That's what she told herself.

When a break in the clouds came, the rain stopped, but her tears kept coming.

11

Maisie knew that Peter Nichols was doing his rounds when the women's chatter reduced to a lower level. As usual, he stopped by her table and asked the same as he did every morning.

'Everything all right with you, Miss Miles?'

Peter was the new production foreman recently arrived from Swindon number four factory. He always addressed her in a formal manner. He also made a point of asking her whether everything was all right almost every time he walked through her department.

Of course, she was all right and told him so.

'New girls settling in?'

Before her meeting with Miss Warburton, she would have used the same stock reply: 'Yes. They're very good, but they've been here a few months so they would be, wouldn't they?' And would have carried on with her work, kept everything on a professional basis.

His interest had been noted by some of her workmates.

'Yer, I reckon 'e fancies you,' Florence Beck had said. Florence had been widowed back in the Blitz and stayed that way. But despite staying single herself, she had become the factory's unofficial matchmaker.

Maisie had noticed the new foreman's interest in her, but up until now, she had always given the same off-pat answer. 'I'm waiting for Sid to come back. We're unofficially engaged.' She said the same thing every time anyone asked if she fancied that chap or that bloke, and did she have a date tonight. Sid was her shield against likely suitors and the curiosity of her workmates. She'd been out on dates but had never got really serious with anyone. But now the possibility of adopting Paula had changed everything.

Peter looked quite delighted when she broke her off-hand habit and smiled up at him. 'Nice of you to ask. Nice to have a foreman who takes an interest.'

'If you're happy, then I'm happy and the factory is happy,' he replied. He asked her about Totterdown and remarked about the wonderful views of the city from up there.

In the past, she'd merely answer his questions without being drawn into conversation and divulging any personal history. Now she wanted him to linger. She had to show interest for Paula's sake.

'It's a bit of climb, but you're right, Mr Nichols, it's a beautiful view from up there.'

'Peter,' he said, leaning into her and whispering his name. 'Call me Peter.'

It wasn't really done to call foremen by their first names – unless there was something of a friendship or more going on. She'd always been careful never to cross the boundary, but things had changed. She wanted to encourage him.

'Right. Peter. My friends call me Maisie.'

He looked awestruck that she'd intimated him being a friend.

Peter was a nice bloke, though a fair bit older than her. Rumour had it that he'd been in the army, but then his wife had fallen ill and he'd got compassionate leave. Following her death, he'd made a conscious decision to move away from Swindon. Wills's, sympathetic to his circumstances, had offered him the job at Bristol.

Nobody knew why he hadn't rejoined his regiment. Perhaps that wasn't an option. Perhaps he'd had a breakdown. Not all injuries were physical. Some were mental. And he did wear glasses. Perhaps his eyesight had deteriorated.

Peter Nichols was still standing there when the bell went for morning tea. Chairs scraped as, en masse, the stripping room headed for the canteen.

As she got to her feet, Maisie was surprised when Peter asked if he could have a word before she went. Perhaps it was because he was always standing over her that she hadn't noticed that his eyes were brown and kindly. His rust-coloured hair was thick but neatly trimmed as was the thin moustache that followed the line of his upper lip.

'Is anything wrong, Mr Nichols?'

'No, no! Nothing at all.' He glanced around him before saying, 'The fact is, and I hope you don't take offence, but I was wondering if you fancy going out for a drink one night.'

'Well...' she began, pretending surprise, but secretly pleased that he'd responded to her increased warmth so swiftly. 'It's nice of you...'

'Don't feel that you have to,' he said quickly. For a moment, she thought he might have changed his mind, but he hadn't. 'I just thought it might be nice, you being by yourself and me being by myself.'

She wondered whether he knew that Carole and her baby lived with her. She'd been careful not to divulge the information. Carole still felt shame.

Maisie took a deep breath. 'Well, Mr Nichols...'

'Peter. Please call me Peter.'

'Yes, of course.'

'Maisie?'

'Well, Peter. I think that would be very nice.'

He beamed from ear to ear. 'That's fine and dandy! On the steps of the Hippodrome at seven thirty? Would that suit you?'

'Not tonight. It would have to be tomorrow night. I've something else on for tonight.'

Carole had asked her to babysit and although she wanted a relationship with Peter to progress as quickly as possible, she'd promised, and that was that.

'It's not that I'm going out with anyone else,' she blurted, keen for him not to be put off or regard her as fast. 'I've promised to read to the old lady next door. She's losing her sight. I hope you understand.'

'Of course. Of course!'

It was an outright lie and harked back to the days when her grandmother had been alive. Worsening eyesight had indeed resulted in Maisie reading to her.

All in all, things were progressing well, though it sat uneasy with her. She'd had a few dates, gone dancing, been to the pictures, but chickened out when things got too serious. One reason for this was that Sid had always been there in the back of her mind, but that was before Paula had been born. Her immediate intent was to rescue Paula from what might befall her. Not that Maisie could easily push Sid from her mind. Scruffy cards sent from the other side of the world had brought them closer. It wasn't beyond belief that they would get together when the war was over – if it ever ended or indeed if he came back. She tried not to think of the latter, but time and distance were having their toll and she had to deal with the here and now.

She smiled up at Peter. 'I've got this weekend free too, just in case you've got nothing on.'

He looked abashed but still highly delighted. 'No, no. Not at all,' he responded, one set of fingers shielding one eye as though blinded by the light, or nervous: just plain nervous. 'Well... I don't know what to... s-say,' he stammered, obviously surprised that she'd so readily agreed.

'As long as you're providing the grub,' Maisie remarked. 'Then I'll do it.'

She prolonged the smile long enough to make his cheeks deepen to almost the same rusty colour as his hair.

'Right. Right,' he said on a wave of exhaled breath. 'Um... perhaps we... could meet up in the canteen? At lunchtime?'

This is fast going, she thought. But it wouldn't hurt to take things further even at this early stage.

'How about the pub? I could murder a cider shandy. The Barley Mow's handy.'

He frowned. 'I don't usually drink during the day. I'm fit for nothing if I do.'

'Then the canteen it is. Liver and onions are today's offering if the smell coming from there is anything to go by.'

'Followed by apple crumble and custard,' he said and laughed. 'I'll see you then.'

He went off whistling, hands clasped behind his back, just as the others returned.

Flo Beck made comment. ''e looks 'appy. Going out with 'im are you?'

'Yes, it'll make a nice change,' said Maisie.

'S'pose you could do worse. Nice bloke Mr Nichols. You could be in there. Got 'is own 'ouse an all.'

Maisie winked. 'Long as he's got 'is own hair and teeth.'

Flo leaned in closer, her voice dropping to a whisper. 'You know he was keen on Ida a while back. Bought 'er the ring and a wedding date was sorted. They'd only been walking out for a couple of months, but she fell head over heels for a Polish bloke. Pilot, I think. But there you are, most women would go for a military uniform over a foreman's brown overall, wouldn't they. Still, there was a

gushed, keen to reassure Maisie that everything was the same as it always was.

'Have a good time,' Maisie called after her.

It didn't hit her until Carole had gone that she hadn't voiced the usual 'don't wait up'. Neither had she wiggled her fingers in a goodbye wave to the baby.

'I think she might have a hot date,' Maisie whispered to Paula and kissed one tiny hand. 'Not that we're worried, are we. Tonight, it's just you and me. How wonderful is that?'

12

CAROLE

Carole was feeling a mix of emotions as she made her way to the bus stop and the centre of town, where she'd arranged to meet her cousin, Shirley Harwood. It had been something of a shock when, three days ago, she'd been out pushing the pram to the park up behind Arnos Court and bumped into her.

'What's this then?' Shirley had asked. Her thin lips had curled up sardonically, suspicion lurking in her eyes.

Carole had gritted her teeth before replying, determined to give as good as she got. Shirley had always been a bit sarcastic. 'Paula.'

'Yours?'

'Well, I wouldn't be out pushing her if she wasn't.'

Shirley had eyed her quizzically. 'Well, ain't you the dark horse. Didn't even know you were expecting. Husband away fighting?' There was disbelief in her eyes, the comment about a husband thrown at her like a lifeline, a challenge to tell the truth or otherwise.

'Something like that,' Carole had answered and wished the pavement could swallow her up. Shirley. Of all people! Why hadn't she taken a different route with the pram? Why not up the Wells Road instead of down past the park?

'Come on, Carole.' A suggestive smile had twitched at Shirley's bright red lips. 'Pull the other leg, it's got bells on. So, who's the father? You can tell me.'

Carole had smarted and turned angry. 'None of your bleeding business.'

Shirley had tried her best to look hurt. Carole had doubted that she was. 'No need to get like that. We're cousins. Remember? So, what's the story? I ain't 'eard nothing about you getting' married. You'd 'ave asked me to the wedding, wouldn't you – seeing as we're related.'

Carole had swallowed the lies she could have told. Shirley was family and it was a pound to a penny she'd heard rumours. 'I'm going for a walk in the park.'

'I'll tag along.'

Normally at this time of year the flower beds would be bursting with flowers. At present, the beds and even the lawn had been dug up to accommodate rows and rows of potatoes, runner beans and cabbages. Carole had told Shirley what had happened, though left out the probability of Eddie Bridgeman being involved in the death of her attacker.

Shirley's eyes had opened wide as Carole had told her about the rape, the perpetrator and the fact that he'd been discovered dead.

'Drunken fight or somethin', I bet,' Shirley had proclaimed before blowing her nose. 'Got 'is comeuppance anyway.'

'Yeah,' Carole had said. 'He did.'

'Oh well. Water under the bridge,' Shirley had remarked dismissively. 'You're too young to be a mum. Got anyone to babysit?'

'Oh yes.' Carole's gaze had transferred to the few pigeons that were left in the city, a little extra to eke out the meat ration. 'I live with a work friend. She adores Paula.'

'Great. Fancy coming out for a drink? Bet you could do with one.'

Shirley wasn't Carole's idea of great company, but she'd seen so few girls of her own age of late, she said yes.

And so it was that she bounded off the bus, waving at Shirley, who was standing outside the Shakespeare Inn on Victoria Street.

There were ruined buildings in Victoria Street, a wide, long road running from Temple Meads to Bristol Bridge, but Carole didn't care. It didn't matter that the air was thick with the smell of dust and grime. Neither did she give a hoot for petrol fumes from buses or fly-covered manure dropped by the shire horses of Georges Brewery and other horse-drawn transport. She was out on a Friday evening with a girl of her own age. She intended having some fun. Tonight, she would not feel guilty about letting Paula go or not telling Maisie what she was up to. *I'll do that tomorrow*, she told herself. But for tonight, there was no tomorrow.

After Tuesday, she could go out any night of the week. After Tuesday, she'd feel better about it all. As Shirley had said, she was too young to be lumbered with a baby. As it was, she was about to tear her life apart, leave Bristol and find a new life elsewhere. Without telling anyone. Financially, thanks to both Maisie and Eddie Bridgeman, she was fine. But this need to begin again was not about practicalities, more about putting the past behind her.

Leaving would break Maisie's heart, but it couldn't be helped. *It's all for the best*, she told herself, just as Mrs Lavender told her it would be. Despite the turmoil Carole was feeling inside, she held on to that belief. If she didn't, she would crack and break like panes of glass in a bomb blast.

* * *

'Time, gentlemen, please!'

The pub landlord's pronouncement was met with a dirge of grumbles laced with expletives. Ten o'clock and that was it.

Carole was knocking back her sixth drink. The night with her cousin hadn't turned out so bad after all. Feeling decidedly squiffy, she gave Shirley a nudge with her elbow.

'It's been a long time since I enjoyed meself as much as this.'

Shirley, her light brown hair styled in a victory roll and her neckline far too low to be decent, laughed. 'Good for you, Carole. You bleedin' well deserve it.'

It occurred to Carole that Shirley's language was a bit coarse and the dip in her neckline was purposely designed to show what was on offer. After a few drinks, her disapproval had turned to amusement.

'Mind you don't drip your drink down there,' she said, indicating Shirley's cleavage with a jerk of her chin and a sultry grin.

Shirley leaned forward. 'It ain't drink I want down there. I'm in the mood for a bit of 'ow's yer father! With 'im there, if me luck's in.'

The smile she pasted on her face was for a good-looking bloke in a dark suit with wide lapels. His eyebrows were just about on view beneath the brim of his trilby hat. A fine moustache adorned his upper lip in a straight thin line, almost as though it had been drawn on with an artist's paintbrush. He glanced at Shirley but seemed more interested in Carole, gazing at her quite intently through a pall of cigarette smoke.

Carole couldn't work out why Shirley was attracted to him. He looked a bit of a spiv; his whole appearance was just too flash. And why wasn't he in uniform? Black marketeer. He just had to be.

Carole looked away. Shirley did the opposite.

'I've made me mind up,' said Shirley. 'I reckon he can get nylons and things. A bloke worth knowing, I reckon. Watch this.'

Hips swaying, she sauntered through the smoky atmosphere towards the man leaning on the bar.

Shirley didn't care about upsetting the group of Canadians who'd been standing them drinks all night. She had always been a bit of a fly by night – flitting from one bloke to another.

It was embarrassing to watch Shirley tip back her head, smile a wide-lipped smile and run her fingers down the man's silky tie. She couldn't get any closer to him if she tried.

Carole fanned her face. Shirley might not care about acting the tart, but Carole found it embarrassing. She looked away and sipped what was left of her drink.

In minutes, Shirley was back looking none too pleased. The man in the trilby hat threw a look in Carole's direction. Not recognising him, she turned away and sipped her drink.

'Bloody nerve,' said Shirley, flopping down in the chair next to Carole. 'Told me 'e don't buy from a shop showing all that's on offer. Should 'ave smacked both sides of 'is face, I should.' She added a few expletives.

'Spicy words, honey.'

The remark was spoken with an American or Canadian accent, Carole couldn't tell the difference. Neither could Shirley, not that she cared.

She laughed. 'Yeah. That's me. Full of spice, I am. Sugar and spice and all things nice.' Her utterance was followed by her shaking her bosom.

Like blancmange, thought Carole. Embarrassed, she turned away. Still, she couldn't condemn her. Like everyone else tonight, she was out to enjoy herself. But the bloke in the trilby had put a dent in Carole's fun.

She looked over to where he had been standing at the corner of the bar, where there was a '*Squanderbug*' poster. She'd always hated that poster, thought it scary enough to give some poor souls nightmares.

The Canadian who'd shown an interested in Shirley was joined by a colleague.

'Have a drink with us. This could well be our last night in Bristol.'

'Don't mind if I do,' said Shirley.

Carole thanked them but pointed out that it was close to closing time.

The Canadians chivvied the landlady for one last drink.

'Mr Churchill don't allow it,' she told them in a loud voice as her fingers curved into the rims of half a dozen pint glasses.

'Bet he's having a few stiff ones tonight,' said one of the Canadians. 'Things being the way they are...'

The second soldier gave his mate a nudge. 'Steady on, Greg. Careless talk costs lives.'

'I hear you, Gary. I hear you,' the second Canadian responded.

'I'd better be going,' said Carole, who was feeling a bit light-headed. She eased herself up from the table, wanting to be home with dear Maisie and the baby she didn't want – or did she?

Shirley, who was canoodling with one of the rugged Canadians, protested, 'Oh come on, Carole. It's only ten o'clock.'

'The pub's closing.' Carole clutched her handbag with both hands as though that might assist her in staying upright.

The second Canadian gave her a bear hug that almost squeezed the breath out of her. 'Sure you got to go home now, doll? You ain't gonna lose your glass slipper and I ain't going to turn into a frog. How about it, huh?' His breath on her face smelt of whisky.

Despite the onset of responsibility, Carole was suddenly torn. The young men were responding to her in the same old way she remembered from before she'd fallen for Paula.

'I've got somebody waiting for me,' she said in a coquettish manner, tossing her creamy white curls as she pushed him away.

'Well, ain't he the lucky one.' He looked put out.

'It's not exactly like that...' she stammered. 'I have responsibilities.'

She looked up at Gary the second Canadian and a full foot taller than Greg.

He smiled. 'I don't mind if you're married, if you don't.'

'Cheeky bugger!' She held up the ring finger of her left hand. 'Do you see a ring on there?'

He looked at her finger and shook his head, his eyes meeting hers. 'No husband?'

'No. An aged aunt who needs looking after.'

Maisie would have had a fit if she'd heard her. She could imagine her saying what a saucy hussy she was to describe her as an aged aunt, then bursting with laughter.

'Don't you fancy going to a club?' asked Gary, spreading his arms around the girls' shoulders.

Carole remained unwilling, her thoughts on the baby she professed not to want. Shirley was drunk and far from being reluctant. Greg was all over her, his hand down the front of her dress.

'Oi,' shouted the landlady, who had resumed her almost constant duty of collecting glasses. 'Cut that out. This is a respectable 'ouse.'

Shirley put up her two fingers in a rude sign behind the landlady's back.

'Come on, Carole. You're out for the first time in ages. Kick up yer heels. Yer only young once.'

'Sure,' said Gary, leaning so close she felt the slight brush of his lips against her hair. 'Young and beautiful. That's you.'

Shirley and their new acquaintances combined to keep up the pressure. What with that and the drink, Carole finally weakened.

'Okay. Okay. But only for an hour, then I'm off 'ome.'

Beneath a star-spangled sky, the four of them made their way down to where the upper storeys of warehouses used to jut out over the river. Thanks to the air raids of a few years back, all that was left was a few tumbled stones and a jungle of weeds through which a path had been cleared. The jagged edges of remaining walls of buildings threw black and menacing shadows. The smell of the river was rank, and the reeds and bushes rustled. Suspecting the rustling was caused by rats, Carole shivered.

The dark was all-embracing. No air raids had occurred for a very long time, but a blackout was still in force. Flying bombs had been dropped on London culminating in yet more destruction.

Carole began to get nervous. 'Are you sure there's a nightclub here?'

The path was stony and edged with fallen brickwork, broken timber and glass that crunched underfoot.

'It's all right,' Shirley giggled. Her breath was sharp with gin. 'I've bin yer before. Not sure where the entrance is though. Along by the river somewhere.'

Carole had little faith in her finding the way and said so. 'You're drunk.'

'Just as well. Smell that river? Stinks to 'igh 'eaven, it does. That's 'ow you find this place. Just follow yer nose.'

With the two Canadians following close behind, Carole reached out to grab Shirley's shoulder. The blackout meant no street lights, and curtains were still tightly drawn across windows. It would be easy to get lost, to sprain an ankle or fall flat on her face.

Shirley began to sing 'Roll out the Barrel' and skip along the uneven path. Fired up with enthusiasm and too much drink, she danced off, still laughing like a drain and staggering over the uneven ground.

Carole hurried after her, though more cautiously, afraid of falling and cutting herself. 'Shirley! Slow down.'

It was no use. Like a whirling dervish was a statement Carole had heard of but never been quite sure what it meant. Shirley was whirling all right, a black figure in blackness, though not for long.

Suddenly, a loud scream ripped through the air.

'Shirley!'

She'd gone. Disappeared.

The darkness was too dense and the path too uneven for running, though Gary and Greg managed it well, their long strides devouring the uneven ground.

From the darkness came a sequence of screams.

'Help! Help!'

The sound was hollow as though shouted from the inside of a bucket.

'Jesus! Where's she gone?'

A strong torch beam picked out the blackness ahead of them. Another joined it.

'Go easy,' said Gary. She felt his hand on her shoulder holding her back. 'This ground isn't firm underfoot. Go easy, dead easy.'

Carole was frantic. The last time she'd been in such a place it was daylight and Reg Harris had been dug out of the rubble.

The two Canadians conversed and decided they needed help. 'I'll see if I can find someone.'

Greg went back down the path, cupped his hands around his mouth and bellowed. 'Hey, anyone! We need some help here. There's been an accident.'

'All right, mate,' somebody shouted back.

Other voices answered, sounds without human form in the dense darkness.

Beams of light danced over the stony ground and blackened walls.

About half a dozen men converged on the spot they were standing. Gary and Greg tried to explain, but Carole's screeching voice shouted out louder.

'My cousin, Shirley! She's fallen down a hole.'

'Right, love. Right. Now stand back and we'll see what we can do.'

Torchlight picked up the letters ARP on a couple of tin helmets. The other men looked to be soldiers on their way home after a night out.

Large flashlights carried by air-raid wardens flitted over the dark, stony ground. Other smaller beams flitted like fireflies. Army boots crunched over broken glass.

One of the British soldiers stumbled. The warden reprimanded him immediately.

'Tread carefully, mate. One down an 'ole tonight is more than enough.'

He turned back to where Shirley had vanished.

'Shirley! Can you 'ear me?'

Shirley's voice came back loud and clear. 'Course I can bloody 'ear you. Get me out of yer!'

'She's not the grateful type,' Carole explained.

The ARP warden grunted something unintelligible, then shouted again.

'We'll 'ave you out of thur in no time. Just sit tight.'

'Just 'urry up! I need a wee.'

'You can go down there. Nobody's going to see you.'

'Bloody charming. Don't come down 'ere until I've been.'

Carole shouted at her. 'Keep shouting. It'll help us locate where you are.'

'I'm in a hole. A bloody great hole! Get me out of yer.'

'Sounds in good spirits,' remarked one of the wardens.

A minute after he'd said it, the pitch of Shirley's voice became a scream and then a series of sobs. 'I don't want to die. I don't want to die!'

More would-be rescuers, attracted by the noise and beams of

light flashing over the remnants of what had been Bristol's finest shopping centre, were coming to give a hand. The news that a young woman had fallen down a hole spread quickly.

'Not another,' remarked one of the crowd, a statement, rather than a question.

'Where's she gone?' asked a newly arrived spectator.

'Fallen down into the cellars,' said the same informed voice. 'All the big shops in Castle Street had cellars. The buildings up top were destroyed, but the cellars are still there. Some of them open directly onto the river.'

Like bats seeking a cave, beams of torchlight fell on the same black spot.

'Bloody 'ell,' murmured one of the wardens.

His flashlight had picked up the hole through which Shirley had fallen. It had also picked out the trickling of loosened and powdery fine earth.

'If enough of that's disturbed, she could be buried alive.'

The statement was delivered in a low voice from one man to another.

'Everyone, stay back,' shouted the warden who had taken charge.

There was just enough light for Carole to notice his worried expression. Without him needing to explain, she knew the trickle could easily become a landslide.

'Can you get her out,' she whispered.

He cleared his throat and looked away. 'She ain't the first to fall down one of these, and not the first I've 'ad to haul out. And the sooner, the better.' Fists on hips, flashlight tucked beneath his arm, he surveyed those gathered. 'Right, lads. This is what we need to do. I need a big bloke to go down there and get 'er out. Someone tall with broad shoulders and strong arms. Anyone good at climbing? Mountaineering or something similar? Any volunteers?'

Gary declared he was willing and was an experienced climber. 'I'll go down. Just tell me what to do.'

Shirley had fallen silent except for the odd sob. All the stuffing had been knocked out of her. This in itself was surprising. Although she told herself she had no need to do so, Carole feared the worst. The trickling earth was ominous and likely to increase.

Thanks to almost everyone having a torch, the place where Shirley had disappeared was lit up like a Christmas tree.

Desperately needing to know she was all right, Carole shouted. 'Shirley! Can you hear me? Are you still there?'

'Well I ain't bloody going anywhere being stuck in a ruddy great 'ole, am I,' she screamed back. 'Get me out of yer.'

A thick rope was obtained and tied around Gary's waist, the rest of the length thrown over a handy beam, once part of a roof truss and overhanging the spot where Shirley had disappeared. Four burly blokes, including Gary's mate Greg, resembled a tug of war team. Their legs were braced, their fists knotted with rope.

The man who'd taken charge gave instructions and used his hands to emphasise what he wanted done. 'Lower 'im slowly now. And when you get down, put the rope round 'er and we'll pull 'er back up. It's narrow and we can only get one of you up at a time.'

'I'll play it by ear.'

Gary's response was ambiguous. Carole wondered if the warden realised that Gary might or might not do as he was told. Not that it mattered. All that mattered was getting Shirley back up before she was buried in dirt.

Heart in her mouth, Carole observed the slow and steady progress of the big Canadian being lowered into the void. A slight fall of earth was disturbed as he bumped against it.

'Be careful!'

'Keep back,' shouted the warden, turning to address the growing crowd of spectators. 'Shine your torches over there, but don't attempt to go any closer. The whole thing is likely to collapse and then we'll all be like pussies in the bleedin' well!'

Lewd comments and laughter were reprimanded with a loud command to be silent.

'This ain't a comedy act at the Hippodrome. Somebody's life is at stake.'

The crowd fell silent as, bit by bit, Gary disappeared.

A few minutes and he shouted up, 'Okay. I'm ready.'

'Right. Get ready to pull.'

The four men holding the rope rebraced their legs, flexed their biceps and began to heave.

'One, two, one, two...'

They kept up an even momentum, leaning into the rope, heaving and leaning back.

Carole prayed the falling earth would remain just a trickle until Shirley was rescued.

A shout of joy went up. 'Here she comes!'

As expected, Shirley's head appeared. She was grinning from ear to ear.

'Whoopee doo,' she shouted, waving her arms in the air just as she'd been waving them when she'd met with her accident.

Shirley was not hanging onto the rope as she should be. Neither was it tied around her waist. Another few careful tugs and the reason became obvious. Shirley was perched on Gary's shoulders. Her skirt had ridden up and her stocking tops were showing. Not that she seemed to care, in fact she looked very pleased with herself. She waved her arms in the air as though playing to a fanfare. 'Da da!'

Carole couldn't help think she looked like a circus acrobat taking a bow.

'Don't nobody obey orders any more,' grumbled the chief warden.

'Depends on the circumstances,' remarked Greg with as wide a grin as Shirley's.

There was clapping as Shirley was grabbed from Gary's shoulders and taken onto firm ground.

'Well, that was one hell of an experience,' laughed Gary. 'Must do it again sometime,' he called out to Shirley as he swung himself onto firm ground.

The clapping reached crescendo level when Shirley gave him a hearty hug and a huge kiss.

'Any time you like, big boy.'

He offered her a silver hip flask and told her to take a big gulp.

She didn't hesitate. 'Ta, very much. Don't mind if I do.'

One, two, three times she tilted up that silver hip flask and rounded it off with a gasp of sheer pleasure. She passed the flask back to Gary and swiped her mouth with the back of her hand.

'Anyone else want a drink?' Nearly everyone indicated that they did, until he held up the hip flask and gave it a shake. His face a mix of light and shadow, Carole saw his surprise. 'Sorry, folks. Not from this baby. The lady was thirsty.'

After tipping the last drop into his throat, Gary slid the flask back into a trouser pocket.

Shirley defended her action. 'I was thirsty. You wouldn't deny a girl a drink after what she'd been through, would you?'

Carole shook her head. 'Of course not.'

'Thanks, Carole. Wouldn't mind another though.'

'I could drink a river,' exclaimed Gary. 'It's getting late. Is this club around here or ain't it?'

Somebody, a British soldier, informed Gary. 'There's one right yer. Right under yer feet. Just walk along the river a bit. Better still, follow me.'

'It is. I've bin there,' said Shirley. 'Can't quite work out where the entrance is, but close by – I know that much. You can drink a river if you like then, Gary. You deserve it,' she said, looping her arm in his. With the other hand, she ruffled the dirt from her hair.

Carole looked towards the river and wrinkled her nose. 'You might want to drink a river, but you wouldn't want to drink that one.'

It raised a laugh. The river was indeed close by and smelt of long caked mud, oil, water rats and rotting timbers. Nobody in their right mind would drink it.

They followed the British soldier, who whistled as he walked. 'The beer cellar is along yer. Ain't bad either.'

'Are you sure you know where it is?' Carole asked.

'Follow the rats,' someone said and laughed.

Carole called to Shirley who was still arm and arm with Gary. 'Can I have a word in private?'

Shirley leaned back and tilted her head, half-hearted attention. 'What is it?'

'I really should be getting home. Can you come with me? I don't fancy going by myself.'

'No! I'm not going home. I ain't ready for me bed even if you are.'

'I hung around for you.'

'Oh,' said Shirley in a shirty and tipsy manner. 'You blaming me for falling down that bloody hole?'

'I'm just saying that we wouldn't have been out so late if you hadn't fallen down it.'

Shirley laughed. 'You might not have done, but I certainly would have.'

In the face of Shirley's selfishness, Carole considered her options. Making her way back by herself was daunting. She considered asking Greg, but he was concentrating on sharing a packet of cigarettes, the orange tips glowing in the dark.

'That's it,' exclaimed one of the soldiers. 'See it?'

Carole's gaze landed on what the soldier had seen. A speck of red light seemed to glow from the very earth itself.

'The entrance is down them steps.'

'Good job,' said Shirley. 'I could murder a port and lemon.'

'You deserve one,' said the soldier. 'Must 'ave frightened you to death.'

'Too right it did,' returned Shirley, laying it on thick in an effort to obtain both sympathy and a few free drinks.

The soldier went down what looked to be only a small flight of steps. There was the sound of knocking, followed by the scraping of a very stiff door opening. Muffled voices, that of the soldier and whoever had answered the door. The soldier's words were more understandable as he told the doorkeeper what had happened.

'A right bunch of 'eroes I got yer, mate.'

Carole held back. She had a funny feeling about this. Besides, she so wanted to go home. The feeling was unexpected. She'd once craved going out and having fun, but now... she wasn't so sure.

'Are we going in or what? I'm dying for a drink,' Shirley moaned down to the soldier.

'The bloke on the door's gone to ask the boss if it's okay. They should 'ave remembered me name, but they don't.'

The soldier had obviously thought himself a memorable figure. Carole almost felt sorry for him. Uniforms made men uniform, alike by virtue of the clothes they wore.

The man who had gone to ask permission returned. 'The boss says for you all to come inside. The first round is on the 'ouse.'

En masse, the crowd, cheering, laughing and still slapping each other on the back – even those who had not contributed to the rescue effort – surged forward, reducing to single file as they went down the steps into the narrow alcove and through the equally narrow door. Carole was carried along with them.

The British tommy led the way. 'Blimey. More bleedin' stairs.'

The stairs were steep. To Carole, it seemed as though they were heading down into the earth. A reddish glow lit bare stonework at the bottom. The doorman pulled back a red velvet curtain hanging in an arched opening. He pointed to another set of stairs. Well, it was a cellar. 'Go on through where that curtain's 'anging and down the next lot of stairs.'

What was it with red velvet curtains? As though they were entering hell, thought Carole, who had stalled, but was pushed onwards by those behind.

'Don't mind if I do,' said Gary.

Greg had taken control of Shirley, so it was now him holding onto Carole's hand and guiding her down the narrow stone staircase. The smell of the river came up to meet them, along with a fug of tobacco smoke, cheap perfume and sweat. She heard jazz playing, though wasn't that knowledgeable to say for sure.

'Didn't this used to be the old Co-op store,' said somebody behind her.

Another man at the foot of the stairs, almost as wide as the stairwell, heard the question and answered, 'Never mind what it used to be. It's the Blue Venus club now and everyone's welcome.'

The two Canadians, Greg and Gary, headed for the bar, leaving the girls to find the toilets and sort themselves out.

'Just look at the state of me.'

Carole helped Shirley brush the dirt from her hair and clothes. 'Hang on. You've got a dirty face.' She wetted a corner of her handkerchief and got off what she could. 'That's the best I can do.'

'Well, it's a bit dim down 'ere, so I don't expect anybody will notice. Blimey, I was lucky though, weren't I? I wondered where the bleedin' 'ell I was.'

'I'm not surprised.'

It surprised Carole that someone who'd been close to being buried alive had recovered so quickly.

'Turned up trumps though, didn't we,' said a totally unflustered Shirley as they headed back into the club. Her eyes were already skimming over the men crowding around the bar. 'Nice club this. And a free drink to start with. Can't be bad.'

Carole narrowed her eyes. She'd never been here before, but she had an inkling of who owned it. Shirley was right though; it wasn't bad.

Candles stuck into old bottles provided a flickering and muted light. The bar appeared to be made from the lower half of a Welsh dresser, the upper half fixed to the wall behind it. Row upon row of bottles ranged along the shelves reflected the stronger light from three bare electric bulbs hanging immediately behind the bar.

The main body of customers were mostly men in uniform. Some wore flash-looking suits. The women were overly made up. The new arrivals were regarded with only the most fleeting interest – except for one face, one set of features that was fixed on her.

Eddie. She'd guessed right.

His eyes stayed fixed on her whilst he talked out of the side of his mouth to the man standing next to him. The brim of his trilby hat half hid his face. She took it he didn't want his face to be seen or remembered.

The conversation finished, Eddie stubbed out his cigar and began weaving his way between a mix of round or square, tables for two, tables for four, all a mishmash of different sizes and styles.

Distracted by the sight of Eddie Bridgeman, the man who claimed to be her father, the man she suspected of killing Reg Harris, she'd failed to notice that Shirley had sidled closer to the bar, amid men, just as she liked to be.

Carole smiled as Eddie approached her and expected him to smile back, glad to see her. He always gave that impression when he dropped off money or chanced to see her out and about.

Not now.

In the semi-gloom, his features were almost demonic, the stuff of nightmares.

'What you doin' out? Why ain't you at 'ome looking after my granddaughter?' His tone reflected the look in his eyes.

She felt like a naughty child told to stay in and do their homework. Homework in this instance was Paula.

'Just having a night out.' Her smile was faltering.

'With a bloke?'

'No. My cousin, Shirley. That's her over by the bar.' She jerked her chin to where Shirley was laughing and joking with a group of soldiers.

Eddie's look darkened. He looked as though he might grab Shirley and throw her out the door. 'Does she charge?'

Carole knew what he meant and roundly refuted such an idea. 'She just likes a good time.'

Just then Gary came over and interrupted. 'I bought you a drink, babe.'

'Thank you.'

Her fingers barely touched the glass, before Eddie knocked it back. The glass flew.

Gary looked shocked. 'Hey! There was no need for that.'

Eddie glowered at him. 'Shove off, soldier. My daughter's thankful for the drink, now clear off.'

'Huh?'

Gary, big, strong and sure of his youthful strength, looked in two minds until Eddie's words sunk in. 'She's your daughter? Sorry. I didn't know that.'

Eddie's hand slammed against Gary's chest. 'Get yerself a drink up at the bar. Tell the barman it's on me.'

Gary was shrewd enough to know that it wasn't so much an offer as a warning. To his credit, he held his ground.

'You okay with that, babe?'

She nodded. 'Yes. It's fine.'

'In The Mood' began blaring out from a gramophone. Soldiers, sailors and airmen, plus women in uniform, began jitterbugging. Girls out of uniform and wearing their best dresses, hair teased and primped into the latest styles, glided around the dance floor. The smooth swing band music changed to jitterbug tempo. Women who had been clasped close to their partners' chests now kicked their legs. It didn't matter that the legs of some of the dancing women were coloured with gravy browning. Some of the girls were lucky enough to have lovers who could get their hands on real stockings.

The jitterbug usually had Carole tapping her feet, but not now.

'Now don't get me wrong,' said Eddie, his voice low, his fingers tight on her arm. I'll do all I can for the little girl – Paula ain't it?'

'Yes,' said Carole. Even to her own ears, her voice seemed a million miles away. She wondered what he would say if he knew she was considering adoption. Best not to tell him. He was possessive enough about her. How would he be about her baby? Yes. She'd be right to leave Bristol and start a new life on her own elsewhere. She didn't like feeling vulnerable so hit back with the only question that might put him off balance. 'Did you kill Reg Harris?'

It was barely a beat before he replied, 'What if I did? Bastard deserved it. Never mind that. You can depend on me, love.' He flicked her cheek with one finger. 'Anything you want, just ask. Did you like the pram and stuff?'

'Yes. Very nice.'

'Who's looking after the nipper tonight?'

'Maisie Miles.'

He gave a deep nod. A dim overhead light picked out the gleam of his Brylcreemed hair. 'Like I told 'er, I own a flew flats and 'ouses. You can 'ave one, you and the nipper, if you like. She told you that, didn't she? Anything you want, you can' ave. Just say the word.'

Carole was struck dumb. She'd no idea about Eddie offering her a flat or house. Maisie had not told her. It angered her that Maisie had purposely withheld Eddie's offer. Not that she would necessarily have taken it up. 'I didn't know,' she said softly.

Eddie took a firm grip on her arm. 'Well, little girl, it's time you were going home to my granddaughter.'

'I can't leave Shirley...'

There was disgust in the look Eddie threw at Shirley. 'You don't want to be out with the likes of 'er. Now come on. Off 'ome with you. Jeff?'

A big guy in an American uniform answered to the name being called.

'Take my little girl 'ome, will you?' Eddie held up a warning and decidedly stubby finger. 'And no funny business or you'll answer to me. Got that?'

Carole was flabbergasted. An American soldier working for Eddie? How had he managed that? Did the army know of it? Her mouth was too dry to say anything.

'Give my regards to Maisie and tell 'er I've forgiven 'er for what she did in the past. I'm just grateful she took you in. A young girl needs someone she can talk to and your mate over there,' Eddie jerked his chin to where Shirley was draped over yet another man in uniform. 'Bit of a tart. I don't like you going around with 'er.'

'Is she too much like my mother?'

He grinned. 'She weren't always like that. Believe me, she weren't. Still,' he shrugged. 'You've landed on yer feet. Maisie Miles is straight as a die, even though she comes from the Dings and her stepfather was a loser.'

Carole wanted to tell Shirley that she was being given a lift home, but Eddie didn't give her chance.

'Come on. Get yer things together. You got a coat?'

She shook her head and suppressed a shiver. It had been warm earlier, but it was late and had been spotting with rain when they'd got here.

'Hang on. I'll get you one.' He snapped his fingers. 'Get this young lady a coat, will you?'

A woman, her features sallow and washed out in the muted light, brought a trench coat. It looked like a man's coat and felt warm when he draped it around her shoulders.

'That's my coat,' said Eddie. 'Don't worry about bringing it back. I'll get it collected.'

More dance music started up. Shirley was swept onto the dance floor, for which Carole was grateful. There'd be too many questions that she had no wish to answer. Rumours would instantly grow into gossip and now, more than ever, she wanted to leave Bristol and her old life behind. Paula too.

Today was Friday. Tuesday, the date for meeting up again with Mrs Lavender was fast approaching. *Best for both of us*, she told herself. After that, the world was her oyster and she could begin all over again. The only fly in the ointment was telling Maisie. It wouldn't be easy, and heaven knows what Eddie's reaction might be once he found out.

A rectangle of light fell out from the club door as Eddie watched Carole get into the jeep. Officially no light should show; the blackout was still in force, but the ARPs were less vigilant than they had been, especially round here. The top rubble of the bomb site had been cleared away, but it was still grim. The only road was a dirt track and there were no street lights. Unless you were extremely familiar with the way through, the ground underfoot was unstable. Carole's friend had found that out and now Eddie was going to deal with her.

Shirley was hot and breathless, boobs bouncing and in danger of popping out of her dress. Sweat trickled into her cleavage.

Eddie grabbed her as she took a breather after she'd ordered one of the soldier boys to get her a drink. 'A word, miss.'

'Sure,' she said, her eyes drinking in a man who looked like he could handle himself. A man of means. 'What can I do for you? Just say the word...'

The slap he landed on her face jerked her head to one side. 'Don't ever go near Carole again. Right?'

Shirley's eyes were round with surprise. Her hand covered the cheek he'd slapped, but she wasn't the sort to be cowed. 'I'm 'er cousin,' she said with a snarl of defiance.

Eddie pressed his face close. 'I don't care who you are. Keep away from 'er. Got that?'

Greg came over with another drink. 'Everything all right here.'

Eddie smiled in a warning, like a snake just before it strikes. He leaned closer and whispered into the Canadian's ear, 'Soldier. The night's young, the girl's wild and willing. Take what's on offer whilst you still can. Live for the minute, son. You're a long time dead.'

At first, the soldier's face was tense, unsure what to say, until the words scythed through the fog in his brain. It didn't take long. The end game of this war was like a breath on the wind, unseen but felt. A nerve flickered beneath one eye. Tension left the youthful face. In the blink of an eye, he looked older and wiser, resigned to a future he might or might not have.

'Got that?' Eddie's eyes blazed.

The soldier looked to where Shirley was waiting for him, arms crossed and red lips tightly clenched. He grinned at Eddie and winked. 'Hell, you're right. Thank you, sir. Much appreciated.'

Eddie went back to the bar. The club was crowded, though not to bursting point as it had been in the depth of war. Things were changing. Rumours of a second front were afoot, and he reckoned that was about right. There'd been drills and mock battles before, necessitating the movement of troops, but never like now. He'd heard from Jeff that the army camps were emptying fast. It was beginning to look as though the whole garrison England had become was heading for the south coast. These Canadians were the stragglers, probably logistics men left to count what was left and make sure it followed the advance guard.

The war had been good to him. The black market had thrived, and he'd thrived with it. Demand and supply had been what it was all about. He'd never given much attention to business – straight business – before. After the war was over, there were bound to be other opportunities. The world destroyed would be a world in need of rebuilding. The secret was to work out the percentages of profit to be made. And he, Eddie Bridgeman, would be there at the rebuilding just as he'd been making money in the thick of it. The future was his for the taking.

He stretched out the hand that held a cigar. The flame of a gold lighter ignited the end of it before the man who'd obliged applied it to the tip of his cigarette. His eyes followed the same trajectory as Eddie's. Shirley's head was thrown back, her throat exposed, her red-lipped mouth loud with laughter.

'George, I've been thinking what 'appens next in business,' said Eddie. 'A bit of black market will still be there, but I'm thinking big. What they going to do with all that scrap metal after the war? They'll want to get rid of it quick and cheap.'

'But if it's cheap, what's the point? Cheap to buy, cheap to sell...'

'Rebuilding! There's going to be rebuilding. Metal for girders, window frames and suchlike. Lorries for hauling gravel. Do you get my meaning?'

'You're the boss, Eddie. You always get the angle,' said George, a broad smile spreading the thin pencil moustache. 'Could make a fortune.'

Eddie drew in another satisfying lungful of tobacco. 'That's what I intend to do.'

He said nothing about why he wanted to be successful. He had a grandchild now. Hard to accept, but at some point, he would die, and somebody would inherit everything he left behind. Carole would get a cut of course, but now there was Paula. He'd never taken to kids, but this was different. Carole was his daughter – or according to her mother she was. And despite everything, Paula was his. He liked that. Made him feel almost respectable.

'All we gotta hope is that this war really is over soon,' said George. 'Fingers crossed, eh?'

'Yeah. Fingers crossed,' returned Eddie, smiling through the smoke. 'Fingers crossed.'

* * *

Maisie had waited up. Her hair was pushed beneath a hairnet, her face was devoid of make-up, and she was wearing a pink candlewick dressing gown. 'You're late. I thought something might have happened to you.'

Carole had no intention of telling her what had happened. Shirley had been rescued so that was all right. Instead, she told her what would worry her the most.

'We ended up at Eddie's club in Castle Green. He insisted I be driven home.'

A strained look came to Maisie's face. 'Eddie brought you home?'

'Someone who works for him.'

Even though the driver, Jeff, was in the armed forces, she guessed he was moonlighting.

'Do you want anything to eat? Toast? A cup of cocoa?'

'No,' said Carole, tight-lipped and offhand.

'It's best you keep away from him.'

'Should I?' Carole's look was fiery. Her hair, tousled by the damp air, swung around her chin. 'He's my father.'

'That may be... but—'

'You didn't tell me he was willing to give me a place of my own.'

Maisie winced. 'Surely, it's best you stay here...'

'Ha! That's what you'd like, isn't it! Me staying here, but not for me, just so you can keep Paula. Fine. How about you giving up work to stay at home with her? I'd like to have a decent job, you know, just as I used to. But I can't. I'm trapped, Maisie. Bloody trapped.'

Maisie sprang to her feet. 'Carole, you can't say that. I'm just trying to do the best for you both.'

Carole's eyes were moist but angry. 'It's for me to make the decision as to what's best for both of us. Me and me alone. So, I'd thank you not to tell me that it's best for me to stay under your roof. It's down to me. Now, goodnight. I'm tired and I don't want to talk about it any more.'

Maisie followed her upstairs. Carole rounded on her at the top.

'Whether you like it or not, it's my choice where I live and whether I choose to give Paula up for adoption. You must accept that, Maisie. You must.'

'But you belong here,' said Maisie, shaking her head in disbelief.

'No. You want to keep me here, Paula more so than me. It's not your decision to make. I've decided, and that's it.'

She saw Maisie's jaw tighten.

Unable to stand this supercharged moment, Carole flounced into her own bedroom, went to the top drawer of the dressing table and fetched out the newspaper and subsequent letters between her and Mrs Lavender.

'I've entered a contract with a reputable organisation to place

Paula with a respectable family. A proper family. Not you and I, Maisie, muddling along.'

Maisie looked down at the paperwork Carole had thrust into her hands. She bit her lip. It wouldn't do to admit that she'd already seen the newspaper article. Reading it left a bitter taste in her mouth, but admitting to snooping into Carole's private box would only make things worse.

'So, this Mrs Lavender will take Paula away and I suppose there's nothing more I can say or do to make you change your mind.'

'Nothing you can say and nothing you can do.'

A cold atmosphere hung in the air in those few minutes before each turned into their bedrooms.

Neither slept, but for different reasons. Carole was apprehensive about her meeting with Mrs Lavender and whether she could go through with it.

Realising she had no power and no real right to intervene, Maisie decided there might be one person who could do something to stop it. Eddie Bridgeman. There was no guarantee, but it was all she could think of.

13

PHYLLIS – MALTA

Phyllis felt a thrill of excitement as she ran her hands down over the satin dress, feeling its silky softness whilst eyeing her reflection in a full-length mirror. Her stomach was flat and her breasts were pert. There wasn't a bulge in sight – not surprising seeing as she hadn't had much chance to overindulge in the past few years. Her eyes were shining. Today she was marrying Mick Fairbrother. Her previous marriage had been a disaster. There was no doubt in her mind whatsoever that this one would be an absolute success.

'How do I look?' she asked. Her voice trembled and butterflies felt as though they were doing acrobatics in her stomach.

'You look beautiful,' said Mariana, her brown eyes lustrous with emotion. 'Just let me fix this straight.'

Her delicate brown hands adjusted the veil so that the fine net was caught by the stems of the flowers fixed in her hair.

'I can't believe that it's me,' said Phyllis, feeling and sounding awestruck.

Beth was sitting in a chair in the corner smoking and looking pleased with herself. 'Told you it would suit.'

'It's beautiful.' The creamy satin skimmed her hips and hugged her waist. The owner of the dress, Lady Dartfield, wife to a senior civil servant, had insisted on meeting her before letting her borrow it. Thankfully, the fact that Beth was known to her had swayed her decision – that and the fact that Phyllis was well spoken for someone from the lower classes.

Phyllis turned from the mirror. 'My mouth's dry.'

Mariana poured water from a jug into a glass. 'Here. Sip some. It's not too dusty.'

There was no way of cooling water, and although covered with a muslin cloth, dust still managed to get through. Like everything else, they'd got used to it.

Beth countered with a hip flask secreted in the depths of her crocodile-skin handbag. 'Better still swig some of this.'

'Think I will. Water and gin. It is gin, is it?'

Beth smiled and Mariana shook her head ruefully, but still smiled. Nobody could condemn a bride for indulging on her wedding day.

The sound of hooves sliding on roads turned glassy from years of hot sun and the polishing of metal horseshoes came from outside. Slats of bright sunlight fell through the closed shutters and striped the stone floor.

'Sounds like the horse and carriage has arrived. If you've finished admiring yourself, it's time to go.' Beth stubbed out the remains of her cigarette and sprang to her feet. Like both the bride and Mariana, she was out of uniform. As promised, Mariana was wearing a lacy dress originally made for receiving Holy Communion. Beth sported a pair of wide-leg peach-coloured trousers and a matching linen jacket with brass buttons that flashed in the sunlight. Since the very first time they'd met, Phyllis had admired the expensive clothes Beth owned.

'Bought before the war, darling,' Beth had told her. 'The

moment it seemed hostilities were really going to happen, Mama, my sister Cressida and I went out on a spending spree.'

Phyllis had been envious, but at least Beth lent her some of the gorgeous things if needed.

She'd had no time to outline the details of her wedding in a letter to Maisie and another one to Bridget. A short note to each would have to do.

I'm getting married. Can you believe it. Regret you not being here, but will have a party regardless once I'm back with the two of you.

'Are you ready?' asked Mariana in her soft, gentle voice. Unlike Beth, she was not from a wealthy family, but a very close-knit Maltese one.

Phyllis took a deep breath, patted her chest to calm the crazy butterflies and nodded. She was nervous but feeling happier than she had been in years and feeling fortunate that fate had led her here. Here, on the island, was where she'd found Mick.

Unbidden and unwelcome, thoughts of her first wedding crept into her mind. She'd married Robert because she'd had to. It was only a few weeks later that she'd told him she was pregnant. Not that the child had anything to do with him. She had been carrying another man's child. Her life would have been ruined if she hadn't taken the plunge and kept her mouth shut.

Everything went downhill from then on. Afterwards, she'd had skirmishes with other men, but none that lasted. Mick was the man she'd been waiting for, but no longer. Today they would marry. It felt as though she was walking on air. Nothing could go wrong. Not now. Not with Mick.

She made her way down the staircase, her hand trailing over the cool stone wall. Other residents of the sprawling villa, one of the many along the seafront and collectively known as Whitehall Mansions, came out of their rooms, clapping and wishing her well.

Inside was far cooler than outside. A dry breeze of sand and salt blowing in from the sea sent her veil flying out behind her like an angel's wing.

Well-wishers going about their daily business waved and wished her health, happiness and many children.

She felt herself blushing as though she were still a virgin – which was far from true. But Mick knew she wasn't. The only thing he didn't know about her past was the baby she'd miscarried. *In time, I'll tell him*, she said to herself. When the time was right.

A horse-drawn vehicle, a traditional *karozzin*, waited outside, the horse's chestnut coat glowing like gold. A white plume adorned its head and a beaded fringe tied between its ears helped to dispel the halo of flies and mosquitoes. Bells tinkled on the bridle as the horse pawed the ground and shook its head. The vehicle had seating for four people and garlands of flowers decorated the canopy the ribbons that held back the curtains at each corner.

A rudimentary chapel had been set up in a section of the old fort that jutted out into Marsamxett Harbour. Built in the fifteenth century, it had once been the warehouses and accommodation for captains of galleys serving the Knights of St John. They were now used as extra storage and official facilities for whatever was currently required, most of it taken over by the military, though not just for weapons. At the beginning of the war, a section of their cool shade had been converted into a chapel.

Once seated in the carriage, Mariana asked if she was ready.

Phyllis nodded and the driver flicked the reins. They were off.

The sea ran parallel to the coast road to Sliema, no more than two miles. The sky was blue, the water a calm turquoise, so calm it appeared flat enough to walk on. The sea breeze was dry. The shade provided by canopy and curtain was pleasant.

Phyllis flicked at a fly that dared keep up with their progress. 'I'm a bag of nerves.'

'Don't worry. You'll be fine,' said Beth. She lit up another cigarette and offered the packet to Phyllis and Mariana. Both declined.

A cloud of smoke billowed out into the air. Beth had been a smoker before she'd become a widow and admitted to smoking more than she'd used to. Phyllis wondered why she didn't find another man and get married again.

Beth rejected the whole idea out of hand. 'I don't fancy being married again. I like being independent.'

'That could be lonely.'

She shrugged. 'Strikes me that if I do, I have two options. I can live in sin or become a nun.'

The first was slightly shocking, the second brought on an outburst of laughter.

'No,' said Mariana, emphatically shaking her head. 'You would have to give up smoking.'

'Okay. So, I live in sin.'

Phyllis tried not to swipe at her eye make-up and ruin it as she laughed.

'Something or someone will turn up,' said Beth with a mischievous grin. 'Are you sure you don't want a smoke to calm your nerves?'

Phyllis shook her head. 'No thanks. I'm too afraid I might leave a burn on this dress.'

'Me too,' said Mariana, brushing off make-believe ashes.

Nerves, impatience, and excitement all combined and Phyllis began to tap her feet in time with the sound of the wheels going round and the drumming of hooves. This was going to be the happiest day of her life. The sky was blue, she was with dear friends and a dear man would be waiting for her at the altar. For once in a long time, the world seemed at peace or more so than it had been for a long time.

'Got something borrowed?' asked Beth.

Phyllis raised the hem of the dress and showed her a sliver of blue silk ribbon that served as a garter. Not that she really needed it to hold up her stocking. Her suspender did that.

'And it's something blue,' added Mariana, her smile and laughter matching theirs.

'A little something extra for Mick to find.' Beth winked and took her cigarette stub from her mouth. It sailed out through the window. At the same time, just when it must have hit the ground, there was an almighty explosion. The horse screamed and reared and the vehicle rocked on its wheels.

Phyllis screamed. Her bouquet fell from her hand and flew out of the window to be shredded beneath a rear wheel.

To save themselves being thrown out from the carriage, each of them grabbed one of the uprights holding up the roof. The curtains billowed, inwards then out again.

Beth was flung from her seat and Phyllis made a grab for her. Mariana's hand was lying flat against her wounded forehead.

Phyllis poked her head out of the window. Their driver had been thrown from his perch and was hanging half in, half out of the carriage, reins in one hand, the horse's tail in the other.

'Whoa,' he was calling to the horse. 'Whoa.'

Once he'd scrambled down onto the road, he grabbed the horse's head.

People were shouting and screaming.

Phyllis's shoulder felt numb. Her face felt dirty. Dust clogged her eyes and nostrils.

They'd been far enough away from the explosion to escape injury, but where was Mick? In the foolish hope that she might see him emerge from the cloud of dust up ahead, she leaned out as far as she could. As she did so, her veil caught on the jagged rail where the curtain had been. A second explosion sounded – closer so it seemed.

The horse tossed its head so violently, that the poor driver was jerked off his feet. Eyes rolling with fear, the animal reared, then shied. The vehicle veered to one side, the wheels cracking against the kerb whilst at the same time lunging forward, then backwards.

Mariana was praying, her lips, parched with dust, moved silently. Her eyes were half closed.

Phyllis fell back into her seat. Her first thought was for Mick. Where was he? How far had he been from the blast?

She was only vaguely aware of Beth touching her hand.

'It's some way off at the other end of Sliema. Nowhere near the wedding venue, darling.'

Her voice was like a breath of wind, only vaguely heard and seemingly a long way off.

Mariana agreed with her and also did her best to reassure. Like Beth, her words were hushed and barely heard.

It was as though the explosion echoed in Phyllis's head, blocking everything else out. As she shook herself out of it, she heard Mariana asking the driver in Maltese whether it was safe to go on. There was a rushed explanation before Mariana interpreted.

'He said that it would be all right to go on once he's calmed the horse down. It's very frightened.'

'The horse isn't the only one who needs calming down,' Beth exclaimed.

The rig intermittently jigged backwards and forwards, the driver could be heard speaking to the horse whilst holding onto its bridle. Through the front opening of the carriage, they could see the horse tossing its head as it sidestepped and skittered with the agility of a prima ballerina.

People gathered and gave advice, shouting as though the driver, who was having enough trouble, was deaf. He shouted back.

In the meantime, the horse continued with its head tossing and dancing steps, the driver holding onto his head on one side, another man on the other. Nothing they did could calm it down. In one head-jerking rear, the feathery plume fixed to the bridle between its ears snapped. The plume flopped onto its face above its flaring nostrils, lifting with each anguished snort.

Mariana asked him if there was anything they could do.

Face glistening with sweat, the driver responded. Mariana passed the details on to Phyllis and Beth.

'He said he needs to get back up into his seat whilst someone holds the horse's head and walks beside it, just for a short way until it's calmed and back under control. He needs to send for his son.'

Phyllis waved her hand at the crowd. 'Won't any of these people help?'

'He prefers someone who knows about horses. I'm not good with horses, but...' Mariana made a move to disembark, one foot already on the iron step.

Beth caught her arm and pulled her back. 'You stay here, sweetie. I used to ride with the Beaufort Hunt.' Slapping her hands together in an act of finality and rolling her shoulders, Beth got down. Approaching from behind the animal, she smoothed her hand over the horse's flanks and from there the length of his body, all the way to his head. 'There, old chap,' she said softly. 'Just listen to my sweet voice and you'll be fine.'

After removing the broken plume, which was likely making him even more skittish, Beth stroked the front of his face, talking softly all the time. She nodded at the driver to get back up onto his seat.

Phyllis and Mariana watched her gentling before taking hold of the head collar. The horse tossed its head and snorted. The dancing hooves came to a standstill. All was calm.

'Right,' said Beth, sounding most definitely that everything was now under control, 'let's get going. We've a wedding to go to.'

'Are you getting back in?' Phyllis asked.

'No. The driver's right. I'll walk beside the poor creature for a while. Anyway, it's been a long time since I was this close to a horse. As I've already told you, I used to ride to hounds with the hunt. Loved the jumping side of it. Loved the horses. Didn't like the hounds very much, and do you know what, I've never seen a fox killed. Didn't want to. It was the riding and flying over five-bar gates that drew me in.'

Phyllis and Mariana exchanged amused smiles. It was so easy to imagine Beth riding to hounds. So easy to imagine her holding her own in a man's world – holding her own with horses too.

The sun was high in the sky by the time they got to the cool, little chapel, where a gnarled tree threw shade over the arched entrance. Although a cloud of dust ballooned some way off smothering the blueness with a yellowish haze, the makeshift chapel was intact.

Guests were gathered outside, mainly RAF, their buttons shining like ingots, the fresh young faces composed, smiling and glad to be there and not on ops. Phyllis knew some, though certainly not all, at least not by name. They were faces who smiled and made polite conversation in a bar, mates of Mick's, good friends one and all. A few of the girls she worked with were there too. There were congratulations of course, but also comments about the explosion.

'Unexploded bombs. Two of them. Hope the UXB bods got out with their lives.'

Phyllis brushed nervously at her hair. 'Is it very dusty?'

Mariana flicked at her own hair and shook her head. 'No more than mine.'

Beth pushed into her hair with both hands. 'That walk with the horse dislodged most of mine, I think.'

They managed to exchange relieved smiles, though Phyllis had the distinct impression that a stone tumbling from a wall, the crack of a horse whip or the sudden stamp of a hobnailed boot would make them jump. They were all used to the explosions that had accompanied air raids. Ongoing danger was still posed by bombs that had not detonated. The opinion was that at least if they exploded you knew where they were. The hidden ones were a different matter and deserved to be feared.

Fragile smiles and warm words helped counteract the shock of the explosion.

One of Mick's Aussie friends gave her a kiss on the cheek. 'You look quite wonderful, Phyllis love.'

'Just a bit dusty. And I've lost my bouquet.'

'Don't you worry. Ole Mick's eyes are gonna be for you. He can pick a bunch of flowers any day of the week, but he can't pick a beauty like you every day. You're one in a lifetime.'

Another Aussie diligently picked some bright purple flowers with heavenly scent from a climber basking against all that remained of the wall of a house. Before handing them to her, he wrapped the impromptu posy in a crisp white handkerchief. 'Have these, love. Don't want to deprive a bride on her wedding day.'

Phyllis took them gratefully, thinking at the same time how generous Mick's countrymen were.

She studied the blocks of stone laid centuries ago to create the inner bastions of the city. Surely if Mick was already inside the church, he would know that she'd arrived. Had he noticed and was inside waiting for her? There was no sign of him out here.

'Has anyone seen Mick?'

She searched their expressions, hoping that someone had seen him.

Heads shook. Expressions were either edgy or puzzled. Nobody wanted to believe he wasn't turning up, but nobody had seen him.

'Probably had to take a detour. Depends on the debris.'

It was a reasonable enough excuse. If a building tumbled, the road could be blocked. This was what she tried to tell herself. However, the butterflies in her stomach became like a coil of barbed wire winding itself ever more tightly. Sicily sprang into her mind, the terrible news that he was missing, probably killed. It had been sheer luck that he'd survived, but, oh God, how sick she'd felt, how devastated by the belief that he was never coming back.

'Where is he?' Her voice was hushed, the question not really directed at anyone. It was a fear. A worrying instinctive fear that something was wrong, the same brand of fear she'd felt when he'd been shot down. He'd come back from that, but what if...?

Beth read her expression and interrupted her worrying thoughts. 'Don't worry. News is that it exploded someway along by the ferry stage. He couldn't have been over that way. He had no cause to be.'

'No. Of course not.' Phyllis tried to sound convinced. This was her wedding day. *Please God*, she silently prayed. *Let him be all right.*

She'd felt so very fine in the cream satin dress. So sleek. So cool. Now, close to midday and after all the trauma of the morning, it clung to her. The veil had ripped to pieces, part of it left on the vehicle that had brought her here.

'Might as well go inside,' suggested Mariana. Her smile was tight. Phyllis was aware of her friends exchanging the same smile, the worried look in their eyes.

Phyllis felt a gentle nudge from both of her friends, who filed in behind her. Behind them, the guests filtered in, conversations muted and respectful.

After the heat outside, the coolness was welcome.

As her eyes accustomed to the gloom, Phyllis took in the details of the small facility. It had been adapted for the weddings of those who wished to keep things simple. The inside of the Pro-Cathedral,

Protestant and so named to separate it from the many Catholic churches on the island, had been built by Queen Adelaide years before and was too intimidating for some tastes. A piece of brocade patterned in gold and blue had been thrown over a trestle table that served as an altar. A rod of sunlight made the two-foot-tall gold cross flash like lightning. It was sudden and beautiful but did remind her of the explosion.

A padre borrowed from the army was waiting. Not so many were dying, and several padres had been ordered to go north into Italy. Thus diminished, all resources had to be shared, and padres were as much a resource as anything else.

The makeshift chapel was too small to have hidden alcoves shadowed in greater depth than the rest of the interior, but Phyllis searched all the same, looking for Mick. Just in case. Her sweeping gaze came to a halt a few feet in front of the padre. He nodded and welcomed her cheerfully.

'Must admit I could stay in here all day. It's delightfully cool, don't you think?'

She agreed with him and thought how untroubled he seemed that the bridegroom had not yet arrived.

They exchanged a reassuring smile before she looked over her shoulder. All she saw was a sea of faces. None of them were Mick. She turned back to the padre.

'He's late.' Fear laced her low whisper.

The padre saw the concern in her eyes. 'I'm sure he'll be here,' he said, though both he and she knew he wasn't sure at all.

The details of that moment of explosion were still with her. Thinking about it was reliving it, feeling its deadly tremor making the very air tremble.

She tensed, swallowed the dryness on her tongue and the fear that would not quite go away.

Her hands clenched the bouquet of climbing flowers more

tightly. It was like holding onto a lifejacket – a symbol of a love shared and a future yet to come.

When still no bridegroom appeared, the congregation became restless, whispering their fears and shuffling feet.

More seconds and minutes ticked by.

The padre glanced at his watch, his fingers tapping impatiently on his prayer book. Every so often, he looked at her and smiled – a wan but reassuring smile. All would be well, it seemed to say. His eyes said something else.

At last, there were no more seconds, only accumulated minutes piling higher and higher like sandcastles built on a beach, stalwart until the incoming tide washed them away.

The possibilities rolled over and over in her mind. Two explosions. The UXB – the unexploded bomb unit – would have been there. Perhaps they'd been wheeling it through a tight alley where no vehicle could venture. The alleys were crowded on either side with ancient houses, their balconies giving shade to the baking ground. Most traffic through these alleys was foot traffic, or perhaps a bicycle, rarely anything horse-drawn. When a bomb fell in such an area and failed to explode, the only way of getting out was to lift it gingerly onto a handcart and wheel it away.

Her breath was an audible gasp in her throat. She remembered Tom Sullivan's chilling words. 'We work on a knife edge. One small upset and we're all blown to kingdom come.'

Tom had filled a brief period of affection in her life in that terrible time when it seemed that Mick was dead. All too brief as it turned out. He was one of those who'd been blown to kingdom come.

Mariana's fingers lightly touched her shoulder. 'It won't be long now.'

'Had to make a detour, I expect,' Beth added, her loud voice full of confidence.

'You said that before.' Alarm was beginning to make Phyllis snappy, but she couldn't help it. Both her patience and her faith in everything being all right had reached breaking point.

'That's because I'm pretty sure that's what happened.'

'Don't treat me like a fool, Beth. You're thinking the same as I am. That's the truth. Well, that's bloody war for you. It's cruel and it's unfair.'

Beth looked surprised by her outburst. So did Mariana and the padre.

Phyllis turned her back on the altar and fixed her eyes on the door at the far end of the building. She willed Mick to enter, to be there, smile in that lopsided way of his and say that all was well. She wanted Mick there at her side and, after that, the next boat back to Blighty, where new postings and the pathway to a new life awaited them.

People were beginning to question what was happening and what they should do.

He's dead! That was the terrible thought that shouted inside her head.

What seemed like a black shadow suddenly filled the entrance to the church. The features of this sudden silhouette were indistinct, but she dared to hope.

'Mick?'

The figure progressed towards her. She took three hesitant steps in its direction, and with them her hoped died.

It wasn't Mick. Alex Dimech who'd been lined up as bet man, had been posted to Italy. The replacement was Joe Parker, a friend of his, the mechanic who looked after his plane and had agreed with great aplomb to be his best man. In the midst of all that had happened, she had quite forgotten about Joe so hadn't questioned why he wasn't there.

His eyes were red-rimmed and his hair, normally a rich brandy brown, looked almost white, thanks to it being thick with stone dust.

Phyllis felt her legs buckle. Beth on one side, Mariana on the other, propped her up. 'No,' she said, shaking her head in denial. 'This can't be happening. He cannot be dead.'

'It's okay, Phyllis. It's okay. He's not dead,' said Joe. His mouth seemed like a gaping red hole in the dustiness of his face. 'He's injured. He's in hospital. But he's all right, Phyllis. Nothing much at all. Just a bump on the head.'

'He's unconscious?'

'Yeah. He's unconscious. Come on. I've got a motor outside,' said Joe. 'I'll take you there.'

Her knees buckled, but Beth and Mariana caught her.

Determination overruled the weakness in her legs. Her light-headedness was alleviated and suddenly she fled the supporting arms of her friends and was running – running despite high heels and the length of her wedding dress.

Such was her headlong flight, that she was only barely aware of Joe shouting after her, repeating again that Mick was okay. His army boots thudded on the shiny sandstone slabs underfoot. Her friends, bridesmaids for the day, were also shouting for her to slow down, their heels clattering and slipping and sliding as they fought to keep up with her.

'Phyllis.'

Beth, having powerful, well-muscled legs, a keen hockey player, horse rider and pretty good at most sports, was the first to catch up with her. 'Phyllis,' she said, grabbing her arm.

'I have to see Mick,' shouted Phyllis as she attempted to wring her arm out of Beth's grasp. 'I'll run to see him if I have to.'

'Phyllis, darling, you're not thinking straight. You're in shock,' said Beth whilst giving her a hefty shake. 'Joe drove here. Didn't you hear him say that he's got a car? Now come on. Be sensible. Bound to be quicker than running all the way to the hospital, don't you think?'

Phyllis regarded the strong set of fingers preventing her from running away. Although her breath still raced, she calmed down.

Many people stopped and stared at the sight of the red-haired bride in her cream satin wedding dress, veil lopsided, flowery crown hanging in front of her face. Their eyes followed her as she headed for the car door, a strong and determined-looking woman holding onto her, leading them to wonder why the would-be bride looked so stunned. Had she changed her mind about getting married?

The day was hot. Flowers, clothes and even people were wilting. Even though it was nearly June, Phyllis felt none of that heat. She would feel as cold as ice until Mick was there in front of her. He had to be all right. She'd almost lost him once before. She didn't want to lose him now.

Beth handed her into the back seat of the car whilst Joe slid into the driver's seat. Mariana was already seated in the back seat, her eyes full of concern.

She gripped Phyllis's hand with both of hers. 'Stay strong, Phyllis. He'll be all right.'

'It's my wedding day. Why did it happen? Doesn't God like me or something?'

Mariana flinched and Phyllis immediately felt guilty for the outburst.

'I'm sorry.'

Mariana shook her head and took on one of her saintly looks. 'God moves in mysterious ways. Perhaps he's planning for you to marry elsewhere. Perhaps somewhere more special than a tin hut.'

All things considered, it was a kind comment, but Phyllis had looked forward to this day. It seemed downright unfair not to get married on the day they'd chosen.

'Step on it, Joe,' ordered Beth as she squeezed herself into the front passenger seat.

A soft clunk of gears preceded the car jolting away over stony ground, skirting heaps of tumbled masonry, bypassing and swerving around uniforms and civilians. Not that Phyllis paid much attention to anything beyond the car and her desperate need to get to the hospital.

'He's tough,' she said, in answer to nothing except her own fears. 'He'll win through. I know he will.' She beat on her knees with clenched fists. Anything to hold onto her hopes. Anything to hold back her fears.

A smiling Mariana smoothed her arm with her fragile, delicate fingers. 'God smiles on him,' she said in a way that made Phyllis think that Mariana had seen the Almighty's face and knew it for certain. It struck her how calm Mariana was in all things, strengthened by her faith. Not at all like her ex-mother-in-law, Hilda Harvey, Robert's mother.

'My ex-mother-in-law was very religious. A right Tartar she was.'

'And I am not like her?'

Despite the seriousness of the occasion, Phyllis laughed at the same time as thumping her knees with her fists. 'Not at all.'

It wasn't a long journey, but long enough. She needed to assure herself that Mick was in one piece.

Beth stopped her from thumping her knees. 'Calm down.'

Easier said than done, a sign of impatience and a terrible gnawing fear. She settled for drumming her fingers on her creamy-clad knees.

The moment Joe stopped the car, she grabbed the door handle with both hands and pushed like mad until the door swung open.

Unfortunately, it swung violently into a passing subaltern. The lowly non-commissioned officer shouted after her. She took no heed. Using her freed hands to lift her dress also freed her legs. Kicking out behind her, she ran up the steps into the cool reception hall of the hospital.

A waggish naval rating sitting in a wheelchair, one leg in a plaster caste, whistled, then called out, 'Here comes the bride. You come to make my day, love?'

Ignoring his cheeky grin and the kiss he blew, she addressed a member of Queen Alexandra's Royal Imperial Nursing Corps.

The QA, wearing battledress rather than the grey and red uniform they were famous for, looked her up and down. 'Oh dear,' she finally said, sighing as she took in the beautiful dress and what remained of the veil. 'That's Lady Dartfield's dress, isn't it.'

'Yes. Flight Officer Mick Fairbrother. Where is he?'

Though the pitying expression remained, the QA pointed the way and gave verbal directions.

'Thank you.'

The clattering of heels from behind her was enough to assure her that Mariana and Beth were keeping pace, not allowing her to see Mick by herself – just in case – it was all just in case.

No matter what, I want him to myself. No matter bloody what!

They weren't to know that and had to be told. She stopped, turned and faced them.

'I want to see Mick by myself. Just the two of us.'

Their expressions betrayed confusion and surprise, both hesitantly replaced by nods of understanding.

'Thank you.'

Leaving them staring after her, Phyllis ran along the stone-floored passages to where she had to be, to where she wanted to be.

Just as she was about to enter the double doors with porthole windows, a QA major came out. Knowing she was about to voice the obvious challenge of why she was there, it was out of bounds, or any other directive that Phyllis would not adhere to, Phyllis spoke first.

'I don't care about the rules. I've been waiting in front of the altar, ready to say I do, but the bridegroom didn't turn up. I need to know how he is.'

The stern look fell from the major's face, her eyes sweeping over the wedding dress. 'I take it you're Flight Officer Fairbrother's fiancée.'

Phyllis took a deep breath. At least she hadn't called her a widow.

'Yes. We would have been married by now. I heard the explosions. Is he all right?'

The woman nodded. 'Yes. He was thrown from the gharry— or whatever it's called. The horse died. So did the driver.'

'A karozzin. A horse cab,' she said, feeling a strong need to explain what she meant. Her voice shook. Driver and horse dead. Mick alive. From behind hands that she'd raised to her tear-streaked face, Phyllis made a half-strangled sigh of relief. 'Is he badly injured?' She held her breath as she awaited the answer.

The major eyed her from head to foot, slowly as though driven by envy. 'That's a beautiful dress you're wearing.'

Her question had not been answered and she couldn't help thinking the worse. This was the man she'd been looking forward to sharing her life with. 'Will he die?' *Please God, don't take him from me.*

'No. He's out cold, but it should be only temporary. No guarantees of course. He just needs to rest, so it might be best if you let him be until—'

Phyllis's response was strident. 'I want to see him. I want him to know I'm here.'

The major fiddled with her watch, frowning at it as though the time and its tiny hands contributed to her decision. 'All right,' she finally said, officiously, stiffly, as though she'd refuse if she could. 'Ten minutes only. No more.'

Without hesitation, Phyllis pushed open the swing door. Although she'd been told he was unconscious, she was careful not to let it bang but let it slide slowly and quietly into place.

He was lying in a bed at the very end of the ward in front of the window. Bars of alternate shadow and sunlight fell through the slatted shutters. An electric fan whirled gently overhead, ruffling her hair as she walked beneath it. It didn't so much cool the air as push it around.

Her shoes squeaked over the shiny brown linoleum floor. It sounded much louder than it really was, here, just after midday. In a hospital. They should have been having their wedding reception by now. The thought screamed through her mind.

White pillows cradled his head. His face had been washed. His colour was as it always was, close to nut brown thanks to the country he'd been born into. His hair, streaked with gold strands in brandy brown, had been combed. He looked, in fact, how she would have expected him to look stood beside her at the altar, though his eyes would have been open of course. He would have been smiling at her, waiting for the moment when the padre would say, 'You may now kiss the bride.' Instead, he was here, alive but lying in a hospital bed.

Letting her satin skirt fall around her like a creamy cloud, Phyllis perched on a chair at the side of the bed, staring at his face. On his forehead, a red gash stood out in a sea of blue and yellow bruising. With trembling fingers, she reached to touch it, her other hand resting on his. She felt the blonde hairs on the back of his hand. His skin was warm. Hers were surprisingly cold.

'Mick? Can you hear me?'

It was hard not to let her voice tremble, hard not to betray the fear she was feeling inside. He had to be made to feel he was still in the real world, would recover and would once again stand with her at the altar.

'Please God,' she murmured but found it difficult to say anything else. Unsaid, she made a promise to light as many candles as it took, recite prayers day and night, if only Mick opened his eyes. 'I'll go to church every Sunday for the rest of my life if you'll just open your eyes, Mick.'

His eyelids flickered. Her heart leapt in her chest. She leaned forward and clutched his hand more tightly.

'Come on, Mick.' She gave a light laugh. 'Just wait until you wake up. I want a word with you, standing me up at the altar like that. Whatever next.' Despite her best efforts, a tear trickled down one cheek. She brushed at it defiantly. Gripped his hand more tightly. 'Get better, Mick,' she whispered. 'Please wake up.'

Ten minutes passed in the blink of an eye. The major came to ensure she didn't linger.

'If I can give you the number at Whitehall Mansions...' Phyllis said and automatically began looking for her handbag. Today, on her wedding day, she carried no handbag. 'Do you have a pen and paper?'

A wistful smile lifted the major's features. 'No need. I know the number there. It's where I was billeted when I first came to the island.'

Phyllis sighed with relief. 'Oh, thank you. If you could let me know the minute he wakes up...'

'I'll leave instructions on the ward, so everyone knows where to contact you.'

'That's very kind.'

'Call it my vocation in life – to ensure that every bride gets wed when she's supposed to. It's difficult when something like this happens, but hopefully not insurmountable.'

'Where there's hope, eh?' said Phyllis. A sudden thought

occurred to her. 'You're not allowed to be married, are you?'

A sad look came to the major's clear grey eyes. 'No. But I did almost get to walk down the aisle.' She looked towards the view outside the window, honey-coloured houses falling in terraced tiers down to a crowded quay. 'He was killed in Sicily, one of the first ashore. I love my job, but I loved him more.'

'I'm sorry.'

The major's shoulders shrugged against the army-style uniform that had replaced their famous grey short capes trimmed with scarlet. 'That's war. But I sincerely hope your man comes round and you get a second chance to declare everlasting love. Someone has to be happy after all this carnage.' There was a bitter edge to her voice and her jaw was tightly clenched.

A throbbing in her head and her expression tense, Phyllis walked away in a daze. She walked quickly but with care, her dress held in both hands so she wouldn't trip over the hem going back down the stairs.

The world was unfair. God was unfair and she would tell Mariana that! She didn't care that such a comment would be cruel to her very religious friend. Today her wedding day had been a disaster and it was hard not to feel bitter.

Beth and Mariana were outside waiting for her. She only briefly glanced at her Maltese friend, preferring instead to keep her gaze levelled at Beth. 'He's alive, but unconscious.'

'Good,' exclaimed Beth in her usual ebullient manner. 'Another day, another wedding. Shouldn't take too much effort to sort out another date. That wedding dress suits you down to the ground. Mick will love you in it.'

The words bordering on blasphemy she'd intended throwing at Mariana were swallowed. Beth was right. Mick was alive. Phyllis determined to wear the wedding dress again, whenever and wherever they happened to be.

14

MAISIE

Despite a lack of sleep, Maisie's mind was made up. It wasn't an easy decision to make. How would Eddie respond? Would he step in and do something or would he laugh and send her on her way?

She sighed and went back to overseeing the shredding of leaves on her particular table, but it was hard to concentrate. Her thoughts continued to flit here and there, so much so that she was slow to notice that Peter was alongside her table and saying something.

'The wedding invitation's arrived.'

Startled from her thoughts, Maisie apologised. 'Sorry, Peter. What was that you were saying about a wedding?'

She fancied he flushed before referring her to the fact that his niece was getting married and that he'd been invited to the wedding.

'They said I could bring a companion if I wanted. 'I wondered...'

Maisie laughed off her consternation. 'Sorry, Peter. I was miles away.'

The fact was, the very word wedding had made her think of planning her own – or at least enticing a proposal.

' It's next Saturday. Are you free?' He had the look of a man who greatly feared being disappointed.

Caught off guard, she found herself gushing. 'Yes. Yes, of course I am. I look forward to it. Might even put me in the mood for getting married myself.'

It was rash, it was cheeky, but hey, she thought, *this is the time to put your cards on the table. Peter is attracted to me. What's the harm in a bit of encouragement?*

'Well,' he said sounding greatly relieved. 'That's good. How about tonight? Are you still on for the pictures?'

She couldn't tell for sure whether he'd taken the bait. Shame about forgetting the pictures. That put a dent in things. 'Oh no, Peter. I'm sorry I can't make it tonight.' She bit her lip and looked as apologetic as she knew how. 'Can we make it another time? Wednesday, perhaps?'

He looked crestfallen. 'Well. I suppose I can rearrange things. Wednesday should be okay.

Maisie drew a sigh of relief. 'Let's just hope that this rain will have stopped by then.'

A sunnier look returned to his face. 'That's good. We'll make arrangements tomorrow, shall we? When you're under less pressure.'

She fancied his gaze skimming over the table and the untouched leaves. She would normally have had them all stripped by now. 'I'll work through lunchtime if I have to.'

'No need.' He smiled. 'Just do what you can.'

She smiled back and nodded. 'I will, and thanks for the invitation to your niece's wedding..'

'Ooow! If you catch the bride's bouquet when she throws it, that means you could be next,' said Doris, her lips stretching into a toothless smile.

'Well wouldn't that be something.' Maisie winked up at Peter.

'Might have to find a man first, though, Doris. It takes two to tango – or get married. You'll be the first to know when I get a proposal.'

'Oooh. Ain't that exciting!'

It was difficult to know whether Peter had appreciated the cheeky aside or not. For her part, Maisie hoped it had planted a seed in his mind. It might pay to be forthright, to at least make half the running.

'Well, 'e ain't a bad catch,' said Doris once he'd gone. 'Ain't love grand.'

'Ain't it just. Now let's get on with some work, shall we?' She said it sharply. If she hadn't Doris would have continued wittering on about romance, men and weddings. Maisie had said enough and had no intention of informing Doris or anyone else that her love was not for Peter but for Carole's baby.

* * *

At the sound of the factory hooter just after midday, it being a Saturday, a tide of people swept out of W. D. & H. O. Wills number one factory in East Street, Bedminster. It was still pouring with rain. May had been wet enough and June wasn't looking much better.

It was usual for her and some workmates to catch the same bus down to Temple Meads and up the Wells Road into Totterdown. On this occasion, Maisie made the excuse that she was off to see Bridget's mother who conveniently lived in the other direction.

Coronation Road was where she was really heading. That was where Eddie Bridgeman lived in a five-storey house overlooking the 'Cut', the overflow of water from the city dock and the river. On the other side was the General Hospital. Above its lofty roof floated three barrage balloons, one of which looked a little deflated, flopping around like a fish out of water. There'd been no air raids since 1941 so they were no longer getting the attention they used to get.

Head down, Maisie clutched her umbrella with both hands, using it like a shield to barrel through the downpour. The hem of the summer dress she wore beneath her overall slapped wetly around her knees and her feet were soaking wet.

Her heart began racing as she left East Street and entered Coronation Road. Puddles of rain had gathered in the gaps between broken paving slabs. Rainwater disturbed by passing vehicles sent waves across the road and splashed up from the grimy gutters.

The news that Eddie had moved into a much nicer and bigger house, had been much discussed by those who knew him. Some said his old place had got a direct hit some time back and the foundations had been weakened. Others surmised that he had the ear of some city councillors and businessmen with their eyes on opportunities likely to come once the war was over. At one time, the caveat of 'if it's ever over' would have been attached. Not so much now. Optimism was in the air.

The houses lining the broad road had once been lived in by wealthy merchants. Despite their imposing facades, some of them were now looking a little battle scarred. Eddie's stood out clean and undamaged. A cluster of bushes formed a barrier between the garden wall and the front of the house. They were overgrown and it didn't look as though they were likely to get trimmed. Eddie's decision was that they provided privacy.

A line of cars was drawn up outside. One of them Maisie recognised as belonging to Eddie. She'd heard tell he was thinking of running for the city council when the war was over. Not for the greater good of the community, she thought. Eddie Bridgeman never did anything unless it benefitted him.

Her footsteps slowed when she heard the slamming of a door. Eddie's door? Would he let her in? And what would be his response when she told him why she was there?

'Come on,' she whispered to herself. 'You can't lose your nerve now. This is for Paula.'

She stood in the gap where an iron gate had once been. Like the railings from Victoria Park and from around the curvature of handsome houses in Clifton, they'd been taken away early on in the war. Saucepans and kettles had also been collected, to make munitions and aircraft. Whether it was true or no didn't really matter. People had felt they were helping defeat Hitler's hordes so gave what they could.

Standing in the gateway, Maisie could see a man stood under the door canopy smoking. He looked up on seeing her standing there. Hesitancy vanquished, she straightened her spine and looked him in the eye.

'Before you tell me to push off, I want to see Eddie.'

He looked taken aback that she'd spoken first, but quickly recovered. 'What do you want to see 'im about?'

Maisie marched defiantly up the path of black and red clay tiles, the bushes rubbing their dampness onto her sleeve. 'Family business, so nothing to do with you. Eddie will want to hear what I've got to say.'

Unblinking, his eyes fixed on hers as he thought it through. Not that he had much choice. 'Family you say?'

'That's what I said, cloth ears.'

Stan, the bloke guarding the door, was unaware of Eddie having any family. He took the view that if indeed he did, then he dare not turn her away. However, Stan was a ditherer, good at taking specific orders but not thinking things through for himself.

Maisie was getting impatient. 'Well,' she said, her voice sharp enough to slice liver – his liver if he didn't watch out. 'Are you goin' to let me in?'

He was tough but recognised determination when he saw it. Inside, Maisie was quivering like a jelly but was good at hiding her fear. Growing up in a tough household in a tough district had made her tough. Don't show fear, be outspoken and the first to threaten, then you'd win through. That's what she'd learned.

As he opened the door, she deliberately elbowed him as she stomped past so he was in no doubt that she meant business. After shaking off her umbrella, she stepped into the hall, spotted an ugly elephant's foot stand and let her brolly fall into it.

Eddie, no doubt having heard her exchange with his man, stood at the bottom of the stairs. His left elbow rested on the newel post. One foot was crossed over the other; a nonchalant pose that he probably thought made him look impressive. A lit cigar dangled from his right hand. The glint of gold flashed from two of his fingers. A gold chain dangled from his wrist. His black eyes were like chips of coal though, without the promise of warmth. His smile was slow and thin.

'Well, if it ain't Maisie Miles. What you doin' in my 'ouse, Maisie Miles?'

She showed no hint of fear but eyed her surroundings with interest. Gilt-framed mirrors reflected the light from a handsome table lamp with a green silk shade. The base was brass and matched the filigree tracery running like gold on the top of a highly polished credenza. The items looked incongruous in a house like this. She could better imagine them in a grand house in Clifton sitting at the top of a hill, looking out on a panoramic view.

She threw him a less than respectful look, her smile crossed with a wince as she spouted a comment. 'Admiring your taste. Didn't know you liked antiques. That's what they are, ain't they?'

'Too right they are. Very discerning of you to notice.'

Discerning? It wasn't a word she'd ever heard him using before. He was striking out!

'Must be worth a packet.'

'I got them cheap,' he drawled. 'Somebody needed the cash.'

'I bet they did,' muttered Maisie. 'Tell me, were they the rightful owners or somebody who just happened to know who found the whole caboodle, and flogged them to you?'

'Finders, keepers,' said Eddie, unmoved by her insinuation, which as far as she was concerned was pretty close to the truth. They were stolen, though looting bomb sites was never really viewed as looting. If the owners weren't around, the great bounty was soon carried off – some of it by those whose job it was to make the site safe and discover ownership.

However, valuable artefacts and furnishings weren't always just the result of stealing from a site. Houses left unoccupied when the air-raid siren wailed were looted. That was one way of procuring good-quality furnishings, though not the only way. Big houses requisitioned for the duration to be used as hospitals or billets for the military tended to store items that would only be in the way. Hospital beds and hobnailed boots needed space and durability, not landscape paintings and gilt-edged mirrors.

She ran her fingers along the brass fretwork of the highly polished credenza. On scrutinising her fingertips, she found them to be spotlessly clean. 'Your cleaner does a good job. I take it you have a cleaner.'

He grinned. 'Well, I ain't gonna do it meself, am I.'

'I'm sure the original owners will be very happy to know how well their stuff's being looked after.'

Eddie's face darkened. 'It's all mine. I paid for it fair and square.'

'Bet you did. It's amazing what you can pick up if you know where to look. Stored for the duration, was it? Or left in an abandoned house up in Clifton?' She'd always been outspoken with Eddie and saw no reason to be otherwise now. Besides, he wasn't the sort to respond to weakness. She knew him of old and he knew her; she sensed a hint of admiration, even respect.

Eddie glanced towards the solid, glassless front door, now firmly shut behind her. It let in no daylight. The sudden darkness unnerved her. Would he let her out again?

'Come into my parlour,' he said to her.

She threw him a flippant look with a comment to match. 'Said the spider to a fly?'

'That's what it is, ain't it? A parlour.'

'Didn't know you knew the word, Eddie. Gettin' a bit posh in yer old age.'

She'd only ever heard older women refer to their front room or even their living room as a parlour.

'You too, Maisie. Don't seem that long ago that you was a scruffy kid in York Street. What a bleedin' dump that was. Now you got old Gracie's 'ouse. Shrewd old bird she was. Must 'ave thought the world of you to leave you a 'ouse. Not known for being generous was Gracie. Sharp as a pin and keen as a knife.'

Maisie didn't like being reminded of York Street. Her early years living with her mother and stepfather had been traumatic. The only light in the gloom had been Alf, her half-brother. She chose to ignore his reference to her grandmother.

'Let's sit in the parlour and you can tell me what you want.' In a flourishing act that reminded her of a circus ringmaster, the parlour door was opened wide. 'Here. Go on in. Take a gander at this room. See what you thinks of it.' He looked proud of himself, cigar clenched in his teeth, head held high.

She reminded herself that Eddie's background wasn't much more salubrious than her own. 'It's a big house for one man.'

'Needs it to run all my business interests.'

The smoke from his cigar followed her into the room.

The walls were painted pale pink. The curtains were a mass of chintz – overblown pink roses and bright green leaves against a cream background. The carpet was a large square of pale green. A red velvet sofa and matching armchairs destroyed the country-cottage look. Red velvet was more Eddie's style, reminiscent of the nightclubs he owned and frequented.

Maisie swivelled on one heel as she took it all in. Mentally she rehearsed words she'd never thought to utter, asking him, almost begging him for help to prevent Carole considering adoption for her baby. At present, all he seemed to want to do was show off a house that to his mind was a palace. Flattery, she decided, wouldn't go amiss.

'Very luxurious.'

'You bet.' He indicated a plush-looking sofa that seemed acquired for comfort, 'Take a pew, sweet'eart.'

She sank into its dark red cushions. It was a big sofa. She only hoped he wouldn't sit too close to her.

To her relief, he remained standing at the fireplace, arm resting on the mantelpiece. The back of his head was reflected in a gilt-framed mirror. She glimpsed a bald spot. Did he know his hair was thinning?

A green marble mantle clock struck the hour.

Maisie interlocked one hand with the other, her fingers strangling the soft leather of her handbag. Asking Eddie for help was alien to her nature. And Eddie helping anyone? Eddie mostly helped himself.

She took a deep breath. 'I'm here about Carole. Your daughter.'

He looked interested, perhaps slightly surprised. 'Oh yeah.'

Maisie too was slightly surprised. She'd half expected him to contradict her, though on reflection, why should he? He'd made his interest obvious.

'It's about Paula.'

'My grandkid?'

Maisie nodded. 'That's right. Your granddaughter.' That too seemed a trifle alien, but she ploughed on. 'Carole can't cope with the situation.'

His elbow came down from the mantelpiece and he looked puzzled. 'If she needs money... I've already told 'er, money's no object.'

Maisie shook her head. 'No. Not money. No. Not at all.'

His brows furrowed. 'So what is it then?'

Maisie felt sick at having to even say it. 'She's mentioned having 'er adopted a few times. I thought she'd accepted her lot and changed 'er mind. I've only just found out that it ain't so. She's made arrangements to hand her baby over to someone she contacted through a newspaper.'

Her eyes flicked up from her clenched fingers to Eddie. His jaw tightened and the amused mockery had left his eyes. Deep lines appeared in his brow. The habitual sneer that turned the corners of his lips upwards now turned down.

'Through a newspaper?' The words were delivered as though he'd eaten something that tasted bad and wanted to get rid of it. 'What the bloody 'ell are you on about?'

Maisie drew up a deep breath and explained about the woman Carole had met, the arrangement she'd made to sell her baby.

Eddie looked at her in disbelief. 'Are you tellin' me that there's outfits that buy babies?'

She shrugged. 'They call themselves adoption agencies, but they're not really legal. All adoption agencies have to be registered with the local council. The rule was only brought in pre-war, and some have slipped through the net, gone round the law. I doubt this one is legal.'

A frowning Eddie looked down at the fire grate, watching as a length of cigar ash fell and scattered onto the carpet. He seemed to think about it for a while. 'You sure of that?'

She detected the anger in his voice. 'Yes. Adoption societies don't ask for money up front. Neither does the local council.'

Eddie's face darkened. 'How much 'as she 'anded over?'

'Fifty guineas. The woman wants another one hundred when Paula is 'anded over on Tuesday. The woman's coming down from London on the train to take the baby away.' The very thought of the event being so close made her feel sick to her stomach.

More ash fell from the cigar as Eddie tapped it with one finger. His black eyebrows were furrowed, hiding whatever she might see in those black pupils. Not that she needed to see anything. His stance, the tense squareness in his shoulders signalled that he was considering doing something, though it scared her to think what he might do. Remembering what had happened to Reg Harris made her wonder if she had aroused evil as well as good.

Her feelings for Paula and Carole overwhelmed her fear. What she wanted of him came pouring out. 'Can you do somethin' about it? Stop Carole from goin' through with it? Warn the woman off?'

Just a single blink, then he stared at her yet in an odd way, as though staring through or beyond, the look on his face unreadable. The corners of his lips curled up in a sardonic smile. 'Why me?'

'Because you're the one with the will to stop this, to persuade Carole not to do this.'

He pointed the cigar at her. 'You want me to get rid of this woman. You can't do it yourself. You think I'm the lowest of the low. Don't say otherwise. I ain't stupid. And neither are you.'

'I'm just asking if you can do anything. She's your daughter. Your granddaughter. I thought you would like to know. I thought you would want to do something about it.'

The words she spoke hid a deeper meaning. In the depths of her soul, she would do anything to prevent being parted from Paula. If only Carole had given her enough time to marry, to supply a home – even though it would be to a man she did not love. A true marriage of convenience, just for her own ends. And now she'd given Eddie reason to act in a way that to him was second nature.

One part of her wanted to blurt it out, inflame him so much that this awful Lavender woman would go the same way as Reg Harris. But how could she live with such a terrible thing? Despite her deep love for Paula, her conscience wouldn't allow her to do that. So, she held it in, asked him if he could use his powers of persuasion on his daughter. It was all she could bear to ask for; to go further was as good as tarring herself with the same ruthless brush as Eddie. And she wasn't like that. She could never envisage being responsible for the death of anyone.

Eddie, however, was a different kettle of fish.

'Just talk to her. That's all. I mean, I wouldn't want anything terrible happening.'

Eddie looked down at the half-smoked cigar still smouldering in the grate where he'd thrown it. 'I can understand the kid. It shouldn't 'ave 'appened. She 'ad the rest of 'er life and that geezer ruined it for 'er.' There was a thoughtful pursing of lips and shading his eyes before he crossed the room and stood over her. 'This adoption lark...the council an' all that. They arrange it proper? Why can't we leave it to them?'

Maisie shook her head vehemently. Hadn't he listened. 'I've already told you she's doing the deal with this woman from London on Tuesday – that's in three days. We don't have time.'

'We?' His eyebrows rose. The sneer once again twisted his thin lips. 'Anyways, you just wants me to speak to 'er and change 'er mind.' He shook his head. 'That's a tall order. She's as stubborn as 'er mother.' Memories smudged the customary hardness of his eyes. Eddie had once been young and so had Carole's mother.

Maisie shrugged. Her mouth was dry and no matter how much she wanted to stop it happening, she could think of no way to do it – except to prevent Mrs Lavender from taking Paula. Eddie wouldn't hesitate to get rid of the woman if he had to. Could Maisie live with such guilt? She knew she could not and regretted thinking he could do something.

'I'm sorry.' She got to her feet, handbag more tightly clasped than when she had arrived. 'I shouldn't have come.' Shaking her head at her own stupidity, she made for the door. Glancing behind her, she saw the gritty damp footprints of her shoes. The pale green of the carpet showed every mark at the best of times, more so in this weather.

Eddie got there before she did, standing like a rock between her and her escape. 'But you 'ave. Got any other idea that might help?'

'Only as already mentioned; adoption through the local council – the children's department. They check things properly. They prefer a baby, a child, to be adopted by a married couple – like somebody who can't 'ave kids.'

Eddie looked thoughtful, then grimaced and shook his head. 'I don't like the idea of my grandkid going to live with strangers.'

Maisie almost laughed. This coming from Eddie Bridgeman? Instead she frowned. 'If I could, I would adopt her like a shot. But I'm not married. It could take some time or it might never happen.'

Eddie raised his eyebrows. 'Ain't you even courtin'?'

She shook her head. 'Well, there is someone, but it's early days. Can't rush these things,' she added and grinned.

'Hmm.' The jagged black hairs of his brows beetled into yet another thoughtful frown. The devil was in the look he gave her when his eyes met hers – an air of wickedness. If her mission hadn't been so important to her, she would have dived around him and gone. 'What time is she going to Temple Meads?'

'She has to be there at twelve noon.'

Emotions that had momentarily clouded those black-fringed eyes disappeared, replaced by purposeful calculation. He nodded. 'I'll deal with it.'

Despite her misgivings about how Eddie would 'deal with it', Maisie felt a great surge of relief and preferred not to jeopardise it by asking for details. However he wanted to handle things was down to him. Instead, she thanked him.

He smiled and just for once gave her a look showing a depth she'd never seen before. 'You love the kid.'

She nodded. 'Yes. Very much.' She couldn't help the tears that came to her eyes.

'Would you marry some bloke if it meant you could look after her, you know, adopt 'er?'

She sniffed, got out a handkerchief and patted her nose and eyes. She would do just about anything to hang onto Paula, to deter Carole from doing this. 'I would do anything. Anything at all.'

It took her by surprise when Eddie laid his hand on her shoulder and gave it a squeeze. 'So would I, darlin'. So would I. Marry if I 'ad to. If I really 'ad to.'

She started. For a moment she fancied he was going to kiss her. Taking just a single step away was not enough to escape the strong scent of cologne. 'I'd better go now. I don't want Carole to know that I've been here. She might be suspicious if I get home too late.'

'Come on,' he said, cupping her elbow. 'I'll get my driver to take you 'ome.' At the door, he turned and faced her. 'I know we ain't always seen eye to eye, what with yer old man and all that—'

'He wasn't my father.'

'I know that. Heard anything from that brother of yours?'

Strange that he should mention him; strange that she'd been thinking of him today of all days.

She shook her head. 'No. I wish I had.'

'Course you do. Blood's thicker than water, and that's how it is with me, Maisie. Blood's thicker than water all right, and believe you me I takes care of me own.'

There was resolve in his look; not outright love for his daughter and granddaughter, but a deadly resolve that he would fix anything and anyone who crossed him. He might not ever show emotion for either Carole or her daughter, but he wouldn't tolerate anyone doing them down. Woe betide them if they did.

In the car going home, the driver kept his eyes on the road. It being early June, darkness had not yet fallen, but the leaden clouds were still chucking it down. The interior of the car should have felt warmer than it did, but Maisie felt cold. In her mind, she went over everything that Eddie had said.

She frowned at the last bits of their conversation. She'd admitted she would marry anyone in order to adopt Paula. He'd agreed with her, said he would do the same. Surely, he hadn't been hinting that he would marry her – had he?

The interior of the car turned even colder. Would she really do anything to adopt Paula? Only time would tell.

15

BRIDGET

On the same night as Maisie had met up with Eddie Bridgeman, Bridget was packing her bags. Fully qualified nurses, those in training and auxiliary nurses had received orders that morning to gather up their things and prepare to travel. All leave was cancelled. The making of phone calls was banned.

Having a premonition that something was going down, she'd phoned Lyndon at his airbase in Lincolnshire around midday but couldn't get through. She'd written a brief note and sent it off. Once assured that the most important letter was on its way, she began writing another one, this time to Maisie.

Dear Maisie,

I hope you are well. Have you managed to visit my mother? I'm sure she'd love to see you. I can't get leave, so won't be in Bristol for a while...

She'd wanted to say that all leave was cancelled, but, of course, the censor wouldn't allow that. All leave being cancelled would be enough of a hint to the enemy that something big was about to happen. And it was.

Everyone was saying it.

As it was, Bridget didn't get chance to finish the letter. There were so many other things to attend to. Efficiently and without comment, bags were packed, wills written, postcards and letters left with an adjutant for posting.

The wills were the hardest to write. Death could happen at any time to any one of them. The War Office was keen to have all eventualities in place. Few of the young women serving alongside Bridget believed they would die. Their youthful energy kept them believing otherwise.

Piled into army vehicles with their things, young women from all walks of life were ferried to the nearest railway station. Pale blue wartime lights gave a ghostly look to both the station and the young women crowding onto the platform. In peacetime, those lights would have thrown a yellow warmth over all they touched. Blue lights were less discernible to enemy aircraft.

Some of the girls were lucky enough to find a seat on a wooden bench. The rest settled where they could, mostly using their luggage. Cigarette smoke wafted skywards. Their laughter was brittle. Their conversation muted.

No one was quite sure of their destination but could readily guess. The troops had moved southwards for onward travel. Doctors, nurses, and other medical staff were following on. It didn't take much to realise that a large number of medical staff preceded the expectation of a large number of casualties.

Like many of their number, Bridget stared across the railway lines to the opposite platform. The throb of aircraft engines came from overhead. Wave after wave after wave.

Eyes looked skyward. Bridget wanted to but found she couldn't.

When she finally braved it, the sky seemed black with aircraft. Lyndon was one of them. That was her instinct. He was bound to be there in amongst such a huge gathering of bombers, like a dark cloud covering the sky.

She jerked her gaze back to the other side of the railway line. Nothing she'd ever seen on the wards had made her feel as sick as she did now. Lyndon, that was all she could think of; Lyndon was up there. She just hoped to God he would come back safely.

The thunder from overhead droned on, heavy and inescapable, rattling windows and unsettling the dust from the platform floor.

Bridget closed her eyes to it but could not close her ears. The huge formation of Flying Fortresses and Lancaster bombers could not be ignored

'Wonder where they're going?'

Thanks to the dim lighting, it wasn't possible to see which of her colleagues spoke, if any. Whoever it was might have been from another detachment, a completely different hospital. More army vehicles had arrived during the time she'd been there. Each one had churned out more medical staff.

Bridget finally made comment. 'Wherever they're going, let's just hope they come back safely.'

'Amen.'

The speaker offered her a cigarette.

A light smoker, this was one of those times when Bridget needed something – anything – to settle her nerves. Her hand shook as she took the proffered cigarette and then a light. She breathed in, then blew out smoke and watched as it drifted upwards. It reminded her of incense, though smelt more acrid and obviously more common.

'Thanks. The man I love is up there somewhere.'

'Good luck.'

'And you?'

'He's in the army. I haven't seen him for over a week. No phone calls. Just a note. *"Take care of yourself."* That was all he said. *"Take care of yourself."'*

'I think we're going to be too busy looking after everyone else to look after ourselves.'

The other young woman sighed and flicked her cigarette into the gap between the platforms. For a while, it smouldered red and then was gone. 'You can say that again.'

They boarded just before midnight, keeping their thoughts and fears to themselves. Once the train was in motion, a strange air of relief descended, though conversation was still nervous and minimal. Cigarettes, food and drink were silently passed round. The compartment was packed with the smell of women, fear and cigarette smoke. Few of them slept.

Bridget found it impossible. She was convinced something big was on. There were so many nurses and other medical staff packed onto this train.

This was it, she told herself. This was the moment the whole world had been waiting for.

Orders were given that on no account were the blinds of the railway carriage to be raised. Not that there would be anything to see. They were travelling at night.

An hour or so into their journey, the news broke that they were heading for a receiving hospital on the south coast. Even this news was received quietly and with a kind of stunned eventuality.

Trains travelled slowly. Even the lights from signal boxes were muted. Care had to be taken. Name signs had been taken down at the beginning of the war. Locations of anywhere important depended on recognising a building or a street. In this regard, pubs, exempt from having their names removed, though blackout was strictly observed, windows heavily curtained, were used as markers.

The George, the Queen's Head, the Tollgate Inn, the Rose and Crown...They ran through Bridget's mind.

Behind her closed eyes, Bridget wrestled with a mix of fear and excitement.

So many planes.

So many people travelling.

She wasn't alone with the feeling that their lives were about to change.

Even that morning when they'd had no firm idea of where they were going, the smell of something big was in the air.

They now knew they were being relocated to a large military hospital. In soft whispers the statement and the consequences were passed from one to another.

'It's the big one.'

They said it breathlessly. Some prayed for all those about to go into battle. Bridget prayed for Lyndon. 'Please God, keep him safe.'

Her eyes blinked open and met those of a compatriot.

'Scary isn't it?' Betty was a cute little person with short curly hair. Her name was Betty Gabbler – the same initials as Betty Grable. Any likeness to the famous film star stopped right there. Betty's hair was bright copper and her face covered in freckles.

Bridget agreed with her. Sighing she folded her arms and leaned her head against the window, eyes half closed. 'I just wish I could sleep.'

'I've got a bloke in the army,' said Betty quietly so as not to disturb those who were taking advantage of the journey to get some sleep. 'I heard from him back last week, but not since. I just hope he's all right. How about you?'

Bridget smiled. In her mind, she conjured up a vision of the man she loved, which actually made her smile wider. 'He's in the US Air Force.'

Betty eyed her with interest. So many girls had met Americans.

Some relationships had lasted, but when a man was posted, it was sometimes a case of never hearing from them again.

'We met before the war,' said Bridget. 'We've been together a while.'

Her statement confirmed she was in a serious relationship. She dared not admit that she was married. Gossip could get out of hand.

Betty looked impressed. 'Do I hear wedding bells?'

A slow smile spread across Bridget's lips. 'Oh yes. Most definitely.'

* * *

It was some time after dawn and they'd arrived at a line hospital just a few miles from the south coast when the news they'd been waiting years for finally broke.

'Normandy. D Day. It's finally arrived.'

Although trying to keep his tone even, the BBC broadcaster was having difficulty controlling an undercurrent of excitement. 'It has been reported that British, American and other allied forces have landed on the beaches of Normandy...'

There was an almost palpable gasp of relief. A few tears were shed.

Nursing corps majors clapped their hands to draw attention.

'Ladies! Tea and toast are being served in the canteen. Get it whilst you can. This day, duty will make great demands on you. After you've been to the canteen, familiarise yourself with hospital facilities.'

For once, the hungry staff who'd trained and learned in double quick time were fast and furious eating toast and drinking tea. Hyped up with adrenaline, everyone wanted the day to move forward and them to get on with what they had to do.

Bridget and Betty pushed open the double doors of the ward and stared. Cleanliness lay crisply on the very air. Unsullied sheets and pillows, pristinely white, looked too perfect to disturb. There was not a crease in sight and the corners of bedcovers were folded tightly beneath mattresses.

Although it looked as if nothing further needed to be done, more and more supplies were being unloaded from trucks.

Like everyone else, Bridget kept busy, which prevented her worrying about Lyndon, though not completely. Alongside her own worries, she steeled herself to the arrival of casualties from the battlefield that was Normandy. They knew little of how things were going. They wouldn't know until the first casualties arrived.

'Ever been there? France, I mean?' The question was put to her by Bernadette, a Catholic girl from Liverpool.

'No. Can't say that I have.'

'Bet some of our more snooty types have been abroad. Not necessarily France, but somewhere. Furthest I've ever gone is Southport on a bank holiday. I'd like to go abroad some day, wouldn't you?'

Bridget laughed lightly. 'A lovely thought, but I'm not sure I could afford to go far on a train, let alone a boat or an aeroplane.'

Bernadette laughed. 'Now there's a thing. Fancy flying away on holiday. I wouldn't mind, I must say.'

'It might be a bit farfetched, but we can only hope.'

'Women didn't have the vote before the last lot – the First World War as they're now calling it. Got it now though, ain't we! So who knows? We might get to visit exotic places.'

Bridget agreed that it was possible as her attention was taken by the scene outside the open window. The rain had stopped some time ago. The dawn sky was a patch of cloud interspersed with splashes of blue. There was a large yard outside the window of the nurses' station, mostly used for ambulances. She'd seen one there earlier. The vehicle she now saw had backed up to the doors of the mortuary. The doors were open. One by one, coffins were being unloaded.

Two men, one over fifty and the other barely fifteen, were talking. The boy's higher and excited voice drifted in through the open window.

'I tell you. It was like thunder. All them ships in the harbour starting up their engines at once was bloody deafening. There were loads of army trucks coming and going, blokes marching and hundreds and hundreds of planes overhead...'

'Now, now, lad,' warned the older man. 'Careless talk costs lives. Get on with your work, son.'

The boy's reference to the planes was like an arrow to Bridget's heart. The confirmation of events stoked her rising fear. She looked up at the sky with longing in her eyes and said softly, 'Please God, keep him safe.' It occurred to her that she'd be saying that a lot during the coming days.

They kept their ears tuned to the wireless. News was passed on with energetic enthusiasm. Again and again the same message was repeated.

'At dawn this morning...'

No matter where they were in the hospital, the words that crackled over the wireless system left some gasping, some stifling a sob.

Bridget's gaze wandered over the neatly made beds in the empty wards. Depending on the speed of hospital ships, those beds would quickly fill with the wounded, the white sheets bloodied and creased by tired, injured men.

The voice of a senior officer of Queen Alexandra's Royal Imperial Nursing Corp, who was in charge of all nurses whether army or civilian, boomed out. 'Come along, sisters. Let's get everything ready. Not a thing out of place. The next few days are going to be busy.'

It appeared they weren't being given time to dwell on matters. The order had been given to keep them occupied. Keep them keen.

There was no real need for the QA major to boom out the same message again and again. Nobody was in any doubt that the injured would be coming in thick and fast.

Bridget had purposely not mentioned seeing the coffins being unloaded. A shiver ran down her spine when she thought of Lyndon ending up in one of those. She forced the vision from her mind, swapping it for one of a smiling Lyndon coming home, wrapping his arms around her, and declaring he would never fly again. That would suit her fine. After this, she never wanted him to fly again, and she backtracked on her conversation with Betty about flying away in peacetime. Who would want to?

This war had to be won before they could enjoy peace. She had no doubt that the fighting would be fierce. Lyndon, his colleagues and everyone else going over there would be fighting for victory. The enemy would be fighting to survive.

During a brief respite, she slipped off her shoes and rubbed at her aching toes and soles. Nobody was complaining about their hours. Nobody seemed inclined to rest. This was the day everyone had looked forward to for so long. Everyone would be putting in their best efforts.

'Tea,' said Helen, one of the other nurses. 'Quite decent too.'

Six of them gathered in the small staffroom used for short breaks. Bridget carefully avoided looking towards the window. Presumably there would be other deliveries of coffins, but hopefully not in daylight.

Betty purposely poured her tea from cup to saucer so it would cool more quickly.

'Bliss,' said Bridget, one stockinged foot rubbing against the other.

'Make the most of it,' said May, a small person of rounded figure and bouncy step. 'We're going to be ruddy busy, that's for sure.'

Everyone agreed that she was right. Once the wounded began arriving, those breaks would become shorter, or even non-existent. Until then, they were all on a knife edge waiting for the horrific sights they would have to deal with, the long hours and increased pressure.

The sudden ringing of the telephone disturbed their silent contemplation and the sipping of decent tea. It was followed by the sound of approaching footsteps.

Gladys, a good sort who had opted to do auxiliary duties – anything to be in touch with the action – came striding into the room.

'A call for you, Nurse Milligan.' She grinned. 'It's a man. Sounds like a Yank.'

Bridget's cup clattered into the saucer as, with inelegant speed, she got up from her chair. Lyndon! How had he managed it? Running along hospital corridors was frowned on even in the face of great emergency. For once she didn't care about receiving a reprimand but raced along to the phone.

It had to be him. Doubts cornered her mind. Or a colleague, telling her that... She blocked out the rest of the thought.

She grabbed the phone. 'Lyndon? Is that you?'

'Yeah. What other guy were you expecting?'

'Lyndon!' She could barely breathe let alone speak.

'You okay?'

'Yes. I'm fine. I got reassigned. I'm at a hospital on the south coast. Obviously...'

'Obviously. London told me you'd been sent south.'

She frowned. 'I thought you'd already been up in the air.' *Though I wish you weren't.* The thought remained unsaid.

'I can't give you any details, but I'll be involved, honey. Careless talk could cook my bacon. These telephone lines can leak information. Did you know that?'

He spoke every word with high-pitched enthusiasm, his excitement palpable.

Fear gripped its iron hand around her heart. 'You're looking forward to fighting.' The words chilled her tongue.

'Honey, we're making history today and, yes, you're right. I want to be part of it. I want to fight. Over a hundred and fifty thousand guys are in this, part of the biggest military assault ever known. Can you blame me for wanting to make history?'

She wanted to say that she wished he was back lecturing the armed forces on adapting to British ways and British life. That was where this had all started, the crazy way he'd hitched a ride in a bomber. He'd told her that none of the crew was more than early twenties. It had made him feel guilty about being in a comfortable 'desk' job. He'd been as scared as them, but excitement had been there too.

'I've heard it said that a man in danger of being killed in battle feels more alive than he's ever felt in his life. I want to feel that, honey. I don't want to miss the opportunity to be part of this momentous event.'

He spoke like a man of many years and much wisdom would sound. He believed in what he was doing and even if she begged, she knew he would not step back from doing his duty.

There was a bitter taste on her tongue. Deep inside, she feared for him, but she needed to have a care how she responded. Lyndon, the man she'd married, and the love of her life, was going into battle and needed her encouragement, not her pleading for him not to go. She consoled herself that at least he would be up in the air, flying a bomber, and not on the ground being shot at. The B17s flew very high. Even the deadly ack-ack had trouble hitting anything flying at such an altitude.

She was scared for him but forced herself to sound encouraging. 'Lyndon, come back to me. Promise you'll come back to me.'

'Just try and stop me!' His obvious excitement was like electricity sparking along the phone line. 'Got to go now. The guys are waiting for me. Take care.' He paused then added. 'No matter what happens, remember I love you.'

* * *

At his end, Lyndon lay the phone down slowly. He'd said all he could say. He couldn't tell Bridget anything about where he was going, but that was only to be expected. She would know that.

'Hey buddy, how about you quit caressing that phone and let another guy get a shot. We all got sweet words and promises to make before we take off.'

Lyndon laughed. Laughter helped all of them cope. He apologised to the waiting airman. 'Sorry, pal. Be my guest.'

There wasn't much time to go before take-off and he needed to get his thoughts in order. It wasn't that Bridget was immaterial, that he could entirely shut her out on this great day. Fighting this war and winning the peace was about her. They were man and wife and intended spending the rest of their lives together. They were happy about being married, but not everyone was – especially his parents.

As he strode across the tarmac to where his plane, part of the third wave to take off that morning, his mind turned to the letter he'd received from his mother. It hurt. It angered. She just didn't get what he felt, how things were between him and Bridget. The words had bit into his very soul.

Bridget may indeed be a lovely girl, but things like this happen in war. Opposites attract, but such relationships are unlikely to last. To that end, I have consulted with Wilfred; you may recall it was your uncle Wilfred who sorted out that nastiness regarding my brother and our maid. The girl lied of course and Wilfred was instrumental in paying her off. I'm sure he could arrange a quick divorce, leaving you free to marry a girl of similar status to your own. Think about it once this war is over, which I for one hope will be soon. I will never forgive the Japanese for attacking Pearl Harbour. We would still be keeping ourselves to ourselves if it hadn't been for them.

Anyway, water under the bridge. I'm just a mother who wants the best for her son. Think on what I've said. In the meantime, I'll run it past Wilfred.

Your father sends his love...

The anger stayed with him. In the absence of his mother, the Germans would get the full force of his fury.

The engines of the B17 Flying Fortress rumbled into life, the whole aircraft vibrating as the propellers spun faster and faster. A shard of light speared through the cockpit window. The gold ring on the finger of his left hand glinted: his wedding ring. He looked down at with sudden fascination and a great deal of love. What an unremarkable wedding it had been, certainly not the kind his mother would have favoured. Just friends and the two of them. He'd loved its simplicity, the fact that it really had been all about just them. He would have hated a society affair with hundreds of guests. All he'd wanted, and all he would ever want, was just the two of them and that's the way it would always be.

Some might think it odd, but in that instant, he felt that Bridget was thinking of him – just as he was thinking of her. Not that he could allow that to happen for too long. Personal thoughts

disturbed his concentration. Charts and his slide rule were the
order of the day. His job was to get the plane and crew over to the
bombing area and back again. Forcing himself to concentrate, he
spread out his charts, took pencil in one hand, slide rule in the
other and began to study the plotted course.

'All okay back there?'

'Ready when you are, skipper.'

Lyndon peered forward in time to see the flare signal from
command shooting up into the sky. Noise and vibration increased
as the brakes were let off and the fierce beast that was the B17, the
strikingly named Flying Fortress, lumbered forward.

They were off. All thoughts of loved ones weren't easy to
dislodge, but needs must. He had a job to do and needed to concentrate. Everything else could wait until he got back, including a reply
to his mother. He'd already composed what he would say to her
suggestion regarding Wilfred – though more politely than the ones
he was presently thinking.

His undivided attention went back to the chart and the briefing
he'd been given earlier. Their destination was Nordhausen – the
place where Hitler's new weapons were made. The RAF had
knocked out the original site in Pennemunde back in 1943. Their job
was to wipe the new site before the rockets got to launch areas that
could threaten the ongoing invasion. Enemy resistance would be
fierce, but as high command had informed them, knocking them
out would save a lot of lives. We must do this. We must give it
our all.

Suddenly the sky outside the aircraft throbbed with explosions,
the sky bright with flak from the ground-based defences. The
aircraft rocked.

'How far are we from the drop zone,' the captain shouted back
at him from the cockpit.

'Pretty close. Can't you tell?'

Lyndon pressed both hands down on his slide rule, which was currently living up to its name – sliding all over the place. Pencil in hand, he did the final calculations.

'We're there,' and gave the coordinates.

The plane banked as it swooped to drop its load into the darkness below and a factory where a weapon was being made that would change the world.

16

CAROLE

Once Maisie had left for work, Carole took deep breaths. She'd expected to feel excited at the prospect of a new beginning away from Bristol, though apprehensive about giving Paula up for adoption.

'You can do this,' she muttered to herself as she packed squares of towelling nappies, feeding bottle, talcum powder – the latter a luxury purchased by Maisie. She had also given her two flannelette nightdresses that she said had been bequeathed by a friend who had lost her baby. They were soft and newly washed. So were the spare bootees and matinee jackets. She bit her lip as she looked down at them, thinking how things could have been so much different if... If. So many ifs. Too many. If only Aggie Hill had come with her to visit Reg Harris. If only she hadn't knocked on Reg Harris's door in the first place. If only his wife had been there. If only he hadn't lied... If only, if only.

I would have loved her, she thought. If the father had died in battle or even deserted her, that moment of conception would still have been a result of love and thus the memory and love would have lingered.

Another vision darkened her thoughts. She'd been there when Reg Harris's body was unearthed on a bombsite, killed by a person or persons unknown. The killer, who may have got someone else to do it, was known to her. Not that she could prove it. Not that she wanted to prove it. Reg Harris had only got what he deserved. It was all in the past. She'd jettison everything just to regain the carefree life she'd once so enjoyed.

Last night she had tended to Paula when she wanted her feed. Usually, she took turns with Maisie, but sleep had been elusive, her mind plagued with guilt and the possible fallout of what she was about to do.

Maisie had awoken to the sound of Paula's demanding cry. She'd looked hurt when Carole had insisted on feeding Paula herself. She'd abruptly closed the bedroom door, leaving her and Paula on the inside. Maisie had been left outside on the landing.

It had been about three o'clock in the morning. The curtains were drawn, and the street outside was quiet with night. All sounds seemed muffled by darkness and sleep.

A strange feeling had come over her as she sat there in the semi-dark room, looking down at her baby. The faint glow of the bedside light picked out Paula's blue eyes looking back at her. There was a smile at first and then a long lingering look that made Carole suspect the child knew of her plan.

She had reprimanded herself. *Of course, she doesn't. She's just a baby.* The feeling had lingered. If she'd cared to think further about it, she would have recognised it as guilt. But she didn't want to feel guilt. She wanted to believe she was doing the right thing, the best thing for her baby. The feelings, the regrets and the likely repercussions had been pushed aside.

Paula had waved her little hands at the sight of the bottle.

Carole had made the decision some time ago to get her off breast milk and use National Dried Milk supplied by the clinic.

'Can't stand all that stickiness spoiling my dress. It's disgusting.'

That's what she'd said to Maisie. Maisie had been understanding about it, and anyway, the bottle meant she could take turns with feeding.

Paula had drunk approximately half the bottle. The blue eyes had continued to stare up into hers, the little fingers touched the neck of the bottle. The pink lips had smiled. The teat had flopped from the rosebud mouth.

There was something challenging in her baby's smile, something she couldn't ignore. The lips looked so sweet, a perfect Cupid's bow and there was laughter in her eyes.

She'd hated breastfeeding, in fact she'd considered it quite disgusting. Blue eyes and a wavering smile had made her reconsider. Before the moment was gone and her daughter was gone, she had a sudden yearning to do it one last time, to have one last intimate moment with her baby daughter.

Her breathing had quickened as she thought about it. Giving in was like falling off a cliff without fear for the consequences. The ground had disappeared from under her feet. She had felt no fear but a great sense of calm happiness.

In the stillness of the night and the privacy of her room, when the only sound was the creaking of joists and door jambs expending their daytime warmth, she had undone the strings of her nightgown.

Despite her best efforts, her breasts, heavy and round, the nipples erect, had retained residual milk.

With careful deliberation, she'd held her breast with one hand and cupped Paula's head with the other. Her heart fluttered. Her breathing quickened.

There was something quite magical seeing and feeling the rosebud lips respond to the insertion of her swollen breast. Both the pursing of those lips over her nipple and the extraordinary intimacy had made her gasp. Why hadn't she experienced this feeling before? Was it because she'd been too tired and too worried in the first weeks and months after the birth? Wounded and sick at what had happened to her, she'd not allowed herself to experience any close intimacy with her daughter. Breastfeeding was the most intimate closeness there could be between mother and child.

With her velvet-soft lips still clamped to her mother's breast, Paula had fallen asleep. Carole had studied her baby's features, trying to see the face of the man who had fathered her child but failing to do so. The downy hair was fair, almost white, like her own, the nose pert, the eyelids, now closed, as perfectly formed as silver teaspoons. Had she been mistaken about seeing a likeness?

Even after she had placed her back in her cot, Carole couldn't stop staring at this small scrap of life that had so affected her own. There was wonder in that look, wonder in what she was feeling and what had happened. For a moment, something overly loving had stirred inside, but she pushed it away. A single mother was frowned on, ostracised, even bullied. Getting a job was difficult, or a place to live for that matter. She'd heard of girls of her age passing the child off as a niece or even sister if their own mother was willing. Carole's mother had remarried and moved miles away. Anyway, she wasn't the sort to be tied to bringing up a baby, even if it was her own grandchild.

'It's all for the best,' she'd whispered when she pulled up the bedcovers. For a moment, she'd lingered, the guilt almost smothering her. The feeling was so strong, that she'd placed both hands around her throat to throttle the threatening sob.

Sleep had remained evasive. She wanted this day to come and go. Once it had, she would feel better. That's what she told herself.

The following morning, she'd poured tea, though neither she nor Maisie took a sip.

As she did every morning, Maisie had stood over the sleeping baby before leaving for work. It was difficult to read the look in her eyes.

'I'll see you tonight,' Carole had managed to say. It was a lie. She would not be here. She would be off seeking her new life and the baby would be in a new home.

Maisie had stood rigidly. There was a paleness to her warm complexion, inherited from her darker antecedents. Her eyes were round and unblinking as though frozen open.

The lie had rolled easily off her tongue. Maisie had made no comment. Carole wondered if she suspected that there would be no homecoming tonight.

The door had slammed with few words being said. Maisie's demeanour made Carole nervous. Had she guessed that this would likely be the last time they would see each other?

Carole now placed both suitcases – one for her and one for Paula – on the wire rack fixed beneath the pram – the place where shopping bags were usually placed. She didn't look back when she left the house. It was too painful and looking back might make her change her mind. She had to be resolute.

Baby, pram and luggage proved a heavy load and she had to put the brake on as she went down the hill from Totterdown. Once on the level Bath Road, she took it off and headed for Temple Meads station.

The roads were oddly empty, even though it was mid-morning. It didn't occur to her that there might be a reason. She didn't care. She'd not turned the wireless on that morning. The pavements were dry, the wet weather finally dispersing. Perhaps the weather was improving from here on – just like her life.

A splinter of sunlight piercing a cloud lifted her spirits and she dared think about the future. No more pram pushing after today. No more changing nappies, feeding her and putting her down to sleep. No more swollen breasts and stained dresses. No more walks like this. Carole blinked at the realisation that she would once more be alone.

She didn't know why she did it, but every so often, she leaned over the pram and uttered excuses that only she could hear and understand. Paula, totally oblivious to the big changes about to happen in her life, carried on sleeping.

Just a little way and they would cross the road to Temple Meads. Carole looked down into the pram once more and saw her baby's pretty lips and a pang of remorse hit her. She lay her hand over her breast. When her nipple reacted, she felt an overwhelming desire to stop the pram, get Paula out and feed her, just as she had during the night – such an intimate moment that had lifted her heart. It couldn't be done of course, not here in public, walking down the road. People would be disgusted. The thought of their disgust made her feel angry. Why shouldn't a mother be allowed to breastfeed her child in public? Wasn't it a perfectly natural thing to do?

Apprehension made her the subject of a sudden tingling sensation. At first it was confined to her fingers, but gradually it progressed all over her body. The world around her became just a hubbub of sound and movement. The bond she'd felt when feeding her baby early that morning took hold of her as though it owned her – owned both – mother and child.

Her breasts began to ache. She'd expected to make more milk and knew it was there radiating from her nipple where her daughter had taken nourishment just a few hours ago. The yearning to turn back was strong, but the yearning to feed her was even stronger. How strange, she thought. What do I do?

She steeled herself to do what she'd decided. In the previous days, it had been hard enough to go through with it. Today, the exact moment when she would hand over both baby and a wedge of money to Mrs Lavender, was harder.

Carole's stomach rumbled. She put it down to having had no

breakfast and she'd only taken a sip or two of tea. Thirst was not enough to persuade her to turn back, but her determination to see this through was not as strong as it had been.

She swiped at the corners of her eyes, willing tears not to spill. Giving into tears would undermine her determination to go through with this. She'd be lost and lumbered with a baby in youthful years that should be given over to going out with her friends and having fun.

Her resolve was weakened. Arguments from opposing camps fought in her mind and even in her throat. Swallowing the lump stuck there proved an impossibility. As a child, she'd swallowed a gobstopper, a huge round sweet that should never be swallowed whole. Her mother had slapped her on the back several times until somehow – she didn't know how – it went down. Her mother wasn't here to repeat the action. The lump stayed in her throat.

Carole bent down to make sure that the small case containing Paula's things was still in situ on the tray beneath the pram. Next, she checked the brown suitcase containing her things, everything she could find room for. Tonight Maisie would come home to a house that would echo with silence. The baby would be gone and so would she.

Guilt plagued her. Guilt for giving up Paula and for leaving Maisie without saying goodbye. She'd left a brief note of explanation on the mantelpiece in the living room. A very short note. She planned to write a letter and send it from London or wherever she ended up. Wherever it was, she hoped to be as far away from Bristol as possible.

Her plan was that once she'd handed Paula over – with the pram if Mrs Lavender wanted it, she would jump on the next train. She didn't care where it was going as long as it was far away from the memory of Reg Harris, his sickening leer, and his probing fingers. She almost choked on far more threatening sobs than she could cope with. She patted her chest, though it did little to still her racing heart.

Paula was sleeping soundly, oblivious to the fact that her life was about to take a path away from her birthplace, her mother, and Aunt Maisie. Not that she knew any of these names at present.

The long walk downhill to Bristol's main railway station seemed to fly. There it was, the Gothic-style tower piercing the sky. She needed to cross the road to get to it.

There were buses, of course, coal lorries, shire horses pulling beer drays stamped with the name '*Georges Bristol Brewery*' along the sides. A long column of army vehicles was being given priority. There were jeeps and lorries, all bursting at the seams with soldiers. One after the other, they came, nose to tail. It didn't matter that she was pushing a baby in a pram, they still wolf-whistled. That was the Americans for you; totally incorrigible. She gave them no encouragement. There would be plenty of time for that sort of thing in the future.

The nearer she got to the station concourse, the more people there were, milling around, trying to push their way up the slope and into the station.

A policeman offered to see her across the road. 'They'll all be in France with all the others soon,' he said, beaming as he held up the traffic and she made her way across.

She didn't ask him what he meant. She didn't care. All she wanted to do was to cross the road.

Folding her fingers tightly over the handle, she pushed her pram up the concourse to the station. Not everyone moved aside to let her pass.

She finally got to the main entrance, where she was forced to manoeuvre the pram through the crowds, saying excuse me all the way.

Inside the station, in front of the ticket offices was as crowded as outside, perhaps more so.

She'd expected crowds all waiting to go somewhere. Everyone had been going somewhere important from the very start of the war. But today, the station was more crowded than usual.

'Excuse me, please.' She kept having to say it.

One or two froze her out. Others questioned what the devil was she thinking of pushing a pram in such crowds. Puzzled glances fell her way from a crowd reluctant to move and it was difficult to push the pram through.

'Excuse me.' She repeated herself again and again and they grumbled again and again.

They grumbled more when the pram wheels bumped into them. 'Hey, watch where you're going, lass.'

An accent she didn't recognise. All around her, accents, male voices, female voices. The smell of humanity outdid that of the coal-loaded smoke and steam.

The pram rocked as a trio of broad-shouldered men in army uniform bashed into it. Paula began to cry.

'Excuse me,' Carole shouted after them. They didn't slow down and didn't look back.

Carole bent low and peered above the pram's apron into her daughter's red face. 'Shhh! Shhh! It's all right, darling. It's all right.'

On seeing her mother, the crying stopped. Big blue eyes peered back up at her; trusting eyes. A small smile curled the rosebud lips.

Something grabbed at Carole's heart. For a moment, she did nothing, just stared back at her baby.

'I'm sorry, darling. I'm really sorry.'

She looked around her and asked herself a question. *Am I saying sorry for all this mayhem, or am I sorry for letting her go?*

The thought rushed in unbidden and was difficult to face. She'd made her mind up to go through with this. She had to see it through, which at present meant getting through these crowds. On the one hand, being late scared her. On the other, it made her less sure that she could go through with it.

She hadn't allowed for this. It was as though someone or somebody had placed these people in her way on purpose.

Fate, she thought. *I did say I would leave it to fate.*

The crowds pressed close. In a way, they seemed without bodies, just a sea of hats, caps, pursed lips kissing, tearful women and orders being barked from the station's loudspeaker system. It was absolute mayhem.

Kitbags slung over shoulders clad mostly in khaki uniforms bumped against her. Bodies pressed around her from all directions. If the walk down along the Bath Road had passed quickly, trying to negotiate the short distance to the station entrance had taken ages. Inside the station was no better, a wall of people prevented her from moving forward.

A man wearing a Great Western Railway cap bumped into her. He'd looked as though he was going to reprimand her in no uncertain terms until he saw the pram. His look softened. 'Sorry, love, but you won't get that pram through yer.'

'But I have to,' she replied, her voice shrill with panic. 'I'm meeting someone – my aunt – she's arriving on the London train.' Another lie but one that might gain sympathy and get her through.

The man flicked fingers at the peak of his cap which had become dislodged in the ongoing melee happening all around. 'Not today, you ain't.'

'But I must. The train will be here shortly...'

'No it won't, love. Not for about six hours – if then. Ain't you 'eard the news,' he asked, with a quizzical sideways jerk of his head? 'The invasion's started.'

'Invasion?'

There was a distinct quivering in her voice. She suddenly had a vision of an enemy army landing on the beach at Weston-Super-Mare. Why there, she didn't know.

'That's right, love. A lot of trains 'ave been requisitioned. Delays and more delays, but then they're more than welcome on this of all days,' he said to her. 'Marvellous news, love. Management can take the whole bloody lot off if they like – begging your pardon,' he said as, with jovial aplomb, he once more grasped his peaked cap as more bodies bumped into him.

Carole frowned and shook her head. 'I don't understand. What invasion?'

Others who'd heard laughed and some almost sang.

'We've invaded France – us and our allies, that is. It's finally happened. We're liberating Europe.'

Unable to move forward or backward, up or down, she was stuck in a crowd of smiling faces.

'About bloody time,' somebody said.

'Three cheers for the Allies!'

A spontaneous cheer went up from the press of people.

Pram rocking from side to side, Paula began to cry.

'Come on, love. You ain't going to get through yer to meet yer aunt. Best come back later. Best leave it till tomorrow.' He jerked his head towards number one platform. 'You've stirred 'em up mentioning invasion.'

The green flags of railway guards and porters waved above the crowds and whistles blew – nothing to do with the arrival and departure of rolling stock, but in celebration and sheer delight that D Day had finally arrived.

Someone began singing 'We'll Meet Again.' Many more voices joined in, singing in time with the movement of people into the station, like a tide, a great, singing tide.

The crowd surged around her and she became an island in the mass of moving people.

Accepting there was nothing more to be done, she tried to turn round, tried to retrace the way she'd come. It was useless. The only way she was getting out of here was if she could float above the throng and fly backwards.

In the meantime, Paula was screaming for her feed, upset by the continuous bumping and rocking of her pram.

'Let me give you a 'and with that pram, love.' The broad brim of a trilby hat hid his face as, without further ado, he lifted the pram from the ground, charging ahead of her to the exit, pushing his way through the crowd.

Carole followed in his wake, taking advantage of the path he'd created.

Whoever he was, he made short shift of the job of getting the pram through, lifting it in strong arms and shouting at everyone to get out of the way.

A newspaper seller shouted the news. 'Allies invade Normandy.'

Finally, she was away from the concourse and in a big enough space to turn the pram round. She sat on a stone wall just down the slope from the station. Paula was warm in her arms. The pram's brake was put on whilst she fed Paula the bottle of National Dried Milk.

'There you are, darling.'

Paula stopped crying. Her eyes locked with those of her mother and she smiled. There was something meaningful in that smile. It was stupid to think she had known that her mother's plan was scuppered, but that was the way it seemed to Carole.

She made sweet gurgling noises. Not quite words, but in Carole's tired confusion, she thought she heard the word 'mmm-mm'. To her it sounded like mum, perhaps just the feverish belief of a confused imagination.

Glad to at last have room to breathe, Carole looked for the man who had helped her get the pram out. He deserved her thanks but found him gone. She caught a glimpse of his retreating back, for the life of her couldn't recall what he'd looked like. She'd been too engrossed and fearful of what was going on, yet somehow, she suspected she'd seen him somewhere before.

Yesterday's rain was no more. Patches of blue were showing through what cloud remained. The weather had changed. Seeing that blue sky and the rays of sunshine slicing through billowy clouds had an uplifting affect.

Someone, she couldn't recall who, had told her that everything happened for a reason. Things happened that made you look at things differently. One of those big billowy clouds reminded her of Aggie Hill. It wasn't that the delayed train was Aggie's doing; Carole wasn't daft enough to believe something like that. No, the delayed trains were down to the need to ferry troops to where they were needed. The invasion of Europe had intervened in her plan to dispose of her daughter. Dispose. Such a dreadful word. She couldn't do it.

Paula looked up at her, eyes big and bright, her smile making her cheeks round and shiny as apples. The bubbles began again. The little pink tongue poked out through equally pink lips.

Carole couldn't resist poking a finger into the warm palm of her baby daughter and feeling the tiny fingers curling around her own.

Carole chose to think that the gummy noises was her baby telling her that she was her mother and that Paula knew that.

Tears sprang to her eyes as she looked down at her smiling child. Was having a carefree life as a single woman that important? The very worst that could happen to a woman had happened to her. It hadn't been her fault and it hadn't been Paula's.

Overcome with emotion and an amazing sense of relief, she burst into tears. 'I'm sorry, Paula. I'm so, so sorry.'

A slightly surprised look replaced the smiles and gurgles. Paula looked a little perplexed. It wasn't so much as though she didn't understand, more so that she was reaching out, wanting to give her mother a pat on the shoulder or a kiss to tell her that everything was all right and that it always had been and always would be.

Taking a handkerchief from her pocket, one of two that Maisie had made her for Christmas from cut down scraps of old pillowcases, Carole dabbed the wetness away.

'We'll be fine,' she said softly to the small scrap of humanity that was part of her and belonged to her and nobody else. 'You and me, Paula. We'll be just fine.'

The baby's smile returned just before her face crumpled, her arms waved.

Home, she thought. Maisie personified home, the type of home she'd never had. There'd been an unending stream of men in the house at Little Paradise, the home she'd grown up in. In time, she might have ended up the same as her mother, having men pay her for services. Maisie had prevented all that happening. She owed her so much and somehow, one day, she would pay her back. Maisie deserved it.

* * *

There was more traffic than usual outside the station, more people hailing taxi cabs, more army trucks and other vehicles offloading provisions and men. Because of that Carole didn't notice the shiny black car coming to a halt some way in front. She also didn't notice Eddie Bridgeman looking out at her, an expression of pure satisfaction on his face. There'd been no need for him to intervene. He would have done the minute the baby was handed over, but as it was, things had worked out just fine.

He grimaced at the dark thoughts crowding his mind. Mrs bloody Lavender indeed. Well, she would have been well sorted, but there'd been no need. General Eisenhower had given the order and done the job for him.

'Good work, George.'

'That pram was bloody 'eavy. It weren't just the baby. She 'ad two suitcases as well.' George grumbled and rolled his shoulders as he said it.

Eddie laughed. 'Course it was. Best I could buy for my granddaughter. Only the best.'

He turned his head to gaze at the crowds. Groups of people were gathered around free newssheets. More detailed news would come later. These single sheets were an interim measure in lieu of the usual midday issue. As if anyone needed to read about what the BBC had already reported. The sixth of June, D Day, would go down in history. He couldn't remember seeing people interacting, laughing, chatting and even throwing their hats in the air for a very long time.

'It ain't all over yet,' he muttered, though conceded that it was the beginning of the end – as long as things went according to plan. The end was in sight and as far as he was concerned, it had been a good war – good for business anyway.

'Wonder what will 'appen next,' said George as he negotiated a route through the traffic.

'I need to plan for the future, old pal. Can't let all I've gained in war get lost in the peace.'

Eddie had been planning for some time, but in the chaos of war, there was still just enough time to get things done before there was no more blackout or rationing. The blackout and rationing had seen a huge expansion in crime and he'd done bloody well. But first things first. He had it in mind to ask questions of business associates – crime bosses – in London. He knew a few shady characters there ready and willing to make a few enquiries about Mrs Lavender. The sooner she was put out of business, the better. Not that he'd ever had any plan to take over the raising of the kid himself. He wanted Carole to raise her. She was the kid's mother. Regardless of the kid's father – and he'd dealt with him all right – it was the mother that counted. His mother had meant the world to him. His father had been a bully, but in time he'd sorted him out too.

'Who'd 'ave thought it,' he said, a plume of cigar smoke rising in front of his eyes and drifting forward into his driver's neck. 'Dealing in babies. I've done a few bad things in my time, but dealing in babies ain't one of them and never will be. Drive on. Let's make sure they both get 'ome okay.'

'Offer a lift?'

'Don't be daft. Where would we put the pram?'

'On the roof?'

Eddie was amused. However, he'd promised Maisie he'd keep a low profile.

'Just keep 'er in sight. Go round the block a few times if you 'ave to.'

17

BRIDGET

The first solitary patient from the beaches arrived at around nine o'clock in the morning, brought ashore by a fast-moving MGB, a motor gun boat capable of almost forty knots. Goodness knows why just him, but his arrival led to a burst of activity.

'A patient! We've got a patient!'

After all the training and waiting about, Bridget and the others were on him like a flock of hungry pigeons. He was covered in sand that had once been wet but now stuck to him in a brittle, irritating layer. In no time at all he was stripped, washed and his injuries assessed.

'I tripped and broke my foot,' he explained. 'Fell straight into the sand. The MGB blokes hooked me aboard and brought me back.'

His name was Corporal Addison and once he was up to muster, he found himself put to bed by at least three nurses between the crisp white sheets which at once became crumpled and creased. No amount of smoothing down would return them to their former pristine brightness, though they did try.

With an air of disappointment, Connie one of Bridget's fellow student nurses, mentioned how many times she'd made and remade that bed until Matron was satisfied it was fit to be seen.

'Let's just hope our boys win through,' Matron added, passing her keen gaze over the rest of the beds for imperfections.

'She's going to be really upset when "our boys" mess up those tidy beds,' whispered Connie to Bridget.

'That's what they'll do,' returned Bridget with just as soft a whisper.

Her smile hid an inner queasiness she just couldn't shift. Lyndon was one of 'those boys', though thankfully in an aircraft and not on the beaches of France.

On receipt of only one patient – whose swift return had had something to do with an accident rather than enemy fire, they would remain light-hearted and even joke about his arrival. Each of them knew that there would shortly be no time to think, let alone to joke. Worse cases would arrive, including those beyond any earthly help.

Bridget tried to keep busy and not think about the empty coffins she'd seen being unloaded, minimal compared to those being put into use on the other side of the English Channel.

Keep busy, she said to herself. So far, she had been occupied doing the more mundane things, but as the day wore on, daylight fading into twilight, then a cloudy but dry summer evening, it wasn't long before she really was run off her feet.

By the end of that first day, what had been an empty ward was full and more injured men were arriving. Time was of no consequence. There was too much to be done and she found herself unable to stop, even for a tea break.

'Come along, nurses. Faint heart never won... whatever it was...'

'Fair lady,' Bridget said softly, so only her immediate colleagues could hear her. She felt no great compunction to be clever or to disagree. There was no time for jollity, and it was doubly hard

smiling at a man with a gaping hole in his torso, a bone sticking out
from his leg, hearing a fearful howling as blood ran from an
abdominal wound around his private parts. She saw the horror in
each man's eyes. One asked through intense pain whether he would
ever make love again or have a family. This kind of question was
more frequently asked than anyone not present would give credit
for. Being and feeling like a man mattered, a life raft that those
who'd been through such carnage held onto. Will I have a normal
life when I get through this?

Swallowing the bile that rose in her throat, she motored on,
indeed moving like a well-oiled machine, not noticing the lights
coming on, the blackout blinds being drawn. She smiled and reas-
sured, though, without letting her emotions run away with her,
have her crumple and be of no use at all.

During a lull, she grabbed yet another cup of weak tea and
swallowed a biscuit whole. In a brief moment of sitting down, she
took off her shoes and rubbed at her aching feet. Blood and pus
erupted from a blister on her heel. Truth of the matter was she
hadn't noticed her heel was so bad. The matron handed her a plaster. She vaguely recalled thanking her but couldn't be sure.

When had she last rested? It was hard to work out and she
wasn't quite sure of the time. It was imperative that medical staff
rested between shifts, but a deluge of casualties arriving had
blurred what they needed and what they could have. Feet ached,
eyes grew dry with tiredness.

Some considerate soul had the gumption to place a bowl of
warm water on the floor. More than one foot had been immersed in
the warm suds, so the water wasn't too clean and was growing cold.

Matron came storming into the restroom, her beady eyes taking
in the tired faces, seeking out those who she considered had rested
long enough. Without being told, a number of them departed
before they caught the edge of her sharp tongue.

Her eyes alighted on Bridget and her sore heel. Bridget attempted to explain.

'I've got a nasty blister. I thought I would clean it before applying a plaster. I'll be fine to carry on once I've done that.'

'You've been on duty a long time. It was me who gave you the plaster.'

Bridget blinked. 'Did you? Thank you. Have I been on duty that long?'

'Since early this morning. You're the only one left from the first shift. It's three in the morning,' Matron added in response to Bridget's puzzled expression.

She asked herself what if Lyndon was injured. She'd want someone to take care of him, to carry on regardless.

'I'm okay, Matron. I *want* to go on.'

Matron's eyes narrowed. Everyone was giving their all, but Bridget impressed her more than anyone. Her blister looked very sore. 'That water must be cold by now.'

'It is.'

Matron snatched the kettle from the gas ring where it had been placed to provide yet another cuppa. Steam rose and hot water seeped into the cold, turning it warm and comforting to her tired feet.

Bridget smiled and uttered her thanks.

Once her foot was dried and a fresh plaster applied, she rolled her stocking up her leg and snapped the suspenders into place.

'Go back if you think you can, Milligan, but don't overdo it. We've no beds for tired nurses.'

Judging by the twitching smile at the corner of her lips, it was meant in a kindly manner. All the same, Bridget surmised that beneath the surface there was serious intent.

Once she felt refreshed, Bridget went back to work.

The ward was a hive of activity, a fervent mixture of sight, sound and smell – the smell of injury and of death. Besides the smell of blood, there was that of the sea and the saltiness of sand, the kind of smell one relishes on a summer beach.

The horrific injuries and agonised groans of men in pain soon wiped out all connection with such warm, homely memories.

In a brief respite, one of the nurses who'd accompanied stretchers coming back from the front related what she'd had to deal with. 'It was hell. Pure hell. Blood. Limbs...' Unable to continue, she shook her head, dropped her cup and dashed outside for fresh air.

Bridget ran after her but, not wanting to embarrass her, stopped when she saw her bent over, heaving up the contents of her stomach.

The next time she saw her, she was laughing and smoking with a medical orderly. He was caressing her face, getting bolder the more she blew smoke and laughed at whatever he was saying.

The nurse, barely into her mid-twenties, suddenly became aware that she was being watched. For a moment, their eyes met. Bridget instinctively grasped the meaning in that challenging look. *I'm alive. I want to feel alive. I want to forget and if it means sleeping with this chap, I damned well will.*

Feeling shaken and immensely sad, Bridget went back to her chores and thanked God again that Lyndon was far above the carnage.

Before falling into bed, she went down on her knees and prayed for him. There would be a lot of prayers in the days to come, even from those who did not espouse to being religious but were desperate for some kind of succour, some kind of meaning in all this bloodshed. The stakes were higher than they had been at any other time during the war and the resultant losses would have to be lived with for a very long time.

Sleep brought some relief. The only nightmare that flitted

through her mind was the very real one that she was due back on duty at eight thirty. She'd had roughly four hours sleep.

In her dreams, the sights she'd seen on the ward that day came back to her. The inhumanity of man to man was unfathomable, the results unimaginable. She'd seen young men, their skins burned and one eye blinking in a shattered face. The physical injuries were bad enough, but judging by their screams and frightening utterances, there were worse things going on in their minds.

'Give me something to make me forget it,' one young soldier had screamed at her, his eyes glazed both with pain and horror. She knew he was asking her for morphine, preferably an overdose so there would be no more pain, no more nightmares in his mind.

Two or three days of sheer hell went by – she couldn't quite recall how many. Everyone was tired. The best news they'd received was that the army had managed to get off the beaches of Normandy and were making steady progress.

There was greater joy when it was announced that letters from loved ones delivered to their old hospital in London had caught up with them.

'Bliss,' was the most uttered word in response to such welcome news.

She looked for one from Lyndon but was disappointed.

It came as something of a surprise when later she was summoned to the almoner's office. The almoner dealt with both staff and patient wellbeing and it was through her that letters and telephone calls were received, sent and noted. It was also her job to break bad news when the very worst had happened.

A cold fist threatened to crush Bridget's heart. Lyndon. It couldn't be anyone else. Was he injured? Was he dead?

'What's happened?'

'I've no idea. I was just asked to relay the message.' Sister Broderick, a firm but fair woman, saw Bridget's face turn pale. Everyone feared unexpected messages and the almoner's office was at the heart of message bearing. 'Best you run along and find out,' she said. 'We can manage without you for a little while.'

The weak but reassuring smile did nothing to quell Bridget's fear. Heart in her mouth, she fled past Matron and neither heard nor cared that she shouted after her that it was forbidden to run in the corridor.

The almoner's office was down one level and halfway along another corridor with walls of Eau de Nil – a colour much favoured by military and hospitals alike. There were rows of closed doors on each side. White letters etched into black proclaimed the nature of the department behind each door. Bridget feared seeing the one for the mortuary until remembering that it was on the next floor down.

The sign for the almoner's office, innocuous as it was, seemed sharp and cold, a precursor of the messages collated and distributed by those within.

Taking a deep breath, she clenched her fists, summoned up what amounted to very little courage. She knocked.

In response to being given vocal permission, she turned the door knob and entered.

Mrs Turner, the almoner, was around fifty years of age and of robust construction, though not very tall. A kind and slightly pink face was surrounded by a halo of fluffy white hair. Her homely appearance made Bridget think she might have been from farming stock. She looked like a farmer's wife, her meaty hands resting on the desk in front of her.

Eyes of the very palest blue looked up at her when she entered.

'I'm Bridget Milligan.'

'Ah. Take a seat, dear.'

Bridget did so.

'You're the Bridget I believe this letter might be referring to.'

She had a kind smile but there was also tightness around her eyes, as though she had a question in need of answering.

Bridget answered evenly, although her heart was fluttering like a butterfly caught in a spider's web. 'Yes. My name's Bridget. Bridget Milligan.' She purposely added her maiden name, yet in a strange way it seemed a betrayal. In reality, she was Mrs O'Neill, but as a nurse she only admitted to the name Milligan.

Her racing heart should have calmed by now, but Mrs Turner's expression made her feel apprehensive.

'Oh yes. Nurse *Milligan.*'

Why such emphasis on her name? Bridget's apprehension intensified.

Mrs Turner scrutinised the letter she was holding. After a brief perusal, the pale blue eyes were turned on her. 'This letter addresses you as Mrs Bridget O'Neill and the only Bridget we have here is you. Perhaps you could look at the form of address and confirm that this missive really is for you.'

She felt the almoner's eyes on her as she read the addressee.

Nurse (Mrs) Bridget O'Neill. Sender was written on the envelope flap as Mrs Luxton O'Neill, Lyndon's mother. Luxton was her mother-in-law's maiden name. Lyndon's mother had insisted on adding it to her married name. 'An old Southern name she couldn't bear to let go,' he'd said to her.

It was as though all the breath had been sucked out of her. Her mouth turned dry.

'Are you married, Bridget?' Mrs Turner's voice was soft and her eyes kindly.

Bridget's blood ran cold as she considered her answer. Should she lie? If she did, the letter would either be returned as addressee unknown or left to gather dust on a shelf. A terrible possibility took hold of her. What if Lyndon was dead or injured? What if his parents had been informed before her? Much as she wanted to deny, much as she wanted to stay in her job, she couldn't bear not knowing. There was no option but to own up.

Feeling embarrassment colour her face, she nodded slowly, eyes still on her name – her married name written in a flamboyant hand by her mother-in-law. 'Yes. It's me.'

She waited apprehensively, fingers knotted, blood running cold. This was it. All that she'd worked for would be for nothing. As a married nurse, she would be instantly dismissed. Nursing and marriage were both serious vocations. A woman could be one or the other but not both. That fact had been drummed into her.

She felt the almoner's pitying though thoughtful look and heard her clearing her throat. The almoner had no option but to pass on what she knew.

She cleared her throat again. Her hands resting on an ink-splattered blotting pad. 'So you've lied.'

Bridget hung her head at first, but then jerked upright. If this had to be, it had to be. She would face her future head on. 'Yes. I lied. I am married. The letter is from his mother. He flies a B17, you see.'

She looked down at the letter, longing to rip it open and read the contents. Her impatience and her fear lessened when she read the date. A week previously. It couldn't possibly contain bad news. Her heart stopped racing. Nursing was all she had to lose. Lyndon was safe.

Mrs Turner's fingers tapped the desk top piano fashion as she thought things through. 'I used to be a nurse. I served in a field hospital behind the lines of the Western Front. I saw all the awful business of war first-hand. Terrible as it was, I wanted to continue being a nurse but I also wanted to marry. I did marry, but like you, I married in secret.' The kindly eyes looked up at her. There was both merriment and sadness in that look. 'I contrived to have both and I got away with it and was glad that I did. We had a few happy years together.' Her eyes moistened. 'War is fleeting. Love lasts forever, which in our case was only five years. He was injured, you see, but, Bridget, I would not have missed having those five years. I'm glad we kept it secret. I'm glad we had those few years together. No children, but we had each other.'

She nodded at the envelope Bridget clenched so tightly.

'Your secret's safe with me. Go on. Live, love and do your duty.'

* * *

Bridget gasped for breath as she leaned against the wall in the corridor outside. The sounds and smells of the hospital were going on all around her. Yet she felt as though she was elsewhere.

Officially she should have gone for a break a few minutes ago, though since the influx of the first casualties, the rules on breaks were no longer adhered to. On this occasion, she didn't want tea, only to be alone so she could read the letter – whatever news it might bring. She made for the chapel.

A few people sat in the rows of light oak pews, their heads bowed in silent contemplation. She fancied she heard the odd sob.

Carefully, so as not to rustle the thin paper, she ran her finger along the join until it was open. Inside there was no letter, but a telegram. The words were direct and to the point.

I am willing to settle the sum of two thousand dollars on you if you give my son a swift and uncontested divorce. I will make all the necessary arrangements. Mrs Luxton O'Neill.

Bridget gasped and her breathing quickened. How dare she? How bloody dare she? She jerked her head upright.

Bottling up her anger – at least for now – she made her way back to the ward. Another long day lay ahead but she felt new purpose. More casualties were expected. It was even rumoured that once a field hospital in France was set up, some of the more experienced nurses would be on their way over there.

Nobody, no matter what service they were in, was allowed leave. She had to work until her feet were sore, but she could share her anger in a letter. Maisie was still in Bristol, still working in the tobacco factory. Maisie would be supportive. She would write as soon as she could.

18

Phyllis looked lovingly at the man she was marrying. Mick had recovered from his injuries incurred on his wedding day. Now here they were on the ship heading for home waters and getting married for real.

The ship's captain looked a little taken aback when Mick asked if it was true that he could marry them.

'Well,' he said haltingly. 'It is, but I've never done it myself, and I don't know whether—'

'Look. Let me tell you about our wedding – the one that never happened. I left Phyllis waiting at the altar through no fault of my own. I got knocked out cold in an air raid. I'm fine now but would like to complete what I set out to do before we get to Blighty. Are you up for that, Captain, or not?'

In response to the captain's agreement to marry them, Phyllis once more adorned the cream satin dress and what remained of the veil. Mick wore his uniform and there were a whole bunch of blokes willing to stand as best man. Two territorial nurses on their way home offered their services as bridesmaids. Both admired the satin dress she wore.

'Wouldn't mind one like that myself,' said one of them and her colleague agreed.

'Sorry I can't let you have it. It was loaned to me back in Malta. Our first wedding was disrupted and due to orders, we didn't have time to arrange a second one there. Her ladyship insisted I take the dress she lent me and once I was finished with it, take it or send it to an address in London. The woman there lends out dresses to other brides in need of a wedding dress.'

The two nurses looked at each other. 'All we need to do is find ourselves a couple of bridegrooms.'

To their great surprise, the chef managed to throw together a wedding cake.

'More like bread pudding instead of fruit cake, but the icing's for real.'

The chef looked proud of his efforts and Phyllis thanked him profusely.

Glasses were raised to the lucky couple.

'Lucky for us we called into Gibraltar on our way back,' said the captain, raising a toast in cheap Spanish wine. 'Spain might claim neutrality, but the border between Spain and Gibraltar is as leaky as a sieve.'

Mick raised his glass and laughed. 'Lucky Mick. That's me.'

The sun had been with them all the way up the Western Approaches. Their cabin had been warm, but they didn't care. They were married at last.

Mick's swift recovery had taken Phyllis by surprise. The doctors back in the military hospital in Malta had advised he rest a while longer before leaving. The bluff, outgoing Australian had insisted that he was 'bonza' – an Australian term he often favoured.

Swept along with his exuberance, Phyllis accepted for the most part that he was fine. Except sometimes she couldn't wake him up in the mornings. When she tried to tell him about it, he just shook his head and told her she was mistaken.

'I'm fine. I bounced back like a kangaroo with its feet on fire.'

The image was a little disconcerting and although it went some way to easing her anxiety, it was still there.

When she persisted, he turned angry. 'Don't keep on at me.'

So, she let it go, told herself that in time all would be well.

The ship was diverted into Bristol.

'Too much happening in Portsmouth and Plymouth,' they were told by a rating. 'A lot of backwards and forwards from the invasion forces.'

'And hospital ships, I expect,' Phyllis said softly.

'You'll be seeing some old friends then,' said Mick.

'And we can have an after-wedding reception – quite a bit after. You don't mind, do you?'

He laughed, wrapped an arm around her, and hugged her tightly. 'Can't wait to meet them. Maisie and Bridget. Have I got that right?'

She told him that he had.

The grey waters of the Bristol Channel seemed bright to her. Everything in her world was bright. She had Mick. They were together and soon she would meet up with old friends.

The port of Bristol was a hive of activity, the arms of cranes lining the docks swinging over to ships, then back again. Ship after ship was being unloaded of supplies, mostly weaponry from North America and food from the vast pampas of Argentina and Brazil. Priority was given to a naval ship to make its way upriver and into the city docks. A tug would guide them around its treacherous bends.

The Royal Navy ship was waved at by people on the land who didn't often see suchlike steaming into the old home port.

Breakfast was provided before they disembarked – along too came Mick's orders.

'A car's coming for me. Sorry I can't meet your friends. I was looking forward to it.'

Phyllis downed her cutlery. 'I don't think I can eat any more.'

He touched her hand. 'I'll be all right.'

She nodded silently before she lifted eyes heavy with moisture and looked into his. 'Promise?'

'I promise.' He glanced at his wristwatch. 'I need to pack. The transport's coming at eleven.'

Back in their cabin, everything he needed was stuffed into his kitbag.

'I think I have everything.' He wrapped the ropes that sealed the kitbag opening around his hands and gave it a good tug.

'Except me,' she said softly, unable to tear her eyes away from him.

'Darling.' He straightened and took her in his arms. 'I would pack you in there if I could. This isn't easy for either of us is it. Just married and breezing off in different directions.' She'd received orders to report to London but had two days to kill before she travelled. He fondled her hair as he held her slightly apart from him. 'Anyway, this kitbag is already pretty full, though I'd get you in there if I thought I could get away with it.'

She smiled nervously, her eyes shining. 'I wouldn't complain of it being cramped in that kitbag, honestly I wouldn't.'

It was a joke of course, but their laughter was light and slightly brittle.

He'd awoke fine that morning and she was grateful of that. The knock on the head had happened some time ago now – at least two weeks. She told herself there was nothing to worry about. Her deepest fear had been that he'd have a blackout whilst in flight, but he'd promised her he wouldn't be flying. He was going to

Oxford to pass his skills onto others. There was nothing to worry about.

'You will check in with the doctor at this base you're going to?'

A slight shadow crossed his face before he said, 'Stop nagging, stop worrying and take care of yourself.' He glanced at the watch nestled against the golden hairs of his deeply tanned arms. 'I need to dash.'

She managed another happy smile intended to camouflage her breaking heart. Not long married and about to be parted.

Mick was off to catch a train cross-country to an airfield in Oxfordshire and was excited about it. He'd told her as much as he knew in the little time they had left together.

'That's where Number One Reconnaissance Unit is based – though perhaps I shouldn't be telling you that.'

She laughed. 'I won't betray you.' Her expression turned serious, though she told herself he would be all right. 'Just keep to being an instructor. Leave the flying to the young bloods.'

His eyebrows arched as he took on an aggrieved expression. 'Mrs Fairbrother, are you saying I'm getting on in years?'

She laughed. 'I hope you are. I hope they really do regard you as too old to go up there.'

The mix of intensity and gentleness in his eyes touched her very soul as he said, in the softest of voices, 'I'll have no choice if I'm ordered.' And with greater exuberance, 'Anyway, we've got this new camera, the F52. It's been fitted into a Supermarine Spitfire or even a Mosquito. I can't recall which. Great planes. Best of the best.'

Despite his attempt to put her at ease, every nerve in her body bristled with apprehension. She knew he hankered to get up there and do what he did best, but it wasn't only that. Mick Fairbrother was born for adventure. He met challenges head on, excited by the moment and the prospect of getting the job done. The trouble was she didn't want him to venture anywhere. That dream of his to plant vines and make wine back in Australia once the world was at peace had become her dream too. She wanted to hold onto it. She wanted it to happen.

'Promise, Mick.'

'I won't inadvertently put myself in danger. There. Satisfied?'

He planted a kiss on her lips, and added one on each of her cheeks and then her closed eyelids.

'I love you, Mrs Fairbrother.'

Tears threatening her eyes, she returned the comment and meant it from the very depths of her soul. 'I love you, Mr Fairbrother.'

'Flight Officer Fairbrother if you don't mind.'

The smile vanished. A single line of worry creased his brow. 'You sure you'll be all right? I hate leaving you here waiting around until your train comes in. You'd think the RAF would be more organised by now.'

Phyllis laughed whilst waving her hands at everything going on around them. 'Come on, Mick. Would you like to be organising this lot? It won't be long. Anyway, I'm looking forward to seeing Maisie again. Luckily, I managed to send both her and Bridget a telegram. The War Office will know where to find me and I've got three days before I catch my train.'

'And then you're off to London. It's rumoured to be sin city. Promise me you'll behave yourself, Mrs Fairbrother.' He said it laughingly, yet she knew in these difficult times, fear lurked just below the surface. Nobody's arms could ever replace his, but she read the other fear he had for her.

On the thirteenth of June, the first of these dreaded 'buzz bombs' had fallen on London. The name was derived from the buzzing sound they made. Once the noise stopped, that was when it fell to earth. They were also called doodlebugs. The weapons were faster than a conventional bomber. Neither fighter planes nor anti-aircraft guns could shoot them down very easily. It was a case of grin and bear it, though grinning never really came into it.

Burying her worries for him just as he was burying his worries for her, she managed a smile. 'I'll be fine.'

His lips were warm and moist on her forehead. 'Of course you will.'

It was hard parting, but Mick had been out of commission for so long and was chomping at the bit like the old war horse he was, desperate to get back into action.

He kissed her lips, her cheeks and both of her hands before he strode off down the gangplank. She'd wished they might have had one more night before his orders took him to Oxford, but his expertise was urgently needed; primarily to teach others he'd said. Phyllis feared he'd be drawn into some dangerous mission.

'Parting is such sweet sorrow,' she whispered as she watched him dash off, kitbag thrown over his shoulder, each stride taking him away from her and back into danger. He'd gone overboard to assure her that he would only be carrying out training. His enthusiasm had been absolute but she perceived a longing in his eyes. She knew only too well that if the opportunity arose, Mick would be up there.

Number One Photographic Reconnaissance Unit was based in Benton, Oxfordshire, alongside the squadrons of Number 106 (Photographic Reconnaissance), which was mostly composed of Supermarine Spitfires with a generous dash of the new and very fast Mosquitos, the only ones which had had some success in shooting down enemy rockets.

Before doing anything else, Mick was shown his billet.

'You're the lucky one. You've got this all to yourself, sir,' said the jolly-faced batman, as a military valet was referred to, who'd been given the job of looking after him.

Mick tipped his cap onto the back of his head and ran his gaze over the single bedstead, a small bedside cupboard and a range of coat hooks that looked to have been hastily hammered into the wall. There was one small window. 'You call this a room? It looks more like a cupboard.'

His batman cleared his throat in rather an embarrassing manner. 'It was, until they put in that window. But you won't be sharing. You've got it to yourself,' he added reassuringly.

Mick flung his kitbag onto the single, iron-framed bed. The mattress didn't give beneath its weight.

'Biscuits?' he asked. Biscuits were three portions of wadding that passed for a mattress.

The batman, who had introduced himself as Evans, nodded. ''Fraid so. I can try to get you something better if you like, sir.'

'Evans, I'm not here to sleep. I'll manage.'

He said this at the same time as taking out the wedding photo some kind sailor with a camera had taken on the ship back from Malta.

'Your wife, sir?' asked Evans as he began unpacking Mick's kitbag.

'Yeah. She's serving in Whitehall – or will be in a few days' time.'

'Oh.'

That one word represented so many that would remain unsaid and all referring to the rockets, the first of which had fallen on London. He'd heard that these unmanned missiles travelled at over six thousand miles an hour. Nothing could catch them. 'A dangerous time for London. Doodlebugs. Whoever gave them that name?'

'Don't know, sir. I didn't think we'd be having any more of that, seeing as the RAF bombed that place in Holland...'

'Peenemunde.' The most prominent launch and factory had been destroyed by the RAF some time ago. The enemy had retaliated by moving the factory to northern Germany.

Evans was going on. 'Thought that was the end of it. Still, we're on the up, I think. Not long now. Oh, nice bit of news, sir, in case you hadn't heard.' Evans slammed the drawer shut on Mick's clean underwear.

'What's that?' Mick prepared himself to hear yet again about the Normandy landings. Everyone on the train travelling up had been enthusiastic to share the news and give their opinions on how it should proceed.

'Don't know who was responsible, but two Zeiss cameras were rescued from a downed JU88. The mechanics have fitted it into a Mosquito. I heard tell the German cameras are better than ours. Sounds a bit unpatriotic to me, but is that true, sir?'

Mick was instantly alert. It was a well-known fact that German cameras, specifically aerial reconnaissance equipment, were far superior to anything the allies had.

He'd been half inclined to keep his promise to Phyllis about not putting himself in danger what with these damned headaches he kept getting. The information given him by Evans changed everything.

He went to the window. Spitfires and Mosquitoes filled his gaze.

'You said they fitted it into a Mosquito.'

Evans replied in the affirmative.

'Fancy a cup of tea, sir?'

Mick gave only a cursory, silent nod. His yearning was not for tea. His yearning was to use the captured camera. The first rocket had fallen on London. It was only a matter of time before they fell on the allies forging ever more deeply into France. The rockets were too fast to be shot down by conventional means. The secret was to bomb the factories producing them and the launch sites which consistently changed to evade destruction. That's where aerial photography came in and despite his promise to Phyllis, he had a passion for doing the job himself.

There were numerous Spitfires and Mosquitoes parked on the flat expanse of tarmac. A crowd had gathered around one plane in particular. Mechanics and officers appeared in avid discussion, their looks both intense and triumphant.

Mick instinctively knew what they were talking about and why they looked as they did. This had to be the plane in which the German camera had been mounted, hence the reason they were looking so pleased with themselves.

He made a resolution then and there. No matter what happened next, what his orders were for the next few weeks, he would go up in that plane as soon as he possibly could.

Photography was his second passion. His first one was Phyllis, but that camera fitted in that aircraft promised a phenomenal experience. Despite his promise to Phyllis, he was overcome with excitement and curiosity. He just had to use this fantastic piece of equipment against the enemy who'd made it in the first place. No matter the danger, no matter where it was headed.

19

MAISIE

'My name's Flo.'

Maisie looked up from her work and her daydreaming. 'Sorry?'

'You called me Paula.'

Maisie blinked herself back to full awareness.

'Oh, sorry, love. I was miles away.'

Flo had retired two years ago but come back when they experienced a shortage of labour. The fact was that so many girls had got married or joined up and Flo's experience was invaluable. As per usual, Flo was chatting non-stop.

'I remember when you first started 'ere. You used to sit with that glamour puss Phyllis Mason and the Irish know-it-all Bridget Mulligan.'

'Milligan. Her name was Bridget Milligan.' Maisie disliked either of her friends being spoken of in such a desultory manner, but bit her tongue.

'That's the one.'

Flo was chewing something with the few teeth that remained in her head – perhaps residual breakfast. Women of a certain age rarely had a full set of teeth, yellowed by smoking and negligence.

Maisie tried not to look at Flo's teeth as she made comment. 'They're still my friends. We've stayed in touch. Bridget's put her intelligence to good use. She's training to be a nurse. I bet she's got 'er work cut out at present.'

'I bet,' said Flo. 'I 'eard on the wireless that there's a lot of casualties but we're winning through. We'll get to Berlin, you just see if we don't.'

'I'm sure you're right, Flo.'

Flo tossed her head in a matter-of-fact manner. 'I wonder when though.'

Maisie shrugged. 'Who can say.'

'What about that flighty one then?'

'She was serving in Malta but is back now. She got married on the ship bringing her home.'

'Is that right? Sailor was 'e?'

'No. An Australian.'

'Oh. Foreign then.' Flo was the sort to whom everyone from outside Bristol was foreign – no matter where they came from.

Maisie just about held her tongue, reminding herself that Flo was of a different generation. It was likely that before this war she'd never come across anyone from outside the area in which she lived, let alone from outside the city. Some people were like that – never trusting or venturing outside their own locale. Rather than snap with frustration, she said roundly, 'She's been through a lot out there.'

She didn't add that Phyllis would be staying with her until reporting to her new post in Whitehall. That was why she was so distracted. It had been so long. Neither of them were the girls they'd been at the beginning of the war, or even a few years ago. So much had happened.

The phone box at the end of the road had rung early that morning. Somebody passing had brought her the news that some woman wanted to talk to her.

'Somebody called Phyllis,' her neighbour had said.

Still wearing her dressing gown and slippers, Maisie had dashed out of the house and up the road, Carole calling out after her, asking if anything was wrong. She'd waved back that everything was fine. Things had become fine a week or so ago when Carole had told Maisie of her decision to keep her baby. And now there might be more good news.

'I'm in Bristol,' Phyllis had declared in a voice breathless with excitement. 'Oh, Maisie, it's so wonderful to hear your voice.'

'You're here! In Bristol?' Excited beyond belief, Maisie slammed her hand against her forehead. 'I can't believe it. How long are you staying in Bristol?'

'I've got three days before I report to London. Mick's here. We're married now. Isn't that marvellous?'

'It is.'

'But look, I wanted to show you my wedding dress and have a party. I won't feel properly married until I've had a party with you and Bridget. No chance that she might have some leave and be in Bristol is there?'

'I haven't heard. Might be a miracle under the circumstances. How come your ship came into Bristol?'

'Normally we would have berthed in Plymouth or Portsmouth, but the south coast is a bit busy and crowded at present – for obvious reasons. A lot of battered ships steaming in for repairs.'

'That's wonderful. Not the battering... I mean you being here! I can't believe it. Is Mick with you?'

'I'm afraid not. His orders came more quickly than expected.'

'That's a shame.'

'I sent a telegram to Bridget before we left Malta. I hope she got it. I wasn't too sure at first where disembarkation would take place, but either way I'd made up my mind to come to Bristol.'

'That would be smashin'. Though I expect Bridget's a bit busy with the wounded,' she added solemnly. 'Still,' a little more brightly, 'Let's hope she can make it.'

'Can I stay with you? I don't mind sleeping on the settee. It's been ages since we've seen each other.'

'There's a spare bed in Paula's room – if you don't mind, or I can go in there and you can have my bed. Or Carole's. Anything. We'll manage.'

'And a party?'

'It goes without saying.'

Words had tumbled out from both ends of the telephone until the pips began to sound.

'I haven't got any more pennies,' Phyllis had shouted. 'I'll see you later, Maisie. Can't wait.'

'No. Can't wait,' Maisie had said. The final pip had sounded, followed by a clunking of telephonic machinery before the connection was severed.

'You look as though you've seen a ghost,' Carole remarked when she'd got back to the house.

Like Maisie, she was still in her dressing gown, Paula suckling at her breast. It was a lovely sight to see from someone who had categorically stated that she couldn't stand breastfeeding her daughter. Things had changed a great deal since the D-Day landings and not just in Europe.

Maisie had given a big sigh as her thoughts drifted into the past. She was almost dreamy. 'Phyllis. I don't think you ever met her, did you?'

'No. I didn't.'

'Such an amazing surprise. She's staying here for a couple of days before going to London. She's married now. Her husband won't be with her, which is a shame. I would have liked to meet him. I'd still like a bit of a party though. I couldn't get to her wedding, but we can still celebrate.'

'We can pretend to be wedding guests.'

'Yep. She did say she sent a telegram to Bridget. Hope she got it. That would be icing on the cake that would – the three Ms back together after all this time.'

'A party! That would be marvellous. I'll go ahead with the stew for tonight.' She'd sighed. 'Wish we did have icing for a cake. Might have to make do with bread pudding.'

'I love bread pudding! And so does Phyllis – at least I think she does. There's a few currants and sultanas left in the tin. It'll be a bit sparse on fruit, but some honey and a teaspoonful of cinnamon should help make it tasty.'

Maisie had clasped her hands together imagining how it would be – all three of them together again after such a long time. She had a yearning to do whatever she could to make this homecoming special. For a start, Phyllis deserved a bit of comfort after all she'd been through.

'The daft thing mentioned about sleeping on the settee, but I'll let her have my bed. I can go in on the spare bed in Paula's room.'

'No need. I'll go in there.'

'Are you sure?'

'Of course I'm sure. I'm her mother. It's only natural, ain't it?'

Maisie had agreed that it was. She couldn't remember a time when she'd felt quite this happy. Her heart soared with happiness. Carole was staying and now her old friend Phyllis was coming for a few days. Her idea about getting married so she could adopt Paula was no longer necessary. In the meantime, what about Peter Nichols? Should she go on seeing him?

Flo went on talking about girls who'd left. All the while, her nicotine-stained fingers continued to strip the leaves. Not once did she look at those leaves, her bare fingers, hardened over time, flew down each rigid stem, golden leaves falling away onto an ever-growing pile.

'Shame about old Aggie. She was a good sort. Knew management she did. Mixed with the big nobs.'

On and on she went. It was like this every day: gossip, tall tales and memories of what might or might not be true.

Maisie let it go in one ear and out the other. It was similar to music on the wireless, droning on in the background. She was too busy processing other thoughts – mostly happy thoughts.

A single word Flo spouted suddenly burst through.

'What was that you said?'

'About little Timmy. They was goin' to adopt 'im, all legal like. Poor little mite. What else could they do?'

Maisie was suddenly all ears. 'Who was this little boy?'

'Charlie found 'im in their neighbour's bombed-out building. It weren't too difficult to adopt 'im seeing as they were a couple, 'usband and wife and with two older kids. It was only natural. An old aunt did offer, but a bloke and 'is wife is best for the kid. That was what everybody thought anyway. But then suddenly, out of the blue, she was in the family way with their own. Well, that was it. They put 'im in an orphanage... Can't blame 'em. Blood's thicker than water. At least the kid will be looked after. There's loads of people wanting to adopt...'

Maisie gritted her teeth and was just about to tell her to shut up when Peter intervened.

'Mrs Beck, don't you ever stop talking?'

Peter was the only person that could make Flo shut up. She had respect for management, even though they were often the subject of her conversation. It was his job to check that each department were doing their job and that production would never be wanting for the basic materials to turn out millions of cigarettes. That included getting the best out of the employees.

She'd enjoyed accompanying him to his niece's wedding, very much a family affair composed of people she didn't know but who he insisted on introducing to her. Each name was accompanied with a shaking of hands. Numerous names and few she remembered. One or two comments were memorable.

'You make a fine-looking couple.'

'So glad Peter has a lady friend.'

She'd parried the comments with a response of, 'We're just friends.'

And that, she'd decided, is what they would always be. Their dates had been sparse and got sparser once Carole had made up her mind not to give Paula up for adoption. A couple of visits to the pictures, a Saturday afternoon sitting in the sunshine watching the factory team take on a team from Frys' Chocolate at cricket.

He gave no sign of having noticed any change in her.

Of late, he spent more time asking Maisie how things were going, was her table up to the mark and how about the rest of the room. She wasn't actually in charge, but his attitude made her feel as though her opinion mattered.

'Miss Miles, do you ever suffer from headaches?' he asked quietly.

Maisie smiled in response to his comment and the wink that accompanied it.

'Not often,' she replied, and winked back.

Totally oblivious Flo, leaves stripped swiftly from stems, had changed the subject.

'Did you know that 'ats aren't on ration? Never 'ave bin in fact. Now, I fer one didn't know that. Not that I could afford to buy a new 'at. 'Ave you seen the prices of a new 'at? I could buy a joint of roast beef and two pounds of potatoes for Sunday for the price of a new 'at.'

Maisie turned away so Flo couldn't detect her amusement. Out of the corner of her eye, she saw Peter do the same before turning to Flo and saying, 'Mrs Beck, do you think you could help out at Maggie Swain's table? There's two off sick and they're falling behind.'

'Course I can.' Flattered to be asked, Flo was up on her feet and off to the other end of the room.

The two girls sitting opposite Maisie were exchanging girlish giggles and whispers with each other. Whatever they were discussing was nothing to do with what Flo had been saying. Neither were they interested in the discourse between Maisie and Peter.

'Fancy the pictures tonight?' Peter asked.

'Not tonight, Peter. My old friend Phyllis has just docked. She's off to a new posting in London in a day or two. We've got a lot of catching up to do.'

20

CAROLE

'Blimey. Puttin' them flags up a bit early, ain't you? We ain't won the war yet.'

The speaker was Doreen Bateman who lived across the road from where Carole lived with Maisie in Totterdown, an area of Bristol that clung like a limpet to the steep hill.

In her early twenties, Doreen had two children and another on the way. Her husband had been in a prisoner of war camp for a few years. The new baby would come as something of a surprise, but Doreen was convinced he'd have no problem accepting the new baby whenever he did get back – 'He's been away for years. What do 'e expect me to do? Become a bloody nun?'

With nails in her mouth and a hammer tucked beneath her arm, Carole concentrated on hanging the flags before making comment. 'It's for Maisie and her mate, Phyllis. Phyllis has been in Malta for the last couple of years and now she's come home. They ain't seen each other for ages. And she got married whilst she was away. Big enough reason for a knees-up, don't you think?'

Doreen agreed that it was. 'Invitin' anyone in particular, are you?'

'No. Just Maisie, her mate Phyllis and me. The two of them got a lot of catching up to do.'

Nails hammered home, Carole stood back to admire her handiwork. Red, white and blue bunting fluttered across the bay window and door. She'd spent all morning getting them sorted plus making a 'Welcome Home Phyllis' banner. The only piece of paper she'd found that was big enough was white butcher's paper and then only one piece. Before the war, the meat had been wrapped in three such pieces. During the war, it had reduced to one piece as inside wrapping and a sheet of newspaper as outer wrapping.

Doreen lingered in the hope she might be invited in for a cuppa and a biscuit. But Carole was thinking of going over the rugs a second time with the carpet sweeper. A few things could do with a dusting too. After all that Maisie had done for her, she felt obliged to pay her back somehow.

No words of recrimination were ever uttered, no harking back to what would have happened that day if the Allies hadn't decided to invade Normandy. June the 6th was a memorable day in a lot of ways.

The very thought of how she could ever have considered having her baby adopted now seemed quite extraordinary. All Maisie had said to her, over a tearful supper that night, was 'It's all over now. Time to move on.' And she would move on, but not from the little house she shared with Maisie. It had become home to all three of them.

Besides making a bread pudding, she'd also made paste sandwiches, cheese, and pickles. There was enough food for three but not four. Doreen would have to remain disappointed.

'I 'ope she's grateful for all you're doing,' Doreen added, swinging her hips and stepping from one foot to the other.

Carole recognised that Doreen was making a last-ditch attempt for an invitation for a cup of tea at least.

'It's my pleasure,' murmured Carole.

'Don't suppose you got a bit of tea I could borrow?'

Resigned to the inevitable, she remarked, 'Better feed Paula before she starts bawling. Fancy a cup of tea?'

Doreen didn't need to be asked twice.

Maisie went inside, followed by Doreen. She made and poured the tea, and then she sat down to feed Paula.

Doreen wrinkled her nose and jerked her chin at Carole's bared breast, Paula's mouth clamped to her nipple. 'Now that's one thing I ain't looking forward to. Think I'll get some of that National Dried Milk. I'm already gettin' the orange juice and cod liver oil.'

Swiftly filled up, Paula fell asleep. Carole placed her in the pram.

'Got a biscuit?' Doreen asked. Her eyes perused the food Carole had prepared that morning, hidden beneath a series of damp tea towels.

'No. Sorry.'

The truth was that she did have biscuits – a pound of broken biscuits fetched from Reynolds in East Street. She'd picked out the less broken for the big event this evening. The smaller pieces Carole had set to one side thinking they would come in handy for making an apple crumble or Brown Betty, scattering it over the top of apples sweetened with a little sugar or dollop of honey. Doreen would have to settle for just a cup of tea.

'So. Any word from your Bill?' asked Carole as she gratefully sipped the second cup of tea of the day.

After pouring her tea from cup to saucer, Doreen slurped appreciatively. She wiped her mouth on the back of her hand. 'Oooh. I can taste the sugar.' She took another sip before answering Carole's question. 'Yeah. I get a letter every so often – about once a month. He ain't much of a writer, but never mind, letters are dead 'andy to light the fire. Do Maisie hear much from 'er bloke?'

'Maisie only gets cards from Sid, not letters, but then he's in a Japanese prisoner of war camp in the Far East and your Bill's in Germany. She don't – doesn't – throw them on the fire. She keeps them.'

If Doreen noticed she'd corrected her pronunciation from her old accent to something a bit more refined, she made no comment. Doreen took another slurp of tea. 'I don't read much anyway, what with the kids and this lump of mine.' When she gave her belly a slap, it moved. Carole assessed that she was roughly seven months. 'Did I ever tell you what 'appened that night I dropped me drawers?'

'Yes. You did.' Carole hid her grimace in her teacup.

Whether Doreen heard her or not, the story was retold. Either Doreen liked the sound of her own voice or enjoyed telling tales of her less than exciting life, making them more exciting in the process. This had to be the thirtieth time that Carole was forced to listen to the story of Doreen's night out when she'd got so drunk that she'd 'dropped her drawers', as she put it.

'I don't know where the bloke was from and couldn't really see what 'e looked like it being pitch black. Never mind though, eh. It 'elped me forget me troubles.'

She smiled as though cheating on one's spouse was the most natural thing in the world. From what Carole had heard from other sources, she wasn't that wrong. In war, lonely women enjoyed a bit of happiness wherever they could. Some were under no illusion that their husband might never come back or when he did, they'd be strangers to each other. Or he'd met someone else.

Bored by the same old story, Carole asked if she'd like more tea.

'I won't say no.'

As she poured, she studied the woman. Doreen's ginger hair was greasy and lank around her freckled face. Carole supposed she must have been quite attractive at one time, though she certainly didn't make the most of herself. Carole vowed that at some point, possibly once Doreen had given birth, she would get her looking good for when Bill, her husband came home.

'Have you told Bill you're expecting?'

Doreen tipped the last dregs from her saucer into her mouth and smacked her lips. 'Yeah. I told 'im.'

'What did he say?'

She shrugged. 'That there's a war on and the world's gone topsy-turvy. Not much else 'e could say is there. And 'e was in France for a while and you know what they say about France. Tarts and dirty postcards for sale on every street corner – so I've 'eard.'

Carole commented that she didn't know much about France.

'Only what I've 'eard,' Doreen repeated.

Signalling that the tea break was over, Carole got up from her chair. 'Better get on. I've got a lot to do before Maisie comes home.'

Though at first looking reluctant to leave, Doreen finally got the message.

'Oh well. Suppose I'd better make a move. Don't want to outstay me welcome now, do I?'

'I'll see you to the door.'

''Ave a nice time tonight,' Doreen got in, just as Carole reached for the latch.

Before she could pull the door open, three sharp raps sounded from the other side of the solid wooden door.

'Looks like you got yerself another visitor,' said Doreen. 'You are 'avin' a time of it, ain't you.'

Carole ignored Doreen and opened the door. Slender and glamorous in her WAAF uniform, her hair the glowing colour Maisie had often described, there was Phyllis.

'Phyllis?'

'Carole?'

'I'm Doreen,' said Doreen, looking hopeful that she could leave the kids a bit longer and enjoy yet another cup of tea and female company.

Carole's attention remained fixed on Phyllis. Maisie had described her hair as fiery, her eyes cool and her complexion near perfect. 'And she always wears red lipstick,' Maisie had added. Yes. This was her. 'You're just as Maisie described you. Come on in. See you around, Doreen.'

Phyllis, complete with kitbag, was ushered into the hallway.

Doreen stood lingering on the garden path until the door closed. 'See you,' she shouted out.

'Just a neighbour,' Carole said by way of explanation. It did cross her mind that Doreen hadn't stuck around for the pinch of tea leaves she'd asked for. Probably because she hadn't really wanted to borrow some. She'd just needed company.

Carole closed off that train of thought and concentrated on Phyllis. My, but she could even smell perfume. Lucky woman.

Phyllis looked around her. 'This is a nice house. Maisie's done well for herself.'

'She deserves it. Maisie's the kindest person I've ever met. We've been dying to see you. Wish we could have been at the wedding. How romantic getting married on board ship. Did you wear a wedding dress?'

Phyllis smiled broadly. She liked this girl and liked where she was. The house *felt* as though Maisie lived here. It was warm but also deceptively strong – just like Maisie. 'I've brought it with me.'

Carole gasped. 'Really? Are you going to wear it tonight? I'd love to see you in it.'

Phyllis laughed. 'How could I possibly refuse?'

'I've given you my bed.'

'That's very kind of you, but really, I don't want to be any trouble. The settee would have done me okay.'

'Oh no. We'd like you to be comfortable in this humble abode.'

'Hardly that,' said Phyllis, taking another look around. The settee was old but well cushioned, the woodwork gleamed and she detected the faint smell of beeswax. 'Even more reason for me to dress up for the occasion.'

'Maisie is so excited. She can't wait to see you. You're Maisie's best friend. Anyway, it's the least I can do. You must need a good night's sleep after your journey.'

Phyllis smiled and took off her cap. 'Carole, you would not believe some of the places I've had to sleep during an air raid. Quite frankly I'm sure I could sleep standing up if I had to.'

The welcome had been as warm as Carole could make it and Phyllis was grateful.

For a moment, these two women who had only just met looked at each other, smiles interspersed with bashful silence.

Carole broke the silence.

'Come on through to the parlour. I haven't long made a pot of tea and am sure it'll stand some more boiling water. I'll get the kettle on.'

The parlour at the front of the house, was rarely used, but on this special day Carole had decided to make use of it. The first thing she'd done was open the windows to let in some fresh air. The second was to place a bunch of flowers picked fresh from the garden into a cut-glass vase. Some of the flowers looked like weeds, but it didn't seem to matter once a few yellow climbing roses and marigolds were added.

'This is nice,' said Phyllis, looking around her. 'And thanks for the welcome home banner by the way. And the flags. I must say, it was totally unexpected. Made me feel like royalty.'

Just as Carole was about to go to the kitchen, the sound of crying came from the pram in the back room.

'Your baby.'

'That's Paula.' Carole smiled. 'She's been fed, but she always wakes up at the sound of strange voices. I'll see if I can get her back to sleep again so you can have a cuppa in peace.'

'No. Don't do that. Can I see her?' Phyllis laid a hand on Carole's arm. Carole noticed the look of longing in her eyes.

Maisie had told her that Phyllis had lost her baby. It was a while ago in the first full year of war. Carole hadn't taken that much notice when Maisie told her, but now, seeing Phyllis's reaction to Paula's crying, she could feel her pain. Adoption was one thing, but losing a baby was quite something else.

Carole smiled. 'Of course you can. Come on through. I'll introduce you.'

The blue eyes that Carole had come to love gazed as if mesmerised by the sight of them both before settling on Phyllis.

'She hasn't seen you before. That's why she's looking at you like that,' said a smiling Carole. She felt a surge of pride in her small daughter. Young she might be, but it seemed to her that intelligence burned like a flame in those bright blue pupils.

'Can I pick her up?' Phyllis pleaded.

Carole nodded. 'Of course you can. Here.' She undid the apron buttons at the side of the hood and rolled back the bedding.

Paula's legs kicked in anticipation and her eyes glowed.

It seemed to Carole that Phyllis held her breath as she carefully lifted Paula out of her pram. Her breathing finally resumed in an ecstatic gasp. 'Oh, you smell so sweet and your little body is so warm.'

Phyllis gazed in wonder at the precious bundle she cradled with both arms. She repositioned the warm and cuddly body onto her shoulder and closed her eyes. 'Oh my God. I wish she was mine.'

Carole winced at the regret and sadness she could hear in Phyllis's voice and pain embedded in her eyes. 'Maisie told me you lost your baby.'

Phyllis nodded as her hand stroked the baby's back. 'Yes. Things would have been so different if she'd lived – my little girl, but there, perhaps they wouldn't have been.'

'I'll make that tea,' said Carole. 'If you don't mind me leaving Paula with you for a moment?'

'Take as long as you like.'

In the lean-to scullery off the room where she'd left Phyllis, Carole thought of how she might have felt if she'd miscarried. At one point, she had hoped she would, but then her circumstances had been different. Phyllis had been married. Dabbling with adoption now seemed like a bad dream. She hadn't been thinking straight. Women did take time getting back to normal – so she'd been told at the clinic.

She sniffed back the sadness as she made the tea whilst recalling the other things that Maisie had told her about Phyllis. Apparently, her marriage had not been a happy one. Still, she might have soldiered on if she hadn't lost the baby.

She could easily believe that the hurt was still with her, the way she'd cradled Paula, the way she'd closed her eyes and wished that Paula was hers. Poor Phyllis. A while back, Carole would have envied Phyllis her freedom, but not now. The baby she hadn't wanted had grown on her. Being an unmarried mother wouldn't be easy, but she would do her best. Her love for her baby had blossomed like the flowers in the garden – unremarkable one minute then full of joyful colour the next. Paula was her daughter; she was her mother. Never again would she ever be so low and unloving.

The kettle boiled. Carole sighed as she added boiling water to tea leaves already used once. Making do in everything had become a habit in wartime. Cups and saucers were placed on a green tin tray, along with a few of the precious biscuits. Pasting a smile on her face, she passed back through the door into the living room.

'I've got biscuits,' she said brightly, her face wreathed in smiles. The room was empty. There was no sign of Phyllis. No sign of Paula.

Beset by panic, she set the tray swiftly down on a table and dashed out into the passageway. The front door was slightly ajar, a strip of sunlight falling onto the green linoleum floor of the passageway.

Half afraid that the street too would be empty, Phyllis gone and Paula gone, a replacement for the baby Phyllis had lost, Carole grabbed the door and dragged it open.

Relief flooded over her. 'Phyllis! What are you doing out here?'

Baby in her arms, Phyllis did a half pirouette on the spot. 'I judged it was time for Maisie to come home.' She spun back on her heels and jerked her chin to the end of the road. 'And I was right.'

The cry from the end of the street was rapturous. 'Phyllis! You're here!'

The cherries on the side of Maisie's straw sunhat bounced up and down as she ran, heels clip-clopping along the pavement.

'There,' said Phyllis to the baby whilst jiggling her up and down. 'It's your Auntie Maisie. Tonight we're going to have a party – a talking party, just you, me, your Auntie Maisie and your mum. Tonight, Paula my darling, will be a night to remember. I just wish Bridget could be here – the Three Ms back together at last.'

21

BRIDGET

Bridget couldn't believe her luck. She'd been saving up her leave – there was no point in having any, what with Lyndon flying raid after raid over mainland Europe. The telegram from Phyllis had landed like a bolt out of the blue – just hours before she was considering swapping her shifts with one of the other girls.

'I'm off to Bristol,' she'd said when somebody did belatedly take up her offer. 'I'm meeting up with old friends.'

She was so looking forward to seeing her old friends and if she could have told the train driver to go faster, she would have. As it was, she barely saw the passing fields, the hamlets and villages, the sidings full of goods trains and station platforms crowded with uniforms. How would Phyllis look? She hadn't seen Maisie for a while. Was she courting? Sid, who she proclaimed to be her boyfriend, had been a prisoner of war for some time. There was surely someone else by now?

First stop was her parents. She hadn't had time to let them know she was coming. They were bound to be surprised, though in a nice way. She hadn't even had chance to buy something special and she did so hate arriving empty-handed. By compromise, she'd piled all the supplies at the flat into her travel bag. Just for once she was out of uniform, so no kitbag, but Lyndon had bought her the leather travel bag in Harrods. Goodness knows how much it had cost. She'd not asked. It was tan and matched her handbag. Her clothes were new too, a lightweight twinset of pale blue cashmere, a panelled skirt in a silky fabric to match. She'd felt extravagant buying them. The quality was like nothing she'd ever worn before, but again Lyndon had written to her and told her to spoil herself. 'If I was there, I'd be spoiling you. Treat yourself, honey, and think of me.'

Bridget maintained a smile the length of Marksbury Road. She was looking forward to seeing her parents' reaction when she knocked at the door.

She passed a group of children, who barely glanced at her before running off towards the Novers, a hill of gorse, wild grass and brambles at the back of the houses on one side of the road. She thought she's seen two of her sisters amongst them – Katie and Mary?

Never mind, she thought with a smile. They were growing up and had their own peer group, and anyway, she'd come to see her parents.

There was no sign of any activity outside the house. The gate was shut and, as usual, not much in the way of flowers was growing in the garden. Her father wasn't keen on gardening. He didn't mind growing vegetables, that to him seemed only sensible. Vegetables were edible.

With great care, she opened the garden gate, praying it wouldn't squeak. On tiptoe, she made her way up the garden path, being especially careful to negotiate the three steps halfway along. On reaching the front door, she stood to one side, flattening herself against the wall, reached for the knocker and rapped it firmly. The brick wall of the house was warm behind her back and she could barely stifle her laughter. Boy, they were going to be so surprised.

Opening the door seemed to take longer than usual or perhaps it was just her impatience. Finally, it was open and her mother's head poked out. She looked straight ahead, then up the road and finally at her.

'Bridget! Oh, Bridget.' Her hand flew to her mouth.

Bags at her feet, Bridget gathered her mother into her arms.

'We didn't know you were coming.'

'It was short notice. Sorry I couldn't let you know.'

Her mother shouted over her shoulder for her father. 'Patrick. Our Bridget's here.'

The interior of the house was unchanged. It still had a clean but busy atmosphere, as though life was going too fast for it and all these people couldn't slow down enough to make it over-tidy. It was clean, but happy.

There were hugs and kisses. Patrick brought out a bottle of whisky that had been a Christmas present from Lyndon. Bridget handed her mother the provisions she'd brought from London.

'It's not much, but I didn't have enough time to buy anything special.'

'This is special enough,' said her mother.

Bridget wanted to say that she looked as though she could do with feeding up. She looked thinner than usual and had a pale complexion.

'A little welcome home,' said her father as he handed her a whisky.

All three drank a toast. Her father led the way.

'To those brave lads over in Europe. May God bless them.'

'And to those flying above them,' Bridget added.

'God bless them all. The long and the short and the tall.'

There was a moment of laughter. Her father asked if anyone wanted a top-up.

Bridget fixed him with a shrewd eye. 'Dad, your measures are worth two or three in any pub. I think I've had enough.'

'The Milligans are a generous lot,' he laughed. 'And so's that husband of yours. He gave me that for last Christmas you know.'

'I know,' Bridget said softly.

Her father nodded, before turning to Bridget's mother. 'Are you going to finish that, Mary, or warm it in yer hands all evening?'

'You know I'm not a big drinker, Patrick.' She handed him the glass, looked at her daughter lovingly, and rubbed her arm. 'It's so good to see you.'

'Your mother's not been too well.' Her father wore a marked frown but kept his smile. Bridget guessed they wanted her visit to be all happiness and light.

Bridget turned to her mother. 'What's been the matter?'

'Oh nothing. Take no notice of him. I had a bit of a summer flu and I've been doing too much – as usual. Now, never mind me, tell me all that you've been up to and why the sudden visit.'

Over tea and cheese on toast, she told them about the telegram she'd received from Phyllis. 'She told me she was heading home with her new man. They were going to get married in Malta, but there was an accident. She didn't go into much detail except to send off a quick telegram before she left saying that she intended visiting Bristol no matter where the ship disembarked..' Bridget frowned thoughtfully. 'I'm thinking Phyllis would have sent like to Maisie. I was also thinking that she's got nowhere else to stay except with Maisie. Even if she's staying elsewhere, I think that's where I must head this evening. Maisie will know where she is.'

'Your bed will be ready when you get home, my darling,' said her mother. The loving look in her eyes was accompanied by fingers lightly stroking the side of her face. They felt like feathers, lacking the flesh and strength they'd once had.

'If I end up staying there, I don't want you to worry. Promise me that you won't.'

Her father patted her on the back. 'My little girl's grown up. She thinks she can take care of herself.'

Bridget smiled. 'This war made me grow up quickly.'

'I'll take that bag upstairs before it gets damaged,' said her father.

'Put it in our room. It's going to be crowded enough with the girls. Wish we had another room we could let you have,' her mother said somewhat wistfully.

Bridget had to concede that what might have been big enough for the family when her siblings were young was now proving a bit of a squeeze. For all that, it was a house full of love.

'I'll put the kettle on,' said her mother, rubbing her hands down over her apron – perhaps a little nervously – as if, thought Bridget, there was something troubling her.

'I'll take a look at the bedroom, Dad, but honestly, I don't mind sleeping on the settee.'

Once they'd reached the sanctuary of her parents' bedroom, she asked her father if there was something seriously wrong with her mother.

'Is there anything I should worry about,' she asked?

Placing her luggage bag on the bed, he sighed and looked at her. She saw a slight frown come and go before he said, 'She forgets she's getting older and tries to do too much. I told her to go to the doctor, but as usual she points out the cost and that I'm being an old fusspot.'

'I'll have a word with her.'

'No,' he said abruptly. 'Don't do that. She's bucked up already with you arriving on the doorstep. Promise me you'll say nothing.'

Much as she was inclined to do otherwise, Bridget promised.

Teatime was a wonderful affair, her brothers and sisters eating everything she'd brought with great gusto. Her mother had made an apple pie and a passable egg custard made from powdered eggs. Her younger sisters chatted; the eldest, Katie, was less talkative; Bridget put that down to the fact that she was thirteen now and did not consider herself a child.

Michael and Sean came in from work, Sean from his job as an apprentice gardener with the city parks department, Michael from his job looking after the milkman's horse until he was old enough to take up an apprentice as a mechanic.

'You won't see horses being used that much in future,' he boasted with the air of a much older man. 'Cars, buses, vans and lorries.'

'No more seeing Mr Grove running out with his shovel and a sack when the milkman's horse has gone by then.'

There was much laughter. Mr Grove grew abundant produce in his garden and in an allotment down by the railway lines.

At seven o'clock, Bridget announced her intention to get the bus into Bedminster and from there walk up to Totterdown to see Maisie.

Her mother's face dropped, but a smile appeared when Bridget reminded her that she hadn't seen her for such a long time.

'What time will you be home?' her mother asked.

'If it gets that late, I'll sleep on Maisie's settee.'

'That won't be very comfortable, and on your first night home,' said her mother, looking taken aback.

'Don't worry. I'll be fine. If I'm not back by midnight, you can count on it that I'm already asleep.'

22

PHYLLIS

It was eight o'clock and the reunion between Phyllis and Maisie had gone extraordinarily well. Carole too had enjoyed herself, and everyone had been enthralled by the details of Phyllis and Mick getting married by the captain on a ship.

'You should have seen the captain's face. He knew he was law on the ship and could marry us, but nobody had ever asked him to do it before.'

'I bet he was shocked.'

'No. On the contrary. He was over the moon. Came over all serene and serious, then afterwards he broke out the rum – and anything else vaguely alcoholic. We had a bit of a do, though those steering the ship remained teetotal of course. After all, we were still at sea. War or peace, the sea is always a dangerous place.'

'And Malta?'

Phyllis's face turned sad. 'There were some pretty hairy times, but also quite wonderful times. I made good friends in the services and amongst the Maltese.' She sighed. 'Dear Mariana. She was Maltese and one of the loveliest people I've ever met. And I loved the island. I'd like to go back there when the world is finally at peace, though if I'm in Australia it would be a pretty long journey.'

Carole, who'd gladly taken charge of the making of sandwiches earlier and was now in charge of cutting bread pudding and making more tea, listened spellbound to the details of Phyllis's life in the services. 'It must have been frightening.'

'It was, though things began to improve once Sicily had been invaded.'

'And Mick. You didn't just lose him once, you lost him twice. Still you've got him back now. So when are we going to meet him.'

Phyllis looked down at the hands that held her cup and saucer. She still had niggling doubts about his health, but as he'd said, it was quite a knock on the head. She pushed away her fears and smiled as though she hadn't a care in the world. 'I'd like to say as soon as he gets some leave, but the truth is, I don't know when that will be. He's at an air base near Oxford and I'm off to London, but...' She raised her head, the light in her eyes as bright as the smile on her face. 'Once victory is finally announced and before we set off for Australia, I want to wear that dress again one more time.'

'Well now's as good a time as any,' exclaimed Maisie. 'How about this being that one more time?'

Phyllis beamed. 'Would you really like to see me in it? It's in my kitbag, a bit creased, but still worth looking at. I loved it from the moment I set eyes on it, even though it was only borrowed.'

'Yes please,' said an overly enthusiastic Carole, her eyes shining at the thought of it. She did love good clothes, though unfortunately they were a bit thin on the ground nowadays.

Phyllis got to her feet. 'Won't be a mo.'

Whilst Phyllis went upstairs, Maisie began to place the cups and saucers on the tray and took them out to the kitchen. Tears of happiness pricked at her eyes. All it needed now was for Bridget to walk in the door. Phyllis had sent her a telegram, but there was no guarantee it had got there.

The invasion of Europe had begun. Victory depended on so much and it wouldn't come overnight. The words of Bridget's last letter from a south coast hospital crowded her mind. *The hours are long, the casualties are high, but we try to remain cheerful. These brave young men, some no more than boys, deserve to see us smiling. Smiling helps them cope with their injuries. In private, we are sometimes sick; that's how tiredness and terrible sights can wear you down. However, we ensure they never see such reactions. Our smiles are as important as the surgeon's skill, encouraging them to win through. I hope and pray for the day when this war is over. We'll never again be the tobacco girls we once were. Too much has happened to change us. All we can hope is for our loved ones to survive in a peaceful and happy future. Much love, Bridget.*

Phyllis smoothed out the creases of the dress as best she could. Her thoughts went back to the wedding that didn't happen and the one that did as she stared at herself in the full-length wardrobe mirror. Her heart filled with nostalgia and love. She felt like a bride all over again.

A deep sigh preceded her descent back down to her dear friend Maisie, and young Carole.

Just as she began singing 'Here Comes the Bride' – the first few words followed by dah de dah's when she'd forgotten the others – a loud knocking came from the front door.

'I'll get it,' she shouted.

Despite that, the parlour door was opened just as she herself dragged the front door ajar.

Phyllis gasped at the sight of the new arrival and Bridget gasped right back.

'My word,' said Bridget as she took in the sight of Phyllis in her wedding gown, her eyes glowing, her hair that same Titian red that she remembered. Yet there was something different about her. Yes, she'd got older, but she looked more of a woman than she ever had, more confident, a challenging look in her eyes.

'Bridget.' Maisie came tumbling forward and once inside the narrow hallway, all three embraced, back together again after such a very long time.

Carole was introduced. Bridget just about remembered her. She'd replaced Phyllis at about the same time as Bridget was promoted to the packaging department.

There were tears before Carole suggested they needed more than tea to toast this fantastic happening.

'I don't think we've got anything to toast the beautiful bride,' said Maisie.

'Yes we do.' Carole ran out to the outhouse and brought in a bottle of champagne.

Maisie and Phyllis were agog. 'Where did you get that?'

Carole grinned. 'Brought round by Paula's grandfather to wet the baby's head. I've had it ages.'

Bet he didn't pay full price, thought Maisie as she dived into the sideboard for glasses. Not that she would mention it. This was an occasion for celebration and for overlooking the marked possibility that the champagne was stolen.

Surprisingly enough, her grandmother had collected quite an impressive collection of wine glasses. She chose four she thought suited the occasion.

'Carole, it's your champagne. How about you propose the toast,' said Maisie.

Carole beamed. 'I'd be delighted. Glasses charged we toast the bride. Oh, and the groom, though he's absent.'

'To the bride and groom,' they chanted in unison.

Glass in hand, Phyllis twirled on the spot. 'So what do you think of the dress?'

'It's beautiful,' cried Carole, her slender hands clasped tightly around the glass of champagne, eyes shining with delight.

Maisie couldn't help but agree. The creamy satin dress was perfect next to Phyllis's colouring and fiery auburn hair. 'It looks as though it was made for you. You look wonderful.' She meant it sincerely. Phyllis glowed with health. Okay, she was slimmer than she had been, though as she'd explained earlier, things on the island had been pretty dire.

Phyllis opened her mouth to say something, but Carole got there first.

'I want a dress just like that when I get married.' Her expression saddened. 'If I get married.'

'Oh you will,' said Phyllis. 'I guarantee it.'

'But—'

'You've got a baby, but let's face it you're hardly the only one.' Phyllis reached out and touched Carole's cheek. 'I lost my baby. You've still got yours. You'll want a lot more from a man, therefore you'll study him more. Handsome is as handsome does, but a good heart is worth its weight in gold.'

Maisie noticed the adoration in Carole's eyes.

Bridget told them about nursing but held back on being too explicit.

'It's going to be a while before they win through, but from what I've been told, they're doing well, pushing further and further into France.'

'Let's hope that by this time next year it'll be all over.'

'Here's to that,' said Carole, tipping the dregs of the champagne into each glass. 'Anyone for any more?' she asked, waggling the bottle from side to side.

'You mean you have more,' said a surprised Bridget.

Carole grinned. 'Paula's got a doting grandfather. We might as well make a night of it.'

More sandwiches appeared. 'Tinned salmon,' said Carole in response to their surprised expressions. 'We need something to soak up two bottles of champagne.'

Over the last of the sandwiches, Maisie asked Bridget about her family.

'They're fine, though surprised when I suddenly appeared on the doorstep. The kids are growing up and the house seems more crowded than ever. There's only the settee for me to sleep on and... Oh my lord. Is that the time? I've missed the last bus. Do you mind if...?'

'My settee is all yours.' Maisie felt happier than she had for a very long time. The tobacco girls were together again. It had taken a war to separate them and who knows where they would be when it ended, but it was Maisie's belief that they would always keep in touch, no matter where they were.

23

BRIDGET

Before Bridget had set off back to the hospital in Southampton, parents and daughter had discussed everything they hadn't had chance to talk about the night before.

Her mother had sat up waiting for her to come home despite her emphasising that if meeting up with Maisie went on late, she'd sleep on Maisie's settee. Bridget's father had insisted she turn in around one o'clock in the morning.

'She's a married woman and capable of looking after herself.' Mary had given in through sheer fatigue.

Most of what they talked about over lunch centred around her marriage, how happy they both were, and how they saw their future once the world was at peace.

'I'll be a good Catholic girl and have four – perhaps six children.'

Mary Milligan had known it was only a joke, but all the same felt pleased as Punch. Her happy laughter had been sincere. She'd felt happier and more energetic than she had for weeks.

Bridget's father had commented that Lyndon was a wealthy man so why not.

Mary had kicked him out of sight under the table. She didn't like money being mentioned. Babies should be born out of love. That was her long-held view, and she stuck to it.

There was also some conversation about Maisie and Phyllis. Mary expressed her pleasure that Phyllis too was happily married. 'Is Maisie courting? She'll be in her mid-twenties before she knows it and left on the shelf at this rate.'

Bridget smiled and shook her head. 'I think she's waiting for Sid to come home.'

She wasn't at all sure about that, but it stopped her mother from going on about it.

Before heading back to the hospital after supper that evening, Bridget went out into the back garden. It used to be something of a wasteland when left to her father. Since then, Sean had begun his gardening apprenticeship and taken it over. Beans, broccoli, carrots, cabbages and onions grew profusely. There wasn't quite enough room for potatoes, but there were blackberry bushes. She guessed Sean had transplanted a few that grew wild up on the Novers.

Her father was puffing clouds of pipe smoke, head tilted slightly back as though studying the clouds in the sky.

'I'll be off now,' she said and kissed his cheek.

His gaze settled on her. 'You know what, Bridie me love, I'm so proud of you. Your mother too. We're both proud of you.'

The look in his eyes emphasised the sincerity of his words, yet there was also a sadness she hadn't noticed before.

'Now you look after yourself. Promise?'

She said that she would.

Parents and five of her six siblings waved her off at the door. Sean had a date with his sweetheart and had said goodbye earlier.

We're all growing up, she thought after the last wave but not the last tear needing to be swiped from her eyes.

The bus took her to the city centre where she took a taxi to

Temple Meads Station – another extravagance she was slowly getting used to. Another part of her life with Lyndon. At times it felt alien, but gradually she would get used to having money. Not this war or Lyndon's mother would break them apart. She'd been tempted to mention the contents of the letter to Maisie, but the night had been so magical, so full of love between friends that she'd held back. She'd married Lyndon not his mother. Their love would last forever. That's what she told herself and was inclined to tear the letter to shreds, but something stopped her. What if he didn't believe her when she mentioned it? Wasn't it best to place it in his hands?

She decided keeping it was for the best. Just in case.

* * *

That night after she'd gone, her parents had talked about her marriage in the comfort of their own bed.

'They're happy. That's all that matters,' Mary said to Patrick before falling asleep.

It was the following morning when the letter arrived, not first thing but in the second post at around midday. The envelope Mary Milligan picked up from the mat was pure white, the paper of better quality than the flimsy stationery currently in use. Just the feel of it sent a shiver down her back. The writing on the envelope was elegant. There was no return address written, just an American postmark. It was addressed to Mr and Mrs Milligan.

After Bridget had left, she'd read her own tea leaves – something she hadn't done for quite a while. In these dire times, it was best not to know what might happen, but yesterday she'd relented.

The leaves had told her she would receive a letter. They'd also told her that she would shortly receive bad news. She'd even seen death mentioned, but seeing as the world was at war that was only to be expected.

Now, Mary gave a little cry of anguish. Nobody heard her. She was alone in the house. Michael and Sean had gone swimming. The younger kids were playing out in the street, taking turns to swing on a rope they'd tossed over a lamp post. Patrick was in his shed putting the finishing touches to a mantel clock he'd been asked to mend. Although totally absorbed in the task, he looked up when her shadow fell over him.

She stood in the doorway of his workshop, which was basically nothing much more than a wooden shed with a workbench and shelving. Tools of one sort and another hung from nails hammered into the wood. Boxes of screws and other bits and pieces were ranged along the shelf.

He smiled as he did whenever he set eyes on her. Although they were long married, she was still the girl he'd fallen in love with.

On seeing her tense expression, he let his glasses slide down his nose and his smile vanished. 'What's wrong, my pet?'

Wordlessly, she handed him the letter. Their fingers brushed lightly. Even after all this time, it still sent a shiver down her spine.

She found her voice. 'It's addressed to both of us. It's from America.'

He glanced at the letter, then back at her; a puzzled frown creased his brow. The only American they knew was Lyndon, their son-in-law.

'You don't think anything's happened, do you? To Lyndon, I mean.'

His look lingered on her. It never failed to amaze him just how little she'd changed over the years. Or perhaps his vision of her was more to do with deep affection and love, the kind that age does not tarnish. Nothing in this letter could disturb him if his beloved Mary was still in his arms.

Patrick sliced along the top of the letter with one of the files he used on clocks. Pushing his glasses back up his nose, he began to read who it was from and informed Mary. 'It's from Lyndon's mother.'

'Mrs O'Neill.'

He checked and said, 'Yes, Mrs O'Neill.'

'Is Lyndon all right?'

He nodded. 'It seems so.'

Mary heaved a sigh of relief. Tea leaves could be very fickle at times. 'Read it. Please.'

Patrick Milligan had only read the first sentence when he looked up at her in alarm.

Seeing his shocked reaction, Mary straightened. 'What is it?'

Her husband cleared his throat, readjusted his spectacles, and began to read:

'I am sure you will agree with me that my son's marriage to your daughter was a terrible mistake. Wed in wartime, their relationship is bound to fade along with the terrible memories of this time. I therefore suggest and am willing to pay for them to be divorced. They may then go their own way and marry within the constraints of their own class to more suitable people. I am also willing to pay compensation to both you and your daughter for this hasty interlude in her life. Perhaps you might all like to take a holiday, perhaps even in the South of France.'

Mary's shiver of apprehension turned to anger. 'The South of France? The stupid woman really has no idea of what's going on over here.'

'Well, the war is a long way off for the likes of her,' said Patrick quietly. Only rarely was Mary roused to anger – the look on her face fiery. He laid the missive on the workbench in front of him and silently reread the words. Finally, he said, 'So she doesn't think our daughter is a good match for her son.'

Mary was tight-lipped. 'Obviously not.'

Patrick shook his head. 'I don't think our Bridget will regard her marriage as a hasty interlude.' His eyes met those of his wife. 'It was plain enough when we last saw them that he loves her and she loves him.'

'But she isn't good enough for him. Well, not according to *her*. You'd think she was a duchess the way she speaks. I didn't think Americans were like that, though I suppose that's me being naïve. Rich people are like that the world over.'

To some extent, Patrick agreed with her, though his voice continued in a measured manner. 'No class system, though I don't think that's strictly true. It's just that their status is based on money rather than titles.'

Mary turned her back on him and leaned her head against the doorway. The tone of the letter had thrown her, reminding her of a young man whose parents had thought the same about her. They'd been from different classes and had been foolish enough to think that love could conquer all. For a time, it had seemed it could, but, as now, a war had intervened.

She felt Patrick's presence behind her, his body warm at her back. 'The answer's no. Isn't it?'

'Of course, it's no. How could it be anything else?'

Patrick paused before reminding her that she'd initially been against the marriage. 'Don't deny it my love.' He pressed her shoulder. 'I understood your reasons.'

'I thought she'd be treated as I was,' she whispered. 'Until they visited and told us they'd married, that was when everything changed. I'm not totally insensitive.' She looked up at him with watery eyes.

An unspoken memory flashed between them. Patrick's smile made deep creases at the corners of his eyes. 'No,' he whispered back. 'You're not. Do you want me to write back, or will you?'

Mary thought about it. 'Not yet. There's someone I must write to first. Someone who should be informed that Bridget exists. I've thought about telling them for a long time. Bridget's always accepted you as her father. I told myself she didn't need that other family who'd shunned the youthful love of a young couple who saw no class divisions.' She gave a little laugh. 'They presumed I'd given birth to a boy. That's how narrow-minded they were. Always right about everything.'

He didn't need to ask to whom or what it might be about. It was about Bridget. Neither did he ask the point of getting in touch with Bridget's father's family after all this time. He knew she heard from the other domestic who'd worked for them, but this was Mary's personal business. A woman should have some privacy in her life. They'd never been joined at the hip, only in the heart.

It was after eleven o'clock at night when he left her to write her letter. Their children were already in bed. She'd specifically asked him to go on up to bed so she could think before she put pen to paper.

'I'll be up soon,' she'd told him as she seated herself at the kitchen table with notepad and pen. 'I have to do this first.'

He knew the basics of what she was writing but would not ask to read it or for her to read it out. He'd rescued her from her past and there was a greater depth to their love than her more youthful love for Harold, but the past still belonged to her and always would; her and Bridget, that was.

24

Bridget's spirits rose at the prospect of Lyndon also getting leave. It had been weeks since they'd seen each other and all the time, she'd harboured the fear that she might never see him again.

Back in the restroom, the kettle was boiling and half a dozen cups and saucers were laid out. There was enough milk, but as usual only a frugal amount of sugar.

Bridget took off her starched cap and pushed her hair back from her forehead.

Edith, a colleague, had been reading today's newspaper, but had finished. She offered it to Bridget. 'Care to read it?'

'Thank you.'

As expected, the push through France comprised the main headline, but her eye was taken by another headline on the right-hand side of the front page.

Air Strike on Rocket Factories.

It went on to say that a squadron of B17s had taken off from an airfield in Lincolnshire and bombed the factory where the rockets were being assembled in Northern Germany. The paper had made a big thing that yet again bombs had fallen on the enemy's heartland.

'The enemy put up strong resistance, but the majority of the attack force made it home...'

Her hands began to shake. 'Oh my God.'

Edith took the paper from her hands. 'What is it, love? What is it?'

Bridget looked up at her, round-eyed and speechless.

Edith got the message – or thought she did. 'Your sweetheart's based there, is he?'

Overcome with emotion, not just fear but anger, she managed a terse nod.

Edith picked up the paper and read the piece that was so worrying Bridget. 'It says most of the attack force got back. That's got to be a good thing. Anyway, your boyfriend will be in touch the moment he's on the ground and debriefed. Have you planned to meet up?'

'No.' Bridget shook her head.

She felt the pity in Edith's cool blue eyes and could guess what she was thinking. He was just another boyfriend and she was just another nurse who had fallen in love. Another one would be along in a minute.

'He means the world to me.'

Edith gripped her trembling shoulder and gave it a shake. 'Give him chance to get himself together.'

Bridget stared at the newspaper.

Edith interrupted her thoughts. 'Come on. Let's get back to our room. I've got some packing to do.'

There was toast and tea once they were back in the room they shared.

Bridget was still worried but determined to maintain that stiff upper lip.

Edith was bustling around, gathering up clothes and placing them neatly into a brown leather bag with a brass buckle clasp.

'Can't wait to see the farm again. My father's got land girls to help him out. Not easy though. Working on a farm is hard work...'

The comment jogged Bridget's memory. Edith had told her where she came from, but if her memory was right... 'Isn't your father's farm in Lincolnshire? Isn't that what you told me?'

Edith stopped folding up a second vest and two pairs of French knickers. The vests were warm army-issue. She'd made the knickers from parachute silk, no elastic of course, but fastened by a button at the side. 'Yes. He does as a matter of fact.'

'I recall you saying that it's not far from an American air force base. You mentioned the name and I recognised it as the one where Lyndon is stationed.'

Edith frowned when she looked at her. 'What are you saying?'

Bridget got to her feet and with a look of pleading in her clear blue eyes. 'Would you go along there and ask if he's all right? I wouldn't ask you, but... judging by that article, he should be back. Would you, Edith? Would you?'

She was aware of her hands twisting in front of her, fingers interlocking tightly enough to break. Lyndon would definitely have been in touch by now, but he hadn't. She was scared. Very scared.

Edith spread her hands in a helpless fashion. 'Bridget Milligan, what the devil do you think I can say to persuade them to tell me where or how he is? As a stranger, I'd be told in no uncertain terms to scarper.'

'They wouldn't say that if you said you were his wife.'

Edith stared. 'Are you kidding?'

Bridget shook her head. 'No. Lyndon and I were married before last Christmas. Please, Edith.'

Looking quite stunned, Edith took a big swallow. Like everyone else, she knew getting married meant instant dismissal. 'Who else knows?'

'The almoner is the only person who knows but promised to keep the secret. My mother-in-law sent a letter addressed to me as Mrs O'Neill.'

'And she hasn't said anything?' Edith looked surprised.

'No. Basically she said she doesn't agree with such an arcane rule and that this country could do with all the help it can get.'

Edith pulled a so-so face of approval. 'Makes sense.'

'Will you make enquiries? Please, Edith.'

Edith broke into a kind smile. 'Don't give it a moment's thought. Of course I will.' Her look turned more sober. 'As long as you're sure you don't want to leave it for a while longer. Just in case.'

Bridget shook her head. 'There's no just in case about it. I'm sick inside. Besides, I might have to leave shortly anyway.'

Their eyes met in mutual understanding. Edith had guessed what she meant.

'How far gone are you?'

'About three months.'

'Darling! Heartiest congratulations.'

They hugged warmly.

'Does he know yet?' asked Edith.

Bridget shook her head. 'You're the first person I've told. I didn't even tell my parents or my friends when I visited Bristol.'

Edith smiled. 'Bridget, I feel so privileged. Thank you.'

Bridget shrugged. 'The moment seemed right. Besides, we've worked together for some time now.' There was as much close-ness in nurses working together as there was for soldiers. You were all in it together, brothers-in-arms, or in their case sisters-in-arms.

'If...' Realising that under the circumstances there mustn't be any ifs, Edith began again. 'When I see him and I'm pretending to be you, do you want me to mention your situation?'

Bridget thought seriously. 'I'm not sure. I'd much prefer to tell him myself, but on the other hand...'

Edith smiled. 'The poor chap could do with some good news.

'You're right. He'll be over the moon.'

25

PHYLLIS

London could easily overwhelm, but although Phyllis had never seen the likes of so many, the crowds, the continuous toing and froing, she managed to take everything in her stride. She was enjoying London but would have preferred Mick to be with her. Oxford would have been a better posting of course. During a recent phone conversation, they'd plotted how best to ensure they got leave at the same time and talked about where they would stay.

'A cosy little inn in the country with a big four-poster bed and a huge fireplace.

She'd pointed out to him that it wasn't yet cold enough for a fire. 'Unless we wait for September,' she'd added.

Mick had laughed. 'I'll do without the fire then. I figure we can work out how best to keep warm – even if the weather doesn't turn chilly.'

They'd laughed at his obvious innuendo. They weren't that long married and they had a lot of keeping warm to do.

A more serious concern momentarily soured her happiness.

'Just you take care, Mick Fairbrother. Don't do anything stupid.'

They'd already had three phone conversations since she

arrived in London, one every other day. She always ended the conversation with the same warning. He always ended his with a fleeting pause before saying that he would only do what he had to do.

Although there were miles between her and Mick, Phyllis chose to believe he was safe and carried on as best she could. He'd promised her that he wouldn't be flying over a combat zone and risk being shot down. One part of her chose to disregard his devil-may-care attitude and believe him. The other part of her that knew him more deeply than any man she'd ever met and worried that he wouldn't be able to resist. There was also his head injury. Was it very much better? He'd assured her that it was. 'Though I get tired. Can't be helped doing my job.'

Serving in the War Office department she'd landed herself in was a far cry from her job in Malta. For a start, no matter that it was ostensibly an English summer, the corridors of power were glum and cold. She shared an office with four other wireless operators in Whitehall receiving direct messages from Normandy for evaluation and passing on to the right sections. Most of it was reconnaissance information that tied up with aerial photography – the very field Mick was engaged in. Everything about it was top secret and the other girls, although very friendly, were not from her part of the world. Nor had they ever worked in a factory.

When first arriving at her new post, a pompous silver-haired gent wearing a monocle and a suit that smelt of moth balls, had told her in no uncertain terms that she wouldn't have got the job if she hadn't served in Malta. 'We prefer girls of a certain calibre. Well-spoken but not too well educated. Filing clerk level at least, coupled with the ability to type. They're women after all, so we can't really expect them to do much more than that. Hardly career material. At the end of the day, no matter their background, they'll all end up as housewives.'

To say that the girls were in danger of exploding was putting it mildly.

The man with the white hair and monocle who wore a suit that smelled of moth balls was Mr Jonathan Snow and he was a Right Honourable.

When he was long out of earshot, one of the other girls had told her that he was the son of a baronet.

The informant was Jacqueline Mautors-Smythe, who sported an upper-class accent, spoke passable French and was more outspoken than any of them. She could hold her own that much was for sure.

'Call me Jackie, darlings. My mother was French and insisted on adding her maiden name to that of Pater. But no need to make things complicated, eh? Jackie it shall be.'

'Have you got a title,' asked Muriel, a vicar's daughter.

'No.'

Phyllis had sensed Jackie wavered slightly before she'd answered.

'So, Mr Snow's the son of a baronet,' exclaimed Phyllis. 'Well there's a thing.'

Jackie had grinned. 'I reckon that in a short time we might be calling the funny old stick the son of another word beginning with b...'

In that moment of girlish laughter, the ice was broken. They had become a team, united in their job, for which Phyllis was glad. She was alone in the city and badly needed friends.

Stuffy Snow, as the girls called him, wasn't to know how much his words had ignited the fire of unity in four female breasts. When he wasn't around and there was time, the girls exchanged acerbic comments.

'He was born in the last century. What can you expect?'

'He's aristocratic. A woman's place is doing the laundry, cooking and having children. And looking pretty,' Jackie added.

Phyllis thought of her old friends at the tobacco factory, especially Bridget. 'The women gave up men's jobs when they came back after the last war.' She frowned. 'Somehow I don't think it will happen this time. We've done too much. Seen too much.'

For the most part, they were silent when Stuffy Snow was around. Phyllis was of the opinion that it wouldn't last. At some point, their inner seething would turn into outright rebellion, then Stuffy Snow had better watch out!

All four girls were billeted in the same five-storey house, owned by a Mrs Fly, a slightly eccentric but friendly old lady of diminutive stature who barely reached their shoulders. She had the face of a cherub and the voice of a child. A pair of twinkling eyes peered from a plump face. Their colour seemed to match that of her clothes. Mrs Fly favoured violet muslin dresses of a style last fashionable in the reign of King Edward the Seventh.

The house boasted a warren of rooms on each floor. Mrs Fly, along with a blue Macaw named Mr Macawber, occupied the ground-floor suite of rooms at the front of the house. The kitchen and the dining room where they enjoyed her fulsome cooking were at the rear, overlooking a garden full of freshly grown vegetables. A tangled mass of honeysuckle and ivy surrounded the vegetable beds, growing in such profusion that they totally obscured the Victorian brick walls they grew against.

'Something smells good,' said Phyllis as they entered the grand old house where they lived.

Jackie remarked that Mrs Fly was a wonder with the rations.

'I don't know how she does it. Hello, Mrs Fly, we're home,' she called.

Mrs Fly appeared at the end of the passageway, where a red velvet curtain half masked the staircase to the upper floors.

'Your dinner's ready when you are,' Mrs Fly called back.

'Tonight we're all off and we're going out on the town, so we'll eat now before we get ready if that's all right with you.' Four more girls, also billeted together in a separate establishment made up the full team that covered both night and day shifts. The war was ongoing and didn't take time off.

Mrs Fly waved her hand. 'Come on through. I'll put a cloth over Mr Macawber so you can eat in peace.'

When Phyllis had first reported to her billet, she'd been surprised at the sound of swearing coming from the back of the house. On seeing her shocked expression, Mrs Fly had apologised.

'That's Mr Macawber. He used to be in a dockside pub. The matelots and stevedores in there taught him some very naughty words.'

Phyllis had smiled and said that she understood, was in the forces and used to hearing bad language. Mr Macawber had continued to swear until Mrs Fly had covered him with a fringed chenille cloth. It was the only way to shut him up.

'He knows when new people are around and can't help himself showing off,' Mrs Fly had explained.

They all sat down, eager to devour something better than canteen sandwiches or Woolton pie. One thing Phyllis had noticed was that Mrs Fly always cooked meat or fish dishes. So far, there was no sign of the dreaded Woolton pie, with its mix of vegetables and dusty pastry.

Jackie made an announcement directed at both her colleagues and Mrs Fly. 'We'll be out by eight o'clock.'

It occurred to Phyllis that Jackie always sounded insistent. Whether she meant to or not was irrelevant. Phyllis and the others just went along with it.

'Coq au vin,' declared Mrs Fly as she set a large Victorian tureen in the centre of the table. She lifted the lid. 'Voila!'

The exquisite smell made their mouths water.

'Goodness, Mrs Fly. You're a marvel. Where did you get the chicken? Where did you get the wine?'

Mrs Fly's cheeks turned pink. 'A bit of port left from before the war.'

She made no comment about where she'd got the chicken.

The main meal was followed by roly-poly pudding and custard.

'Oh my,' said Phyllis, patting her stomach after devouring her portion. 'That's a pudding that always lies heavy.'

Jackie scooped the last spoonful into her mouth and laughed. 'Mrs Fly's roly-poly pudding must be the true origin of that old saying about there being a bun in the oven.' She rubbed her stomach. 'It certainly feels like it – not that I'd know what it feels like of course.'

Phyllis laughed with her newfound friends but refrained from admitting that she knew exactly what being pregnant was like. Time had passed; living in Bristol and losing her baby was behind her, but still the memory bit deeply like a sore that would never quite heal.

Food was devoured and plates were cleared away. Excitedly, they trooped upstairs, talking about what they would wear and how much they were looking forward to going out.

'Right,' said Jackie, bringing everyone to a halt at the top of the stairs. 'First thing is to sort out the bathroom timetable. Come this way.'

Like a line of obedient ducklings following their mother, they trooped along to the far end of the landing and the one and only bathroom in the house.

There were white tiles on the walls and black and white ones on the floor. The bath could passably accommodate three people at once, four at a push.

They all had their own towels allocated once a week by the well-organised and kindly Mrs Fly.

Jackie pointed. 'There it is. All above board.'

A line had been drawn in crayon around the bath indicating regulation depth.

Phyllis and her friends eyed the line with derision.

Phyllis sighed. 'I was really looking forward to having a bath. I'd forgotten how little water we're allowed.'

Rosina grimaced. 'Well, hen,' she said in her Glaswegian burr. 'That is not going to cover much.'

'Mrs Fly's got a rainwater barrel out back for the garden,' said Phyllis. 'I'm half tempted to dip myself into that.' She shivered. 'Bit cold though.'

'I suppose we can sit in it and sluice ourselves down with a face flannel,' said Muriel, hugging her towel to her narrow chest. Being slight, she could probably manage fine like that. However, the others, Phyllis included, were not convinced.

'I've an idea, dahlings,' said Jackie, one beautifully manicured finger resting on her scarlet lips. 'I suggest we allow two inches for each of us. Two multiplied by four is eight inches. A reasonable amount in which to take a bath. Two of us bathe first, then two when those are finished.'

Muriel, the vicar's daughter, didn't look convinced.

Jackie, her face close to the other rather whey-faced girl, spoke more slowly. 'Two by two. Just like on Noah's ark. One at the plug end, one against the taps. Do you understand what I'm saying?'

Muriel stared at her wide-eyed before nodding, the bath towel now hiding her chin as well as her chest.

On seeing Muriel's consternation, Phyllis added some encouraging enthusiasm. 'That's a grand idea. Let's do it.'

'I do hope we don't get into trouble,' said Muriel. 'Do you think we will? I mean, seeing as we're only allowed two inches, and really, are we allowed to share?'

'Dahling,' said Jackie in her plumy voice. 'It's perfectly fine.

We'll draw lots to see which two get in first...'

As the penny dropped so did Muriel's jaw. Her cheeks turned bright red. She looked at Phyllis as though for sympathy. 'I've always bathed alone. How about you?'

Phyllis shrugged. 'A bath was rare in Malta. We needed the water to drink, so we mostly swam in the sea followed by a quick rub-down with a flannel to disperse the salt.'

Her comment resulted in another round-mouthed 'Oh', from Muriel.

A coin was tossed to see which pair would use the bath first. Muriel and Rosina won the toss.

Jackie ordered them to be quick. 'Leave a bit of warmth in the water for us. Let's get us a cuppa,' she called to Phyllis over her shoulder.

Phyllis had laid out clean underwear and the petrol-blue dress Maisie had insisted on buying for her. As she retrieved the light-weight wool dress from the wardrobe, ideal for an English summer, the silky sheen of her wedding dress drew her attention. Back in Malta she'd been given the address to where it must be delivered. So far she hadn't been given enough leave to make the journey into the West End of London. But she would. She'd promised and there were other wartime brides in need.

Mrs Fly called to them to join her in the parlour. 'I've made a fresh pot,' she explained as they entered the handsome room mostly frequented by her and the royal blue macaw.

The tea was indeed freshly brewed – first brew, not second or third. Phyllis exchanged a look of surprise with Jackie. Thanks to rationing, it had become usual practice to dry tea leaves before reusing them. There was no doubt that these were fresh and infused with something decidedly aromatic.

Phyllis made comment. 'Lovely tea, Mrs Fly.'

'Are you a hoarder or a black marketer?' Jackie asked jokingly.

A look of alarm came to Mrs Fly's doll-like face. 'No! No! My darling brother was in the Indian army. He brought me back a very generous supply on his return some years back – 1937 I think it was.'

'Your brother was in India? So was my father. He worked in the viceroy's office.'

Mrs Fly's expression brightened. 'Oh, I say.' She was obviously impressed. So was Phyllis come to that. She'd never known anyone with quite so illustrious a background as Jackie. It occurred to her that it might be the reason why their boss appeared at times a little in awe of the raven-haired girl with model looks. She obviously had connections.

'I think I impressed her,' Jackie whispered to Phyllis as they made their way back along the landing to the bathroom.

'You impressed me too,' returned Phyllis with a grin.

Jackie banged on the door of the bathroom. 'Your time's up,' she shouted.

A muffled response came from a small voice within that they wouldn't be much longer.

With their towels around their shoulders, they leaned against the banister.

'Will you ever marry?' Phyllis asked.

Jackie pulled a face. 'I'm expected to, but that doesn't mean that I want to.'

'What if you don't? What will you do?'

'Carve out a career for myself. I quite fancy being a politician. There aren't enough women in the House of Commons. I think it's time there were.' She grinned suddenly. 'I can imagine myself now, ready to crack my handbag round a few heads.'

Phyllis laughed. 'I think they'd expect you to do more than that.'

Jackie's confident features, usually set for fun, became quite serious. 'I've met people – especially women – from all walks of life during this war. Before the war, I'd hardly met any apart from my own class, except for servants and suchlike.' She frowned. 'I'd never really got to know any of the lower classes as people with rights as important as anyone else. I'd like to champion their causes, do some good before I die. That's the other thing about this war, it forces you to face your own mortality. So might as well get some brownie points, yes?'

'We're coming out,' came the cry from behind the bathroom door.

'What's the bet they put the bolt on,' Jackie whispered.

Sure enough, there came the sound of a bolt being pulled.

Phyllis beamed as the other two came out. 'Thank you, girls. I'm looking forward to this.'

Once inside, they both stripped off without showing the slightest embarrassment. After all she'd been through in Malta, Phyllis did not feel in the least bashful about being naked with another woman.

'Do you mind taking the plug end?' asked Jackie. She looked pointedly at Phyllis's scrawny frame. She'd lost pounds in Malta. 'Fact is my backside is wider than yours so I need more room. Is that okay with you?'

Phyllis laughed and said that it was.

They washed their own bodies and poured water over each other's shampooed hair. The shampoo was a couple of packets Jackie had hoarded. 'Bought in a posh West End beauty shop.'

'West End?' Phyllis's ears perked up at mention of the very place where she was to return the wedding dress. She told Jackie about the dress she'd borrowed and where she had to return it. 'I've got the address. I phoned the other day hoping to speak to the woman I was to take it to, but she was out on brigade business – at least I think that's what was said. Off in the country and won't be back for at least a week.'

'A woman high up in the army. Well, there's a thing. Once she's back, let me know and I'll go there with you. I know my way around London. Are you enjoying it?'

Phyllis's eyes sparkled. 'London is amazing. It's so busy. I love getting the underground. Love the red buses more though. Ours back in Bristol are green. They seem so dull in comparison.'

'Your Mick won't mind you going out on the town, will he?'

Phyllis's wide smile lessened. 'No. He trusts me and I trust him – well, as far as the opposite sex is concerned. What I don't trust him to do is to keep out of danger. If there's a chance to pilot an aeroplane, he'll do it. All I hope is that he won't fly over enemy territory. He did promise me, but...'

'Sounds like a born warrior,' Jackie said with a resigned sigh. 'The sort this country and every other war-torn country depends on.'

Once out of the bath and dressed, Phyllis twirled on the spot in the blue dress which she'd teemed with a pair of navy-blue court shoes she'd bought in Oxford Street.

'Almost ready,' she cried excitedly as she squirted some perfume around her neck and in her hair. 'Tonight I'm going to enjoy London.'

'I'll make sure you will,' said Jackie, giving her back a hefty slap.

Mrs Fly waved them off and told them to take care. They said they would.

Once away from the house, they headed to a very crowded pub, where men in uniform offered to buy them drinks. So did other men of obvious wealth and smooth confidence.

It was one of these latter men, his hair gleaming with lotion, his shirt ultra white and his suit charcoal grey and well cut, who offered to take them dancing.

'My chauffeur is outside.' His voice was as refined as the way he held himself, cigarette holder posed in one hand as though about to conduct the London Philharmonic.

Jackie flashed Phyllis a secret wink. 'That's kind of you. I'm afraid I've left my chauffeur at home, so I will by all means take you up on your kind offer.' Phyllis noticed that her finely pronounced vowels were on a par with the man's own.

Phyllis could barely believe Jackie's nerve. The man who'd offered her his car and driver was obviously of a different class to herself. Jackie, however, was his equal so not in the least put out.

The four of them piled into the plush cream leather seating in the rear of the car fully expecting their host, whose name was Michael Throckmorton, to sit in the front with the driver. Instead he squeezed in with them.

'You married?' Jackie asked him.

'Sometimes,' he said with a leering grin.

'So are we. And totally loyal to our beloved boys.' As if to prove the point, she dabbed at her eyes with a spotlessly white handkerchief. 'We will dance tonight, but we've sworn to all go home together. It's as our husbands would wish.'

Jackie wasn't married. Rosina was engaged and Muriel was not at all interested in men. There were rumours about her preferring girls, but as far as they were concerned that was her business.

The nightclub they went to was packed with men and women. Those in uniform, as though scenting birds of a feather even though they were in civvies tonight, bought them drinks, danced with them, and didn't protest too loudly when they bid adieu and headed out into the night.

Michael Throckmorton had consoled himself with a curvaceous blonde in a red silk dress that exposed more than it covered. He didn't offer them a lift, which was a shame seeing as their feet were aching.

'It's a fine night,' said Phyllis in response to the rubbing of heels and kneading of aching toes. 'I don't mind a walk.'

'My feet are aching,' grumbled Muriel.

'So are mine. I can manage without.' Phyllis took off each of her high-heeled navy blue court shoes. Muriel followed suit.

The clouds had lifted enough to allow a silver-faced moon to relieve the perennial blackout. Black buildings were outlined in silver. Dark windows reflected spangled clouds gleaming like jewels with borrowed light.

They sang snatches of the music they'd danced to. It surprised Phyllis to see that they weren't the only ones wending their way home through moonlit streets. They passed canoodling couples in dark doorways. Tipsy sailors home from the sea, three abreast holding onto each other. If one went down, they would all fall like skittles, thought Phyllis.

'What a beautiful night,' she breathed. 'Just look at that moon.'

The words were barely out of her mouth when a burst of searchlights flashed in arcs over the indigo sky. The powerful beams picked out ragged clouds but nothing else.

Phyllis felt her stomach cleave to her spine. 'There's nothing,' she said.

'Yet,' warned Jackie. 'It's another of those bloody doodlebugs.'

Barely were the words out of her mouth and the siren sounded.

For a moment, it was as though time stood still. They were figures able to move but stiff, taken off guard. They glanced from one to the other as though seeking an order or advice as to what to do next. Being frozen in time lasted barely a minute before an unspoken agreement was reached and they all began to run and seek shelter.

The sound of feet pounding pavements was all around. A few screamed. Some shouted. There was fear but also defiance and the uncalled-for sharing of one stark detail that everyone already knew. 'Doodlebug. Another of the buggers!'

'The sixth today!'

'Who says so? I ain't 'eard any go over.'

'Dartford. Essex too.'

'Come on. Run. This one might be heading our way.'

'Bugger, bugger, bugger.'

'Sod doodlebugs. Sod Hitler.'

'I'd like to send one of them bloody things right up his...'

Phyllis and Muriel, still in bare feet, ran regardless of scattered stones, uneven pavements, just praying there was no strewn glass.

Everyone chose to believe that it couldn't possibly be their name on the bomb that would explode and tear the air asunder. But still they ran, all encouraging each other to go faster.

'Come on.'

'The searchlights are up. Won't they shoot them down?'

'Travelling too fast.'

A continuous droning sounded from overhead, a dead and menacing sound vibrating downwards, filling their heads and setting their nerves on edge.

Suddenly the dull drone was split by a monstrous whooshing as though a high wind had been whipped up from nowhere.

'Down here.'

They fell down the steps into an air-raid shelter, bouncing against the piled-up sandbags the whole length of the steps into safety.

Phyllis gasped as the air she breathed in suddenly became like powdered glass in her mouth.

A loud booming noise made the air vibrate. They seemed to race just ahead of it, the floor shaking beneath their feet as they tumbled through the door and onto the concrete floor of the shelter.

To Phyllis, it felt as though a huge hand cuffed her head, hitting it sideways with the force of the explosion. Through the whirling dust, she saw Rosina's lips forming words she could not hear. Her ears ached. Her head also ached, and her mind seemed void of clear thinking.

In the dim light, she saw that Rosina's lips were still moving, but still she could not hear.

Phyllis made circling movements with her fingers around her ears and tried to say, 'I can't hear you.' She couldn't hear herself.

Like a brick tumbling from a wall, the barrier to sound cracked and broke. Rosina's words came through.

'That was close.'

'Too close.'

The all-clear sounded. They made their way back up the steps and onto the street. The air was thick with dust, and it was difficult to breathe.

They all began coughing, Muriel more so than everyone else.

Covered in dust and the feet of their stockings punctured by stones, they decided to call it a day. The platform on the underground station was packed, though not so much as back in the Blitz. Most people now stayed in their houses. The more nervous still headed for the safety of being deep underground.

They were close to home when the next one fell. Their eyes gazed fearfully skyward as it passed overhead. Some way in front of them, it stopped flying and fell to earth. Just as before, there was that same sucking of air from the lungs, the force of the explosion hot on their faces.

Muriel began to sob. 'Oh, my God.'

Phyllis took a deep breath and voiced her fears. 'I don't think we have a bed for the night.'

Jackie swore. 'Poor Mrs Fly.'

Phyllis groaned as another grim thought hit her. 'My wedding dress'

'That's the least of our worries. We've only got the clothes we're stood up in.'

26

BRIDGET

Lyndon had stood there in the doorway looking thinner. There were circles under his eyes but a ready smile on his face.

'You're here!'

During his phone call prior to meeting up, he told her how hard he'd had to press to get just one day of precious leave.

'Me too. I swapped a few shifts. I did it.'

Bridget had sounded disbelieving.

'I told them you were expecting our first child. That helped.' He'd grinned. 'What a clever girl you are, sending your friend to get the message through. Can't tell you how much it lifted my spirits.'

'How long?' he said now as they lay in bed, sheets tangled around their naked bodies, his hand gently caressing her stomach.

'A few months yet.'

He kissed her forehead. 'How long before you pack in nursing?'

She grimaced. 'I love nursing, but...' She looked into his eyes. 'I love you more.'

The touch of his fingers running through her hair sent tingles down her spine.

She hesitated before she voiced the question uppermost in her mind. 'Will your parents be pleased? About the baby, I mean.'

'Honey,' he said, 'how could they fail to be pleased.'

His mother's letter remained like an open sore. She'd kept its arrival to herself, but she wondered about telling him. Would it divide his loyalties; family and her?

Their apartment was an oasis of calm, an island in a violent sea. They made love and, in its aftermath, Lyndon outlined his mission.

'The rocket factories in northern Germany. I know they're the enemy, but I can't help thinking that our bombs are dropping on the innocent as well as on the guilty. They use slave labour.'

When he closed his eyes as if trying to blank out the dead and injured, she ran her finger across the lid of each eye. Not that it would go far to soothing away the imagined visions of destruction. Nothing would ever do that, but at least he hadn't seen them first hand. She had. Men destroyed by terrible injuries. All she told him was that she'd been very busy.

They slept clinging onto each other for dear life as if that would keep the nightmares at bay. Maybe it did.

The morning sun picked out the breakfast Bridget had set out on the table. Toast and fried Spam. It smelt better than it looked and certainly better than it tasted – at least as regards the bread. Two ounces of butter, part of her ration she'd brought from the hospital helped, dripping through and moistening the toast. Despite a hint of morning sickness, she managed to eat. The coffee was quite wonderful, Lyndon's donation from US catering.

'I'm phoning the hospital today. Once I tell them I'm married *and* pregnant, it's purely a formality. I don't have to go back there.'

His fingers caressed her hand as she looked down into her tea. She deeply regretted not going back. She'd made some good friends, but that was how things worked. She would be automatically dismissed.

Lyndon took both her hands in his. 'I'm sorry you have to leave your job.'

She laughed. 'I've got a far more important profession lined up. I'm going to be a mother.'

'Your parents are going to be over the moon. When do you plan going down to tell them?' he asked as he buttered his toast.

'Just after I say goodbye to you. I can't wait to tell them and now I'm without a job, I can tell them in person rather than just writing. Writing is so impersonal, don't you think?'

He smiled at her from above his slice of toast and tipped her a wink loaded with enough meaning to make her blush. 'Yes. Surprises are best declared face to face.' He met her steady gaze that came without a smile and tensed. 'Something wrong, baby?'

She looked away, wondering if it was best not to mention it, then looked back at him again. 'It's a letter. Seeing as we're on the subject of surprises, I think you should read it.'

She'd kept the letter from his mother without mentioning it to anyone. Now, with new life growing inside her, it seemed the time had come. She fetched it from her handbag where it had remained safely hidden.

'I received this letter two weeks ago. It's from your mother.'

Returning his unfinished slice of toast to his plate, his eyes met hers. Soundlessly, he took the letter and began to read.

She looked at him as he read, loving the tilt of his head, the hairs on the back of his hands, the soft hair flicked away from his brow. A frown line deepened before he refolded the letter and put it down on the table.

He said nothing but pushed it to one side. There was something about the silence and the action that rang alarm bells. She'd expected an outraged reaction, part of the process of defending her corner – loudly. Or the opposite – defending his mother. To her mind, this could only mean one thing and she was drained, angry.

'You already knew.' Her voice was just above a whisper.

Head bent, he fixed his gaze on the plate in front of him.

'She wrote to me too and I wrote back.' He looked lovingly at her. 'I told her how it was between us and that there was nothing she could do to break us apart.'

His words were mellow, gently spoken and thus she was soothed.

Her anger, and also her fear, melted away. 'Have you told her about the baby?' Her voice was soft.

'After the visit from your friend Edith, I sent a telegram and told her if she wanted to disown our child, then she could disown me too.'

'What about your father? Does he want us to divorce?'

Lyndon's face clouded. 'I knew he wasn't well, but I didn't know how serious it was. He dictates his letters to his secretary, but my mother scrutinises them before they're sent – if they're sent at all.' He tossed his head in consternation.

Bridget frowned. 'Why would she do that?'

'To punish him.'

'I don't understand.'

When he gave her that melting look as he was doing now, she could forgive him anything. There was no need for forgiveness in what he said next, certainly not from her.

'My father had an affair. There was a love child. She was paid off and the child provided for, but my mother continues to make him suffer. That's the way she is.'

'And us?'

His hand reached for hers. 'I don't care what she says or what she does. You've got me forever.'

* * *

His looks, words and touch travelled with her all the way to Bristol. She'd never met his father but decided she would like him once she did. His mother was a different matter.

Bridget rubbed her hand protectively over her stomach. In her mind, she practised what she would say to her parents.

The path to the future lay full of hope and happiness. Nothing could now upset that wonderful image. The war would end. She and Lyndon, plus their newborn, would make a life together. Nothing and nobody could prevent that – except perhaps Adolf Hitler.

27

Bridget was coming home!

Ration coupons Mary Milligan had saved over several weeks were spent on putting together some party fare. A great deal of time had been lost queueing for what was needed. Before the war, such items would have been regarded as ordinary. Nowadays, the most basic ingredients for a cake were a luxury.

In one of her letters, Bridget had sent her a recipe for carrot cookies, a concoction of margarine, sugar, vanilla essence, flour (mixed with some rolled oats to eke it out) and of course carrots. There'd also been a fruit cake, a large pinch of cinnamon making up for the fact that the fruit consisted mostly of currants and dried apple rings broken into pieces. The kids had been particularly looking forward to the butterfly chocolate cakes and she couldn't blame them. Bridget had brought a whole box of chocolate bars, providing real chocolate for those cakes rather than just cocoa.

This time there was no lingering at the door in the hope of surprising them. Bridget was aching to tell them the news.

The house was full of the family and Maisie was expected to call in.

'Everyone sit down. I've got something to tell you,' Bridget cried above the din. She herself remained standing and all eyes turned in her direction. She smiled broadly. 'The news is that I'll probably be visiting more often.'

Happy expressions became inquisitive.

She took a deep breath. 'I've resigned my nursing course.'

Nobody said a word, though there was a joyful spark in her mother's eyes. It occurred to Bridget then and there that she'd guessed the reason why.

She looked straight at her mother, then at her father.

'I've a question to ask you.'

Her father looked puzzled but urged her to go ahead. Her mother too.

'How do you fancy being grandparents?'

In the ensuing hubbub, she managed to ask her siblings how they felt about being uncles and aunts to her baby. Hugs, cries of joy and clapping confirmed their pleasure and acceptance of their new status.

Her mother was crying. 'Oh, my darling,' she said, throwing her arms around her daughter's neck. Her father did the same and her two brothers and four sisters crowded in.

'This is like a rugby scrum and the breath's knocked out of me,' cried her father.

Amid that scrum, Bridget noticed that her mother's arms felt almost weightless. Like her hands, they were far thinner than they'd used to be, even thinner than the last time she'd been here and she worried she might be ill.

The sudden knocking at the door broke the scrum, and there was more noise, more laughing and happiness as Maisie broke into the room and was told the wonderful news.

Cake and glasses of Bristol Cream Sherry were handed round, though the younger Milligans were supplied lemonade.

'So that's the reason for all this commotion. Here's to the new baby.' Maisie raised her glass. 'You look wonderful,' Maisie added. 'I've never seen you looking so good.'

'I feel it now the sickness has stopped. Absolutely on top of the world.'

'When can I expect to see you again?' Maisie asked her.

'A couple of months perhaps – unless you decide to get married, then I insist on being your bridesmaid.'

Maisie laughed. 'I'd have to find a man first.'

'There's always Sid.'

'Yes, there's always Sid. I do 'ope 'e makes it 'ome. He deserves to survive.'

They silently agreed that he did.

'Come and take a look at our back garden. Our Sean has worked wonders with it when I last saw it. Bet it's even better now, eh, Sean?'

Sean assured her that it was. 'Can you look at it by yourself, only I'm going to 'ave to shove off shortly.'

Ruby and Katie immediately sang, 'Sean's got a girlfriend, Sean's got a girlfriend.'

'I want a word with Maisie anyway. We've got some personal things to talk about. I want to know about Maisie's boyfriend.'

'I told you I ain't got one,' said Maisie once they were out in the back garden.

'I know,' said Bridget. 'I wanted to talk to you out of earshot of Mum and Dad.'

Maisie frowned. 'Go ahead.'

Bridget glanced over her shoulder before continuing. 'I don't think my mother is very well. I could feel every bone in her body when I hugged her.' She shook her head. 'And she looks so pale. I've told her to go and see the doctor. I even offered to pay for her. You know how it is with older people. They're all scared of doctors' bills.'

Maisie said that she did.

'Is it too much to ask you to keep an eye on her?'

'Of course not. Do you think it's serious?'

Bridget's eyelids fluttered. 'She's very pale. What with that and the weight loss, I'm worried. Very worried.'

'Did you mention it to her?'

Bridget nodded. 'Yes. Last time I was here.' She shook her head. 'I worry.'

'I'll look out for her. What happens next?'

She smiled. 'I go back to London and wait for Lyndon to come home on his next leave.'

'And when the war is finally over?'

A sudden dry breeze disturbed the leaves of the kidney beans. The sky was dark with clouds and a rumble of thunder sounded in the distance.

'America, except...' She told Maisie about the letter she'd received from Lyndon's mother. 'It made me feel cheap.'

'Oh Bridget!' Expression full of compassion, Maisie placed her hand on Bridget's shoulder. 'That's so cruel.'

Young Katie came out to ask if they wanted any jelly.

'I'd love a couple of spoonfuls,' Maisie declared, patting the little girl's head.

Later, once they were partied out, Bridget offered to walk with her to the bus stop.

Maisie shook her head. 'No need. Stay yer with your family. The war's 'ad enough of yer time, and I'm not in need of it. Enjoy yourself. You deserve it.'

'And you will do me the favour I asked you?'

'Of course, I will. We're two of the three Ms, one for all and all for one.'

28

To Mary Milligan, her family was everything. She wished them no harm, no pain and a happy journey through life. The doctor had told her she was ill, but she would not tell them. Not even Patrick, her darling husband. However, she would prepare herself for the inevitable. The doctor had told her there was no hope. The cancer had invaded her body with the same purposeful speed as Hitler had invaded Europe.

A day after Bridget had returned to London and Patrick was out delivering a clock he'd mended, she decided to go through her papers.

Despite it being summer, Mary felt cold. She felt cold all the time nowadays, though that wasn't the only reason she'd lit a coal fire.

Sitting in her favourite armchair, she began sifting through old photos and letters. Both writing and images were faded, the paper crisp and curling with age. She picked up the poker and prodded the fire. In response, flames licked around the piled coals. The under-surface of the coal began to glow enough to burn the letters and photos that constituted her life.

It was hard not to read again the sweet letters he'd sent her, hard also not to study his image which had never faded from her memory. He was there. It was still him, the man she'd loved all that time ago, yet oddly enough she couldn't recall how she'd felt back then. Patrick had taken his place. Patrick was the love of her life.

The sepia photograph was creased, one white ridge following the same route across his chest as his Sam Brown, the leather strap that was part of his uniform.

Her aim had been to consign photograph and letters to the fire. It was time. In fact, she should have done it years ago.

So why didn't you?

Even now, it was a difficult question to answer.

She steeled herself to do it at last.

One last read, she thought, *and then they're gone.*

My beloved Mary, I awake each morning thinking of you and each night before I close my eyes...

She clenched her jaw, determined not to be moved by either the words or the photograph. She'd sworn to herself she would only glance, but it was hard not to rake over the past. What was the point of keeping them? She had no intention of letting her daughter Bridget know that Patrick was not her natural father. Neither did she want Lyndon and that family of his to know. They already looked down their nose at her daughter. How much more if they were ever to learn that she'd been born illegitimate, the daughter of Irish aristocracy? No. They must never learn of it.

With great resolve, she screwed up this letter, the third so far. She'd been married to Patrick for many years. During all that time she'd not once fetched these old letters from their home in a battered old suitcase gathering dust on the top of the wardrobe. Neither had she ever admitted to Patrick that she still kept *his* letters, Captain Harold Hennessey. Patrick knew about him of course. He couldn't help but know about him. She'd been pregnant when they'd met and unmarried, though she had hoped for so much more.

How naïve I was, to think the son of the great house would marry a lowly parlour maid. But I was young then and anything seemed achievable.

Gradually, the pile of letters diminished, the paper curling and turning to blue and gold in the fireplace, gone up in smoke, sacrificed to the past and at the same time to the future.

Why now? some would ask. Because she was ill and her mortality was staring her in the face. When she died, as she would, the thought of Patrick finding these letters was unbearable. He'd no idea she'd kept them – everything tied with blue ribbon, including the telegram addressed to Mr and Mrs Hennessy saying he'd been killed in action. The telegram had arrived at the Queen Anne house on the outskirts of Dublin. She'd seen the telegraph boy pull up on his bicycle and guessed what it would say. Once the master and mistress had read it, she'd taken it from the bureau in the living room when they were out. She'd almost fainted when she'd cast her eyes over it. Harold was dead, killed in battle. Her hands had shaken as though she'd had a palsy. The longing to slide it beneath her crisp white blouse had been very strong. It had been hard, but she'd done what was right and put it back. Later, when everyone was asleep, she crept down and took it.

The pain she'd carried in her heart immediately after that was further exacerbated when she found herself with child. Panic-stricken, she'd gone to church and prayed fervently that the Virgin Mary would take the child from her and look after it up in Heaven.

'I can't, you see, Holy Mother. The father is dead. It's best for everyone that the child goes to you.'

She would work until the bitter end – that was her plan, but her burgeoning belly became more and more noticeable. Summoned to the drawing room, the mistress had looked at her with ice in her eyes.

'What is it with you girls around here that you rut like hogs?'

Appalled at the harsh words, Mary had hit back with the truth. 'The hog you refer to is your son. We fell in love. I'm unsure whether hogs do that.'

Cold eyes had glared from a face grey as granite. Her harsh voice, cold as ice, had ordered her from the ostentatious luxury of mirrored walls and thick Turkish rugs.

Sitting up in her room, Mary had counted out the little savings she had. She didn't need the mistress's stony glare to know that she would be turned out. She would go now of her own accord. The decision made, she'd packed her things and crept down the servants' stairs to the back door.

As she opened the door, a blast of wind and rain had hit her in the face.

She heard the soft rustle of a skirt hem over the flag stoned floor followed by a voice.

'What are you doing?' Molly, the kitchen maid, asked where she was going.

'Dublin,' Mary had replied, though wished she wasn't going. Wind, rain and the darkness of night were deeper in the countryside than in the city. It would be a long walk in such filthy conditions.

'Write to me, Mary. Please.' Molly's eyes had been wide with alarm. 'I'll write back, just as you taught me to.'

Mary smiled as she recalled the lessons she'd given the illiterate girl and how pleased Molly had been when she'd written and then read her name and then her first sentence.

'I'll write to you as soon as I'm able and give you my new address. I promise.'

She'd kept that promise and Molly had written back, her hand-writing improving with each letter she wrote. In them, she'd told her about events at the house. The last letter had arrived only a year or so ago.

Sir Charles died but her ladyship clings on. She's getting old and suddenly very religious and keen to get her affairs in order. She spends more time in church than she used to and when she's too sick to go, the pastor visits. I heard her asking him to hear her confession, even though she's no Catholic and he's a Protestant minister. 'I have a great need to repent of my sins,' I heard her say to him. She was going on about not having seen her grand-child. Should I tell her where you are, or would you prefer to tell her yourself? Or perhaps you'd prefer to say nothing. Let me know. As I said, she's not far off entering heaven – or hell. Which-ever of them will have her!

An aching mew had escaped Mary's throat. Her life would have been very different if she hadn't been ordered from the house.

Now it was her who had to set her affairs in order, though good-ness knows hers were far smaller and quite insignificant compared with her ladyship.

For a while, Mary stared into the fire as the flames licked at the paper curling its edges until it fell as ash. That's how her life had felt when the doctor had told her that she was suffering from breast cancer. It had spread all over her body. There was nothing they could do. As a Catholic, she wouldn't dream of being cremated and being like that paper crisping and curling until no sign remained that it had ever been. All the same, that's how she felt, that all she was, all she ever had been, would no longer exist except in the memories of those she'd loved and those who'd loved her.

Her fingers played with the letters and old photo she had left whilst feeling a terrible emptiness inside. The doctor had been vague about the prognosis. 'Some people soldier on for a year or so. Some only months. Individual constitution's got a lot to do with it.'

Just keep living until the end. That's what he'd told her and that was what she was telling herself. *Just keep living.*

Having some firm idea of when death would take her mattered. It mattered to her and would matter to her husband and to her family. She couldn't imagine not being here, not running her household and looking after her children as she always had.

Patrick was her main concern. It wouldn't be easy looking after the brood they'd had together. Sean, Michael, Molly, Mary, Ruby and Katy. She couldn't count on Bridget, the child of her heart, to help. Bridget's allegiance was to her husband, Lyndon and the expected new addition to the family. Their happiness would be complete, just as it had when she had given Patrick their firstborn, though Bridget had remained there too. It was as things should be.

She consoled herself that Sean was at work and bringing in some money. Michael would be leaving school before long, another off her husband's hands.

Closing her eyes and clasping her hands above the items remaining in her lap, she said a heartrending prayer. 'Please, Mother of God, help him to cope.'

Patrick Milligan's heart was as big as the ocean. He loved her. He loved their children. He also loved Bridget, the daughter fathered by the captain, a member of an English/Irish aristocrat family and one of the brave who'd gone over the top in the first big war of the century and never came back.

Focusing on the shapes made by the bright fire and black nubs of coal brought pictures to her mind of the old days, the sad days. Branded a sinner by mores of that time, she'd been entirely alone. Her money had quickly run out and as she'd got bigger, it had become harder and harder to get a job. All she could get was a bit of bar work or washing and ironing laundry for those that could afford it. It was hard work. The rim of the washtub had dug into her belly.

Backwards and forwards she'd gone, from poor houses black with soot to fancy white ones with pillars out front. Two different worlds. Black and white. Dark and light. Dirty and clean.

On one particular morning beneath an overcast sky, she'd staggered off to deliver a heavier pile of laundry than usual. Most of it she carried in the wicker basket as she usually did. The rest she'd tied up in a sheet and balanced it in front of her, resting its weight on her growing bump. Unfortunately, it got in the line of sight of her feet. As a consequence, she tripped over a loose flagstone and went flying.

She'd cried out in frustration on seeing a number of items from the top of the basket lying in the dirt.

'Can I help you up from there?'

It was the first occasion she'd heard Patrick's voice. The hand that helped her up was strong, though he'd had a funny way of reaching down for her, one leg bent at the knee, the other stretched out behind him. She hadn't known then about his injury.

Not only had he helped her up, but he'd also dusted off the dirt from the pile, retrieved it and stacked it back into the laundry basket.

'I know, I know,' he said when she looked at him with such surprise. 'I'd make somebody a good wife!'

She'd burst out laughing and he'd joined her. It was right in what he said. Few men would lower themselves to handle laundry. From the first, he'd been there to help her. He'd come with her to deliver the laundry to one of those white terraced houses with pillars either side of the door. It was Patrick who had made sure she got back to her dingy room safely. He'd seen her all the way up the stairs and didn't bat an eyelid when she'd opened the door. The rent was sixpence a week and it showed, though she'd done her best to brighten it up. For a start, she'd scrubbed the dirt and cobwebs from the small window and stuffed all around the frame with paper to stop the draught. A piece of Victorian lace cut from an old-fashioned mauve dress hung at the window, tied back with ribbon that had once formed part of the hem. The table had wobbly legs. She remembered apologising for it when she'd asked him to stay for a cuppa, and tea had sloshed into the saucer.

'When confronted with a problem such as this, it's up to a man like me to sort it out.'

His blitheness had yet again made her laugh, even more so when he'd jammed a piece of folded-up newspaper under the offending leg and made the table solid.

He'd looked around the room with its meagre furniture and single bed. She'd read his mind and was proved correct when he said, 'You've no man?'

Shame had bowed her head. 'No.'

He'd barely missed a beat before he'd said, 'And you look in need of a friend. I do believe it's going to be a fine day tomorrow. And it's Sunday. We could go for a stroll, you and I, if you've nothing else to do, that is. And have no other man ready and willing to sweep you off your feet.'

She'd stared at him then. 'You know I'm unmarried. Walking out with me will ruin your reputation.'

There'd been kindness in his eyes when he looked at her and said, 'Looking at you, your hard work and the way you've cheered up this room, I'm willing to take that chance. I reckon I'm a good judge of character. Sure I am in fact.'

His smile had lit up the whole room. She'd seen so many of his wonderful smiles over the years and had hoped to see many more.

Patrick Milligan wore his honesty like a placard around his neck. He was what he was, did what he did and cared little for the proprieties of the sanctimonious.

Over a number of days, they'd met up either in the park or the snug of the local pub. Neither visited their respective rooms, maintaining an aura of respectability long after the time for doing so was gone. He'd stuck by her, told her about losing his leg and suggesting that as they were both at a bit of a loss, they might marry and share their burdens. She'd told him about being a maid at a great house and making the mistake of falling in love with the son and heir.

'So he let you down?'

'No. The war let me down. He was killed.'

She'd told him everything. One fact stood out above all others for both of them. They were both all alone in the world. Her parents were dead and so were his. Like pieces of flotsam caught in the stream of life, they had crashed together and became entangled.

The early days together had whirled past. He'd insisted on marrying her not long after Bridget was born. It had been an easy decision to make and she'd never looked back. Patrick was a good man and what was more important was that he'd taken Bridget on as his own. Over the years, the two of them had become close and were somehow alike, though not a drop of Patrick's blood flowed in Bridget's veins.

An ember sparked from the fire brought her back to the present day and the history of her life sitting on her lap. Just the remnants now. Gazing at the photograph aroused no passion in her breast, only a reminder of what he had looked like.

Determinedly she screwed up the last letter and watched as it caught, flamed and gradually turned black.

Aside from a letter, a postcard and a photo, the only items still nestling in her lap were photographs taken once she'd tied the knot with Patrick. One was of Bridget as a baby. Another was of her and

Patrick on their wedding day, Bridget in his arms. A tear-filled smile came to her lips as she looked at him, remembered how loving he'd been, the most caring man she'd ever met. Even if he'd survived the war, it seemed obvious to her now that Bridget's father would never have married her. She'd been convinced that Lyndon too would desert her daughter, but she'd been proved wrong and was glad that she was.

She sighed and placed the photos of Patrick and Bridget to one side.

The last letter was from Harold's parents and had arrived a year or so after giving birth, passed on to her by Molly before she and Patrick had relocated to Bristol. As she read the words, she questioned why she'd held onto it.

Having lost our son and heir, Sir Charles and I have carefully considered our options with regard to your disgraceful behaviour that has unfortunately resulted in the conception of a child. In this regard, we are willing to take on both the financial and practical care of this child. We are only willing to do this if you revoke all claims to said child, never mention him to anyone else or ever see said child ever again. In lieu of this, we are willing to settle one hundred pounds on you to do with as you wish. Perhaps you might like to consider emigrating to America where, so we hear, many more people of Ireland have already gone.

We await your response.

Moistened by tears, the pale blue ink became more indistinct. Her first instinct had been to tear the letter to pieces, but something had held her back. Patrick also suggested she keep it.

'In case Bridget should ever need to know about her father's family.'

What surprised her about this letter was that they always referred to the expected baby as male. Girls never counted so much as a boy, even in the lowliest households, more so in upper-crust families.

Together with a sepia print of Harold in uniform, all that remained was a postcard, his last postcard from France.

Great chaps here and from all walks of life. They grumble sometimes and although they might wonder why we're here, nobody says it out loud. We're here to fight until victory is achieved and we will win. See you at Christmas.

He wasn't to know that he wouldn't be around for the last Christmas of the war. He'd been killed just a few months before victory, the armistice signed in a railway carriage at twelve noon in France, at the eleventh hour in Great Britain. She placed it with the original telegram that had told of his death.

It was hard to accept that she would be leaving her family behind, that she was going somewhere they could not go. *But at least my affairs will be in order*, she thought.

For now, her beloved Bridget would continue to believe that Patrick was her father. There was a strong bond between them and she wanted that to continue. It was the least she could do for him after all that he'd done for her.

All she had to do now was find the right moment to tell Patrick what the doctor had told her. Tomorrow, or perhaps the next day, she would tell him then.

One more look at the last letter, the last photograph. Holding one in each hand, she caressed both with her thumbs. The nostalgic part of her wanted to hold onto them, keepsakes of the girl she'd once been, the love she'd long lost. The more pragmatic side of her insisted it was only sensible to consign both to the flames.

She decided to leave it for now. *Tomorrow*, she told herself, *I'll throw them away tomorrow.*

29

PHYLLIS

Stuffy Snow adjusted his spectacles as he took in the dusty, bedraggled sight of four of his operatives.

Phyllis, tired, fed up and on the verge of tears, finally snapped. 'Before you tell us to get into uniform and tidy ourselves up, we haven't got a uniform. Every piece of clothing we had went up in last night's raid. Everything we owned in fact.'

'We've put in a chitty so at least will get uniforms,' Jackie added. 'And a bed for the night. A more permanent billet might take a bit longer.'

He pursed his lips. Thick spectacle lenses made it difficult to read what he was thinking.

Phyllis was ready to punch him if he said anything to upset her. At present anything could. Never mind the wedding dress. Much as she pitied the demise of Mrs Fly, she also pitied herself. The address she'd given Mick was no more. Letters from him would take time to catch up with her. It would also take time for her to write back once she'd found a new billet.

'You still have your lives.' It was very matter of fact and all he said before he stalked off.

Glenda, one of the other girls billeted elsewhere, whispered across to them, 'His mother's house got hit too.' She shook her head. 'I heard about it, but he hasn't mentioned it.'

Phyllis hid her eyes behind her hand and sighed. 'Poor man.'

Although it was hard not to dwell on things, it was best to move on.

'Come on. Let's get ourselves sorted. We look like scarecrows.'

New uniforms were found from somewhere, along with everything else they'd lost. The new billet was in a fine house in Hampstead. Jackie was in her element on recognising the people who owned it.

'I knew their daughter at boarding school. Helen Champion. Champion by name and by nature. She could send a hockey ball into the net every time. Nobody could come close to her.' Jackie rubbed at her shin and frowned. 'She was a hard hitter. I can still feel it.'

They never heard about the dress, but they did hear that the large tins of tea hidden away in Mrs Fly's downstairs larder had indeed come from India – though via a West End store. A rival to Fortnum and Masons, the store had suffered a direct hit. Tins of tea, chocolate, jams and preserves had disappeared overnight. If Mrs Fly really did have a brother, he'd likely never set foot in India. It was more likely he had looted the bombed-out upmarket store where tea was stored in large tins and ladled out with a scoop into brown paper bags – a quarter pound at a time.

The biggest surprise was being told by the billeting officer that the billet was only temporary.

Phyllis slumped onto the bed, head in hands. 'This is ridiculous. If I don't get something more permanent, Mick won't know where I am.'

Jackie was more forthright, tackling the officer head on. 'You came round here to tell us that? Come on, Beattie, you and I go back a long way. Surely you could have found something more permanent. We do have a life to lead, you know. Phyllis's husband is going to wonder where the devil she's got to.'

Beatrice was yet another of Jackie's old school friends. *They're everywhere,* thought Phyllis wryly. She knew everyone and thank goodness she did if Phyllis was going to keep in touch with Mick.

As it was, Beatrice came up trumps. 'I'll make sure he gets to know where you are. Trust me. I'm on your side.'

Phyllis sighed and ran a hand through her hair. 'I much appreciate it.'

The billeting officer stood silently and a little too stiffly for Phyllis's liking. Something was up.

Jackie was standing next to a very fine chest of drawers in front of an equally fine mirror. There was something about her expression, the way she was looking at her old friend that made Phyllis feel nervous. 'Is there anything else we should know?'

Beatrice wasn't the sort to be guilty about anything, but she did look a bit guilty right now. 'I shouldn't be telling you this. Not until you're got your orders in writing.'

Phyllis got to her feet. Together she and Jackie stood there, shoulder to shoulder. They'd known each other long enough to sense they were about to be given bad news – or at least news they didn't want to hear.

'You've both had experience abroad in a battle zone. You're being sent over to France. It's where you're needed. That's all I can say.' She looked directly at Phyllis. 'But I will get word to your husband. I promise.'

After she'd gone, the pair of them remained standing in shocked silence.

Phyllis slumped back down onto the bed – an iron-framed army-issue bed that looked totally out of place in the fine Hampstead house. 'It doesn't sound as though I'll have time to see him before we leave.'

'Use that.'

When Phyllis looked up, one of Jackie's long slim fingers was pointing at an ivory-coloured telephone. Never had she seen such a fine-looking phone in real life, only on the big screen used by a female film star in a Hollywood film.

'Have you got his number?'

Phyllis nodded. 'In my handbag. Thank God I took it with me the other night.'

'Don't tell me, you carry it everywhere.'

'You bet I do,' said Phyllis, retrieving the piece of paper on which Mick's number was written, and diving onto the telephone almost as though it was a living thing and likely to fly away.

He wasn't there, but she left a message.

'Tell him a rocket landed on my billet. I've lost everything. Please also tell him that I'm being posted. I'll get my new address to him as soon as I can.'

The person on the other end assured her that her message would be passed on. 'Hang on a minute.'

For one giddy moment, she believed Mick had been spotted walking by. The phone would be passed to him. He would speak...

'Hello. Is that Mrs Fairbrother?'

She didn't recognise the voice and didn't catch the officer's name and rank.

Formalities were instantly cancelled out when he said, 'He's been trying to get in touch with you. Didn't you get the message?'

'No.' Her voice wavered before repeating what she'd said before. 'My lodgings got a direct hit from a rocket. All my personal things went up in smoke. It's taken a while to get things sorted out, so no, I didn't get a message. What is it? Is he all right? Is he there?' Sweat stuck her hand to the phone. Her blood had turned cold. *Not again, please not again!*

Her head spinning, she didn't at first catch the words. She felt Jackie's hand laid reassuringly on her shoulder.

'He's been transferred to an airfield in Northern France.'

France! The front line – or at least close to it. Her panic intensified and so did a sudden surge of excitement at the thought of them both being stationed in the same country.

'So how do I get in touch with him?

She felt Jackie move away, head for a chair. Today's newspaper rustled as she transferred it from chair to table.

'Send your new address here and we'll send it on.'

Unsettled and feeling helpless, Phyllis put down the phone. 'Oh my God. I don't know when or where I'm going to see him again.' Hand still resting on the phone, she turned to Jackie, eyes blazing. 'What if it happens again? What if he gets shot down? He promised he would leave the dangerous stuff to somebody else.'

'Perhaps he felt it needed experience to do what was asked of him.' Jackie was sitting in the chair, the newspaper flattened on her lap. She stabbed her finger at one particular headline. 'Could it be this?'

Phyllis took the newspaper from her and read where she pointed.

ENEMY ROCKET SITES TARGETED

The probability that Mick was involved couldn't possibly be corroborated. Details of top-secret operations were kept just that – until the danger was destroyed and another headline declared victory. Or Mick came home and confirmed he'd been involved.

As it turned out, they were taken over by events. Stuffy Snow confirmed their new posting. 'Northern France. Close to the

Belgian border. Forward telecommunications operations. They'll have anyone who can type and use a wireless. It's important. Good luck.'

He was as abrupt as usual, though it was a first for him to wish anyone luck.

Phyllis's mind whirled with possibilities. 'The rockets. This is all about the rockets.'

Jackie shrugged and lit up before offering her opinion. 'Understandable. Mr Churchill won't want the army worrying whether they're going to come back to a home or a pile of ruins. It's all about morale.'

Phyllis was only half listening. In her mind, she imagined the surprise on Mick's face should she run into him. Her spirits soared.

Before leaving, she phoned the kind woman who organised gowns for brides and explained what had happened.

'How terribly sad. Well, never mind. I dare say we'll manage without it. Thank you for letting me know.'

A sharp click and she was gone.

'What did she say?' asked Jackie.

Phyllis told her. 'She didn't sound that worried.'

Jackie shrugged. 'Why should she? What's done is done. Make do and mend. Carry on regardless. It's all we can do.'

'It's all we've ever done,' Phyllis said somewhat bitterly. 'I'll do this. But it's my last effort. I want a life, Jackie, and I want Mick.'

* * *

Two days later, they'd been given their pick-up time. New uniforms and personal items had been supplied. Everything was packed.

Phyllis looked sombrely at her kitbag. She'd hoped that Mick might ring before she left, but there'd been no word. She was very disappointed.

'Seeing as we're off tomorrow, I'm going to take a bath whilst I can.'

Jackie nodded. 'You carry on, darling. Make it four inches and I'll get in after you.'

The great delight of their new billet was that the bath and hand towels were made of the finest Turkish towelling. A bath was soothing but wiping oneself with a luxurious Turkish towel was quite delicious.

A heavy flow of water started from the taps. Scented steam filled the air. She did her best to pull the bolt across, but this was a house of women. It didn't matter.

Having already washed her hair once this week, Phyllis wrapped it in a small towel so it wouldn't get wet again. Once undressed, she lowered herself into the warm water lay back her head and closed her eyes. So much had happened since the start of this war. Her life had changed so completely. Looking back, she hadn't been quite sure of what she'd wanted from life, but she did now. For better or worse, she wanted Mick Fairbrother, her husband.

Was the weather in France as warm as this bath? She'd heard it was better than in England and sincerely hoped it was true.

Dreamily she drifted, enjoying the warmth, and comparing it with that of Mick's body. At first, she discounted the sounds outside the bathroom door; the tread of feet coming up the stairs, footsteps along the landing. Voices too.

'In here?'

Because the door was thick, the voice was muffled. Even so, she perceived it being male.

'Phyl?'

She sat up so quickly that the towel around her head fell into the bath.

'Mick?'

Without giving it a second thought, she stood up stark naked.

The door swung open. And there he was.

'Mick! It's you.'

After taking his cap off, he looked her up and down and grinned. 'Who were you expecting?'

'I'm wet,' she cried as she was lifted by his strong arms and swung out of the bath.

'I don't care,' he said as he took her in a crushing embrace. 'I swung it for us to be together. Tonight, we paint the town.'

'I think I'd better get myself respectable first. They don't let naked women into pubs and nightclubs, even in London.'

'Then get yourself dressed. I've got a lot to tell you.'

In double quick time, Phyllis was ready to go out on the town. The girls she roomed with grinned once she was dressed and sparkling.

Some of their admiration was for Mick.

'Hi there, handsome.'

He played along, though Phyllis sensed he had some serious things to say.

He guided her into the quiet of the saloon bar of a pub. Most people of their age headed into the public bar, but that was always noisy.

'Cheers,' he said, raising his glass. 'Our destination is a village named St Orme – or at least I think it is. My French isn't that good.'

She felt a pang of fear at his message but countered it with her own. 'I've been ordered to France too.'

He grinned. 'I know. The area we're going to is safer than it was. You're being attached to my division. What do you think of that then?'

Phyllis's jaw dropped. 'We're being sent to the same place?'

She saw the amused smirk on Mick's face.

'You arranged it?'

He nodded. 'I've even swung us a nice little place to call our own. There are a few other girls from your division going over. Every photograph we take has to be catalogued. It's a tiresome job, but I didn't think you'd mind.' He clutched at her hand. His eyes smiled into hers. 'It's about time we spent more time together.' The smile was swiftly replaced by a worried frown. 'You don't mind leaving the wireless set behind, do you? I told them we were man and wife, and I wasn't going up on reccies again unless they put us both together – just as we're meant to be. You okay with that?'

Choking on happiness, she nodded soundlessly.

His expression turned more serious. 'Just a bit of top-secret information – courtesy of my analysis of the situation, this war won't be over until next year, but we're well and truly on the road to victory. Trust me, I know we are.'

'If you say so, then I believe you, Mick Fairbrother.'

30

MAISIE

D-Day had happened in June. It was now August and a massive army had retaken Caen and was moving across Europe.

Maisie had a new friend at work. Dolly Meadows was a young widow with two children. In her late twenties, she was still good-looking and at one point Maisie thought she might make a good match for Peter – replacing herself of course. The guilt at letting him down was eating at her.

Dot had laughed at the very thought of it. 'I'm enjoying myself. I've got a good job and Lil, my mother-in-law, is happy to look after my kids.'

Dot Meadows was a good sort whose priority in life was her family.

Hearing that one of Dot's children was named Alfred brought tears to her eyes.

'That's my brother's name.'

'Is he in the armed forces?'

'Merchant marine. I haven't seen him for ages. But he is off all over the world. The last letter I had from him, he mentioned South America.'

The contents of his last letter had surprised her. She hadn't been sure he was being serious, but if he was, then she wasn't likely to see much of him in the future.

'He said he might never come back to England. Fancies becoming a gaucho,' Maisie exclaimed.

'What's that when it's at 'ome?' asked Dot.

'A cowboy in Argentina.'

'Didn't know they 'ad them. Thought they was all in 'ollywood, you know, like Roy Rogers.'

Maisie burst out laughing. 'Alf riding Trigger and singing like Roy Rogers. Can't see it some'ow.' Out of the corner of her eye, she saw Peter Nichols looking in her direction. 'Foreman's on 'is way,' she muttered under her breath.

'Better look sharp then,' Dot murmured in response.

It had always been Peter's habit to make a beeline for Maisie's table, lingering there whilst exchanging small talk. He'd always been complimentary and smiling. Not so of late. He flicked his hand through the pile of tobacco leaves lying on the table and grunted. 'That's a small pile.'

'It's all we were given,' Maisie responded. She knew he was picking fault for the sake of it. She'd snubbed him, opted out of dates until it became obvious she wasn't interested.

He was less scathing with Dot. 'How's the family, Mrs Meadows?'

'Fine thank you, Mr Nichols.'

'Think he fancies you,' whispered Maisie once he'd gone.

Dot laughed. 'No chance. He doesn't like kids. Lil told me that he was one of seventeen raggedy kids and vowed he'd never live like that again. So, I'm safe enough.'

Maisie's jaw dropped. 'I never knew that.'

'I tell you my mother-in-law knows everything and everyone. Including Peter Nichols, mainly because Auntie Flo lives in Swindon. Both she and her old man used to work in number four factory, that's how come she knows it all.'

'But he was married.'

'Yep. He was, but that was until his missus went off with a younger bloke. Had a kid with 'im. She was still married to Peter at the time. Auntie Flo said that when the young chap joined up, the kid was left with his parents. Better than adoption, I suppose.' Her face darkened. 'I'm glad I've got Lil and me job. I've 'eard of kids being taken away when there's only one parent and put into children's 'omes. I couldn't stand that. I'd top meself if that 'appened.'

'You reckon kids are being taken away when there's only one parent at 'ome?'

'So, I 'ear. Mostly mothers being told that they can't manage – even though they can.'

'What about you? Have you been approached?'

Dot shook her head. 'No.' she frowned. 'It's got something to do with Australia and Canada, about building up the population. Not many people live there.' Dot shook her head. 'Whatever the reason, I don't think it's right that kids can be taken from their mothers without a by your leave.'

Maisie fell to silence, aware that Peter was still eyeing her, though not once did she chance raising her eyes to meet his. She'd thought all was well now Carole had given up her idea about adoption. She did her best to shake away this new threat. Paula was well looked after, and Carole had become a good mother. However, it made sense for both her and Carole to be on their guard.

* * *

'Here is the news... Following the taking of Caen, units of British and Canadian troops are now pushing ever deeper into France and although meeting stiff opposition...'

It was Saturday morning and Maisie's regular once a month day off. She was listening to the wireless as she sipped the last of the tea ration. The same leaves had been used the night before, then left to dry in a saucer. It was still palatable, but if they had to use them a third and fourth time, the tea would likely be indistinguishable from plain water. Especially without sugar. She hadn't got her hands on sugar for two weeks. The larder was looking bare. 'Like Mother Hubbard,' Maisie had quipped.

There was no mention on the wireless of the Far East, and she wondered whether that had something to do with keeping up morale. The Allies had gained a foothold in France and were pressing the enemy into retreat – or at least that was the story they were hearing. Surely it couldn't be too much longer before the prisoners of war were liberated. There was already talk and a great deal of hope around that subject. But what about Japan? What about Sid and all those others? Had they been forgotten about?

It had been some weeks since she'd received one of the all too familiar postcards from Sid. She missed him being in contact. She missed his drawings of matchstick men and cryptic messages of what life was like as a prisoner of the Japanese.

Swallowing the last mouthful of tea, she got up and made her way to the back door. Runner bean flowers climbed up their supporting sticks. She was proud of her garden efforts, which included onions, leeks, carrots, and lettuce. Early cabbages grew at the very rear of the garden. If she didn't pick some of them very soon, they would go to seed before she had chance to plant the winter variety. Perhaps she could shred some of the leaves and fry them with bacon. It might just work.

As she stood in the back doorway, musing on some very basic recipes, the sound of the letterbox clattered behind her. The morning post had arrived, or so she'd thought. There was no post lying on the coconut matt used for wiping their feet. The letterbox rattled again.

We do have a knocker, she felt like saying, but instead shouted, 'Coming.'

There was something instantly recognisable about the small woman standing there. So was the reason she had not used the knocker. She simply wasn't tall enough. She had a strong face and wore a cloche hat looking left over from the twenties. A tall feather sprouting from it added to her height. From her features, it was easy to imagine her as a kind person with a ready smile. But not now. There was pain in her eyes. Her voice when she spoke faltered a little.

'Are you Maisie Miles?'

Maisie said that indeed she was. The feeling that she knew this person persisted.

'I'm Sid's mum.' She delved into her handbag and brought out a card. 'It's from Sid. He's been ill.'

When she burst into tears, Maisie shelved her plan to dig up some vegetables. 'Oh, Mrs Powell. Come on in, please.'

Cupping Mrs Powell's elbow, she guided her into the passageway and took her into the room adjacent to the kitchen.

'I'll get you a cuppa.' She steered the small woman into one of the tapestry-covered armchairs placed in front of the back window.

The feisty feather trembled as Mrs Powell did her best to stem her tears with her handkerchief.

Mrs Powell handed her one of the instantly recognisable cards of which she'd received quite a number. 'His mate wrote it for 'im. He wanted you to know.'

As she took the card, Maisie felt a cold clinging sweat fall down her back.

Heart in her mouth, she began to read.

Dear Ma. I'm ill so a mate is writing this. The doc says I'll be lucky to survive. I hope I'm lucky. I just wanted to prepare you for the worst. It's one card at a time, so can you let Maisie know? I can't expect her to wait for me. Just tell her to be happy. Love, Sid.

Maisie made a determined effort not to have her hands shake as she passed the card back to Sid's mother.

Poor Sid. She'd always been blithe about her relationship with him, but looking back, she'd enjoyed writing to him and him writing to her. A world without him didn't seem possible.

'He's telling you to get on with your life.' Mrs Powell seemed to caress the card before returning it to her handbag. The sound of the clasp snapping shut was like the shot from a gun. Just as final, just as frightening.

Old memories came flooding back to her: their first date, him getting fresh at the pictures, eating fish and chips on the seafront at Weston-Super-Mare. And all those cards with their telling scribbles designed to get past the Japanese censors. She smiled easily at those old memories. Strange as it might seem, they'd become closer via the written word, more so than in person. She reminded herself that they'd been writing to each other for some years, far longer than seeing each other in the flesh.

'One of the girls at the factory told me where you lived.'

Maisie looked at her glassy-eyed. 'I vaguely recall you live in Stokes Croft.'

For the first time, Mrs Powell's face lost its tension. 'I used to. It got a direct hit. I'm living with my sister now in St John's Lane. She's got a shop there and both of us being all alone... well, it seemed the best thing to do.'

They sat there in silence until Maisie remembered offering a cup of tea. She sprang to her feet. 'I'm so sorry. I'll get that cup of tea... it won't be very strong...'

'No need.' Mrs Powell held up a shiny palm criss-crossed with lines. Her skin had a polished look about it, the look of someone who'd worked hard all her life. It just didn't seem fair that she'd lose her son.

'I don't recall Sid saying that he had any brothers and sisters.' She felt obliged to mention it, hoping that talking about other children might ease Mrs Powell's pain.

Mrs Powell shook her head. 'No. He was the only one who survived.'

At those words, it felt to Maisie as though her heart had become too heavy to hold inside her body. Imagine, she thought, holding a baby to your breast, and having that same baby snatched from you by circumstances beyond your control.

She thought over the sad words Sid had written. Reaching across, she placed her hand on that of Sid's mother.

'The doctor did tell him that if he's lucky, he will survive. Sid always did consider himself lucky. Let's hope he's right.'

After handing Maisie her new address, Mrs Powell made ready to depart.

She paused by the front door. Maisie felt her kind eyes studying her. Finally, she said, 'I would have liked you as a daughter-in-law. Can we 'ope that one day it might really 'appen?'

Words were a long time coming for Maisie. Mrs Powell needed both strength and sympathy. Breaking down in the middle of a sentence, whether of sympathy or hope, wouldn't help Sid's mother cope with her loss.

'I'd like to keep track of things. Would you mind if I called on you?'

Mrs Powell nodded.

As Maisie opened the door, there was Carole turning the pram into the front garden.

'Hello,' Carole said merrily enough.

'Carole lives with me,' Maisie hastily explained. 'She lost her husband.'

Mrs Powell didn't appear to hear but asked Carole if she could look at her baby.

Carole's eyes met Maisie's questioningly as she gave her permission.

A look of silent pleasure passed over Mrs Powell's face. 'We've all lost so much in this war. Let's hope this little one reaps the benefits and never sees another.'

Maisie and Carole watched her totter off down the road.

'Sid's mother,' Maisie explained.

'What's happened?'

Maisie took a deep breath before the words came, stumbling and sharp with pain. 'He's ill. Very ill.'

She didn't need to say any more. As the tears overflowed, Carole's hand patted her shoulder. 'I'm so sorry. So very sorry.'

* * *

After lunch, Maisie headed for the Milligan household in Marksbury Road. It was a long walk, but the air was fresh and the day sunny and as Paula was almost sitting up, she decided to use the pushchair rather than the more cumbersome pram. Carole had met up with Eddie and told him she needed one. As usual, Eddie obliged.

Mrs Milligan was sat on a dining chair in the front garden with a piece of knitting in her hands.

Maisie waved. 'Mrs Milligan.'

Mary Milligan waved back. 'Maisie. It's been a long time. Would you like a cuppa?'

'I'd love one.'

As she'd suspected, the pushchair was easier than the pram to manoeuvre up the steps.

'I've got some orange juice,' said Bridget's mother, smiling at the baby. 'Is she allowed?'

'No need. She's just had a feed. That's why she's sound asleep.'

Mary Milligan continued to smile down at her before saying she would go and make some tea. 'Patrick's gone to the football match with the boys. The girls have gone to the park.'

'Nice day for it.'

Bridget was right, thought Maisie as they talked and drank tea. Her mother looked ill.

'You're still working at Wills?'

Maisie replied that she was.

Paula chose that moment to wake up. Her bright eyes immediately latched onto Mrs Milligan and the eyes of Bridget's mother latched onto the baby.

'What big blue eyes,' she said, wonder lacing her voice. 'May I pick her up?'

Maisie said that she could.

Mary Milligan hugged the baby against her chest and looked down into her face with outright wonder. 'So beautiful,' she whispered. 'I wish she was mine. I've always liked babies.'

She said all this without taking her eyes off Paula's face.

Maisie felt the urge to be cheerful. 'Never mind. You've got grandchildren to come along yet. Won't that be wonderful?'

When Mary Milligan looked at her, the ashen greyness of her face was obvious. There was also something in her eyes, a misty disjointed look that ached with tragedy. But what tragedy?

Maisie leaned forward. 'Mrs Milligan, is everything all right?'

A weak smile crossed the tired-looking face. 'It will be. Not for a while yet, but it will be.'

Her meaning was difficult to work out, but Maisie couldn't help thinking that Bridget had been right to be worried.

Maisie being Maisie was always forthright. There was no room for waffle. 'Mrs Milligan, you look ill. Am I right in thinking that?'

The skin of the once beautiful face was taut. Her cheeks were sunken, and her eyes lacked lustre. Her eyelashes fluttered. Maisie guessed she was thinking something through, something very serious.

She gave Maisie a very direct look. 'You've always been a very good friend to my Bridget. You know her husband too, don't you?'

'Yes.'

Mary Milligan sighed. 'I've only just got round to telling Patrick my days are at an end. He's strong. He must be for the children's sake. I haven't told my children. I haven't told Bridget.' Her hands trembled; her arms grew slack. 'Please,' she said, handing the baby back into Maisie's arms. 'I've no strength in my arms. No strength full stop!' She sank slowly down into a chair, her breathing shallow, her eyes half closed.

Maisie put Paula back into her pushchair and gave her a bottle of juice.

'You must know that my daughter is going to discover things when I go that she never knew before. I would like you to be there for her. Will you do that?'

Maisie's mouth and throat seemed suddenly devoid of moisture. 'Yes,' she said.

Mary Milligan sighed deeply. Her pale, tired eyes settled on the now sleeping baby. 'I won't be around when the baby is born. I only wish I could be. I'm glad she's got you. I'm also glad she's got Lyndon.' She smiled directly at Maisie. 'They'll always be together. I've made sure of that now. Their future is assured.'

Maisie wondered what that assurance might be but held her

tongue. Whatever it was, she sensed it would make Bridget happy. And that was what they all wanted.

Maisie noted the wandering look that had come to Mrs Milligan's eyes. How like Bridget she was, very much so in fact. Bridget bore some resemblance to Mr Milligan but not a lot.

'There are two letters in the sideboard, fetch them out for me will you. I want you to have them to give to Bridget when I'm gone. You could say that one of them is my confession, my life story that Bridget knows nothing about. I want her to read it when I'm gone. The other is from a firm of lawyers in Dublin.' She smiled weakly. 'It explains who Bridget is.' She smiled wanly and even managed a weak chuckle. 'Just wait till her high and mighty mother-in-law hears the news.'

Maisie fingered both letters without asking what was in them. It wasn't for her to know. Besides she had a fearful instinct that what was inside wasn't good.

Something about her expression must have struck a chord.

'Can you keep a secret?'

Maisie responded. 'I think so.'

Mary Milligan's look was steadfast.

'I have cancer. It began as a lump in my breast but has taken hold. The doctor did mention treatments – all expensive of course.'

'But couldn't Lyndon—'

'No. I won't allow it. I still have my pride. Anyway, I've lived to see my children grown big enough to survive. I promise you won't have to keep the secret for long.'

* * *

Leaves were turning scarlet and burnt sienna when Bridget's mother died. The funeral was at Arnos Vale Cemetery, there being little space left in the graveyard of their local Catholic church.

The whole family attended. Bridget held the hand of the man she'd always regarded as her father. Lyndon held those of the younger children.

Phyllis and Mick had not been able to get leave but had sent flowers and a card expressing their sincere sympathy.

Maisie had handed the letters to Bridget some days before the funeral. Bridget's face had paled. After reading each one, she'd passed it to Maisie.

Silently they had sat there, both knowing an astounding secret that would change Bridget's life.

After they'd sat like that for some time, Bridget sat bolt upright. 'I don't want anyone to know about this. Any of this.' Her serene grey eyes met Maisie's darker ones. 'My father is the man who brought me up. He loves me and I love him. As for the other matter... well, it will certainly put Lyndon's mother in her place.'

'Will you tell her you've inherited a title – and everything that goes with it?'

Bridget looked thoughtful. 'No. Not yet. Not until Lyndon and I go over to the States. That's when I'll tell her. Tell them all!'

There was triumph in her eyes and love; love for her departed mother, her husband, her family, and the baby growing within her. Also for Patrick Milligan, the father who'd brought her up.

Maisie had always admired Bridget's serenity, her ability to cope with any situation. Strength was embedded in that serenity. It shone in her.

Maisie's voice pierced the eerie silence. 'You know I'm always there for you.'

A slow sad smile crossed Bridget's face and her eyes were liquid.

'We're all there for each other. That's how the Three Ms began and will continue until the end of this war, whenever that might be, and hopefully for the rest of our lives.'

MORE FROM LIZZIE LANE

We hope you enjoyed reading *Marriage and Mayhem For The Tobacco Girls*. If you did, please leave a review.

If you'd like to gift a copy, this book is also available as an ebook, digital audio download and audiobook CD.

Sign up to Lizzie Lane's mailing list for news, competitions and updates on future books:

http://bit.ly/LizzieLaneNewsletter

If you haven't yet why not discover the first in the series, *The Tobacco Girls*.

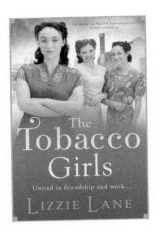

ABOUT THE AUTHOR

Lizzie Lane is the author of over 50 books, a number of which have been bestsellers. She was born and bred in Bristol where many of her family worked in the cigarette and cigar factories. This has inspired her new saga series for Boldwood *The Tobacco Girls*.

Follow Lizzie on social media:

[f] facebook.com/jean.goodhind

[twitter] twitter.com/baywriterallatı

[instagram] instagram.com/baywriterallatsea

[BB] bookbub.com/authors/lizzie-lane

Sixpence Stories

Introducing Sixpence Stories!

Discover page-turning historical novels from your favourite authors, meet new friends and be transported back in time.

Join our book club Facebook group

https://bit.ly/SixpenceGroup

Sign up to our newsletter

https://bit.ly/SixpenceNews

Boldw⚬⚬d

Boldwood Books is an award-winning fiction publishing company seeking out the best stories from around the world.

Find out more at www.boldwoodbooks.com

Join our reader community for brilliant books, competitions and offers!

Follow us
@BoldwoodBooks
@BookandTonic

Sign up to our weekly deals newsletter

https://bit.ly/BoldwoodBNewsletter